BRIGHT WICKED

BRIGHT WICKED 1

EVERLY FROST

Frost, Everly
Bright Wicked

Cover design by Claire Holt with Luminescence Covers
www.luminescencecovers.com

Illustration by fantasybookdesign.com

For information on reproducing sections of this book or sales of this book,
go to
www.EverlyFrost.com
everlyfrost@gmail.com

DISCOVER THE EVER REALMS

Seven series set in the same world.

Suggested Reading Order:

Bright Wicked
Storm Princess
Assassin's Magic
Soul Bitten Shifter
Supernatural Legacy
Dark Magic Shifters
Kingdom of Betrayal

For everyone who brings starlight to someone in their darkest night.

CHAPTER 1

$\mathcal{T}$onight, I'm the prey.

I lean low over my thunderbird's neck as he sweeps his wings and carries us toward Bright's border, where the danger awaits.

My indigo armor absorbs the moonlight, turning me into a shadow on his back. But his heart is powered by lightning, and with every beat of his blue-gray wings, electricity sizzles around his body and mine, lighting us up in the dark, making us visible for miles.

That's the way I want it.

On the other side of the border are the Fell creatures. Monstrous cowards who lurk in the foggy marshes that stretch along their side of the border, waiting to strike.

Tonight, I will draw them out.

I will strike first.

Sparing a quick glance upward, I register the faintest signs of the squadron of thunderbirds and riders concealed within the clouds high above me, ready to fight if I'm outnumbered.

Every thunderbird has the ability to dim their power, and

the armor the riders wear can absorb the moonlight, allowing them to become mere shadows in the night and making them nearly impossible to see.

Among them is the Captain of the Border Guard, my adoptive brother, Evander of the Frost.

I sense his worry and know his focus on me will be unwavering.

He didn't want me to volunteer tonight.

But it's my last night as our Queen's Champion. Tomorrow, as is the case every year at the end of the Winter Ascending, my position will be challenged.

I will fight to retain my place at the Queen's side.

I must prove that my strength and skill are unshakable.

I'm determined to spend what could be my last night as the Queen's Champion protecting her and my people—the fae.

"Go, Treble," I whisper to my thunderbird, gripping his back with my thighs and leaning my weight in the direction I want him to fly.

My bond with Treble is absolute, and I trust him with my life.

Far below us are the vast fields that sit between Bright and this side of the border line.

I shudder as we pass over a large patch of scorched earth. It's littered with the crumbling skeletons of the outpost that had once stood there.

That's where the Fell staged their last deadly attack fifteen years ago.

My family lived in that outpost.

I was the only survivor.

Whatever happened that night, the attack was too vicious for my young mind to cope with, leaving me with no memories of my family or of my life before the attack.

My people fought back—our Queen herself saved me—and drove the Fell back into the darkness where they belong.

Since then, the Fell's attacks have grown less frequent, and I intend to keep it that way.

Leaving the burn site behind, Treble banks in the direction of the foggy marsh on the Fell side of the border.

Far behind me, a mountain range forms a line of defense for the enormous city that shelters behind it. Ahead, the air is thick with mist, creating a nearly impenetrable darkness.

My skin prickles as we draw closer to it. Even the air on that side of the border is sour, pressing in on my chest.

What I've learned about the Fell is that they only attack if they believe the odds are in their favor.

So, each night, one Bright rider flies across the open sky below the clouds to draw the Fell out of their hiding places.

Some nights, it's quiet.

Other nights, it's a bloodbath.

It's the brutal ones that Evander is worried about.

Despite every battle he's seen me fight—despite the number of Fell I've killed—he's old enough to remember the scared seven-year-old orphan I was when the Queen sent me to live with him and his father. Ever since then, he's watched over me like an older brother.

But as the Queen's champion, I rank higher than any other fae in Bright, including him. Which gives me the power to override his wishes, and as much as he worries, I know he understands my choice.

As we near the border, I scan the glitter field that forms our first line of defense.

It's a three-mile-wide field that stretches along the entire border between Bright and Fell country.

Every blade of glitter grass is made of a tall, crystal stem with a tiny glass bulb of a different color at its top. The bulbs are no bigger than my pinky finger.

In the moonlight, the grass is deceptively pretty, but when disturbed, no matter how gently, the grass hums. Even a humblebee landing on a glitter bulb would make the bulb sing.

And when bumped... the explosion of sharp fragments cuts down anything in its path.

Sailing across it, Treble's lightning casts flickers of light that reflect off the glitter field, creating rainbows of color in the otherwise dark sky around us.

It's a beautiful display as we finally cross the border.

Up ahead, a faint swirl of movement within the dense fog draws my attention to a group of trees on my right.

"Treble," I whisper, leaning close to his neck. "Take me down."

He understands my instructions, even if he can't speak back to me.

Shifting my weight in that direction, I lean low, prepared for the sudden drop as he soars safely clear of the glitter field and dives toward the muddy ground at the edge of the trees.

I take my last breath of fresh air and brace for the cold mist that envelops me as we descend. The trees are sparse, their silhouettes like misshapen bones jutting from the ground, so there's plenty of room for Treble to land and fold up his wings.

Evander won't like that I've disappeared from sight, but Treble can make a cracking sound with his wings if I need help. After all, the thunderous sound his wings make is how the thunderbirds got their name.

Sliding from Treble's back, I drop softly to the ground, sensing the mud squelch up around my boots. My heart hurts every time I see these trees, victims of the darkness around them. If they grew in Bright, they would be nurtured and lush with emerald leaves.

I remain at Treble's side, one hand resting on his neck, pressing a little—the signal that I want him to dim his lightning now.

Even though I want to make my presence known, I don't want every aspect of my armor, or my concealed weapons, to be visible.

My armor covers my body from the top of my neck to my ankles, extending down beneath my calf-high boots, which are made from a similar light-absorbing material.

My head and face are also completely covered with a hood and a facemask that allows me to breathe as well as to see out, while others can't see in.

I take a moment to survey the area, waiting for the movement I saw before to repeat itself.

The fog shifts again. This time near an oak tree whose branches are pulled to one side as if it once battled a gale force wind and lost.

I twist sharply in the direction of the movement, pretending to stumble a little as I turn.

"Who's there?" I call, injecting a tremble into my voice to make myself sound more vulnerable.

I wait as the silence stretches.

Hmm. This Fell wants me to come to it.

The Fell creatures are not 'him' or 'her' to me. I'm not even sure if they have genders. They present as fae-like in shape: standing upright with two legs, two arms, a head, and most importantly a neck, which is their most vulnerable spot.

But they always conceal their faces and bodies in the fur of slaughtered animals—the face of a fox, the skin of a wolf, the claws of a bear.

I touch them as little as possible, never trying to see their faces, and never using my power on them in case I become tainted by the contact.

It's an unbreakable rule of combat: We never use our power around the Fell. Darkness lives within them, so much darkness that even standing in their presence is like teetering at the edge of a bottomless pit without a single spark of light in it.

Taking a careful step away from Treble, I deliberately place my foot on a brittle-looking twig, exaggerating a twitch when it cracks in the silence.

I pause, but the sharp sound doesn't draw the Fell out.

I want the creature to come to me. The fact that it hasn't tells me it's smarter than most.

What I don't know for sure is how many there are. Sensing one Fell's darkness is the same as sensing many. I can handle ten on my own. Any more than that could be a problem.

Step by step, I make my way toward the tree's outstretched branches, my hand brushing my hip and the liquid dagger that is melded to the side of my armor. A sword, also liquid, rests across my left shoulder.

The Fell won't know I carry weapons until I pull the sword and dagger off my armor and they solidify in my hands.

With every move I make, I expect the creature to leap out at me. "Show yourself!" I call.

Still nothing.

I stop three paces from the tree's trunk and sigh into the dark fog. I've stepped beyond the circle of Treble's light now, and the mist is thicker here.

I can see only two paces in front of myself, and after that, my surroundings are murky. The creature could be four paces away, and I wouldn't know it.

Five seconds pass as I remain in position. I count out each moment while the silence remains so complete that I wonder if I imagined the movement before.

Maybe the darkness is only that.

The shifting fog could have been a moth beating its wings. While Bright has butterflies of every color, giant moths live in Fell country with wings as wide as a crow's.

I press my hand against the tree's coarse bark.

A shiver runs through me on contact.

Despite the eternal fog in which it grows, the tree is alive. I don't have an affinity with nature like the Springtime fae do, but I sense the life I'm touching. It isn't flourishing like it would in Bright, but the air around it is...

My forehead creases. I'm confused by what I sense in the fog. A presence that's stronger than it should be.

Bravery. Resilience. Unwavering determination.

Oh... damn.

What I sense has nothing to do with the tree.

My gaze shoots left just in time.

I duck, barely avoiding the sharp blade that slices through the mist and lodges in the tree with a *thud.*

My eyes widen as I identify the gleaming weapon. It's a halberd. Two sharp blades sit on opposite sides of a pole that's the height of a fae.

The blade embedded in the tree is curved, while the blade on this side of the pole is a wicked spike that can be used like a dagger.

It's undoubtedly a warrior's weapon. The Fell creatures I encountered before never carried a weapon like this.

Jumping back, I reach for my shoulder, drawing my sword. It peels off my body and solidifies just as the Fell creature rips its weapon from the tree.

His dagger slices through the air toward me, though the Fell's body remains concealed in the fog.

I duck again. The blade follows my path as if its wielder anticipated my move, sweeping downward.

My sword clangs against it in a defensive move, preventing the blade from impaling the top of my head.

I prepare for more blows, but the creature pulls the weapon back and finally steps from the mist, gripping the halberd in two enormous hands that match the proportions of the rest of his body.

I've been trained to assess my enemy within a fraction of a second, to make decisions in the space of a heartbeat, and to swing my sword even faster, but when the fog parts to reveal my attacker, I freeze.

The Fell creature stands taller than the average fae, his broad shoulders held back and bare arms corded with muscles that glisten with dew. Stealthy and light on his feet despite his bulk.

Black leather pants cover his powerful thighs and legs, while a charcoal-gray fur pelt rests across his shoulders and falls down his back, drawn together at his chest by a golden chain.

Strands of walnut brown hair fall past his ears, accentuating his strong jaw, which is shadowed with growth across his jawline. His full lips are drawn down in unforgiving determination, and his brown eyes carry no hint of mercy.

He.

It is definitely a *he.*

He isn't covered up like the Fell usually are, and his face is more striking than most fae.

Without taking his eyes off me, he reaches across his chest and unclasps the pelt, balancing the heavy halberd in one hand and allowing the pelt to drop to the ground before he rapidly closes the gap between us.

He can't be a Fell. Surely.

He is far too strong. Far too beautiful...

Far too un-*creature*-like.

His weapon swings at my chest and my senses return to me in a rush.

As my training kicks in, I block the strike with my sword.

I fight back hard, my weapon clashing with his in a quick succession of hits. When he attempts to drive his halberd into my neck, I lunge forward, blocking with my sword while snatching my dagger from my hip.

I push against his halberd, then drive the dagger toward his stomach, a savage move that will disembowel him.

He shocks me by pulling my dagger arm farther forward, harmlessly past his side, while at the same time pushing my sword arm back so far that my shoulder nearly dislocates.

A scream rises to my mouth as I end up plastered against his alarmingly bare chest.

I've never come this close to touching a Fell, not skin on skin.

Shockwaves scatter through me as he continues to push against my sword arm and simultaneously wrenches my dagger arm even further forward, forcing me so close to him that my head spins.

I need to escape, but it's more than just needing to survive.

He smells like burnt caramel, a startling scent that dulls my senses and confuses my fighting instincts.

Curse the stars. He smells like comfort food, with a strong dash of bravery smothered in determination.

Desperate to get away from him, I kick his knee.

I can't get my leg up enough to do any damage, but it propels me away from him and his distracting scent. It also forces me to abandon my dagger, which drops to the ground with a soft crackle on the dead leaves.

That's okay. I still have my sword.

He doesn't attempt to pick up my dagger, instead lunging at me, the dagger side of his halberd arching toward one side of my face and then the other as I dart left and right to avoid the blows, my mind working fast to plan my next move.

I sense Treble's growing agitation, his twitching talons squelching in the mud. His glowing form is a dim blob of light ten paces to my right, growing brighter as he shifts closer. I won't call for him unless I really need him, and I'm certainly not defeated yet.

I retaliate with a quick succession of deft stabs that would gut, dismember, and behead any other Fell, but this one skillfully blocks each blow, matching my speed and strength to swiftly push me farther away from the oak tree.

Another set of misshapen branches enters my field of view as the Fell backs me toward the next tree.

With a final swing and shove of his halberd, he locks it against my sword, turning his weapon into a prong.

Forcing me hard up against the tree, he pins my sword against its trunk while the length of the shaft allows him to stay outside the reach of my fists.

My chest heaving, I struggle to free my weapon, but he was clever. He caught my sword across the grip and beneath the cross-guard so I can't slide my weapon downward to free it.

My only option is to reach across with my left hand, grab it by the blade, and risk slicing open my hand when I pull it upward. It's a choice between wounding myself on my own blade or abandoning my weapon altogether.

My breathing is rapid, but my facemask is designed to handle my quick inhales.

If I lose the use of my hand, I'll be in a worse position, so I let go of my sword and launch myself forward, counting on the moment it will take him to wrench his weapon from the tree.

He dodges the fist I aim at his face, the kick at his stomach, and the next fist at his chest, all while hanging on to his weapon.

Damn. He's agile.

I try another kick, but before I can get my leg up, his free arm whips around my stomach and forces me up against the tree again.

The breath whooshes from my chest so fast that my vision blurs.

He finally lets go of the halberd, but a silver blade glints in his other hand, this one much smaller, not much more than a knife I'd use to peel fruit.

Where the stars did that come from?

"You wanted me to show myself," he says. "So I did. Now you can do me the same courtesy."

His voice is deep, like the growl that the old Vanem Dragon makes when he's angry. It tells me that this Fell creature isn't used to being disobeyed.

It occurs to me then that the jabs he'd made at the sides of my face might have been intended to cut through my mask, not injure me. He also used the flat of his arm to push me back against the tree instead of his fist, which could have knocked me out.

He wants me to remove my mask. In fact, he commanded it.

Except that it's in my nature to rebel against the things I can't control.

I struggle and kick with my legs as he continues to pin me against the tree with the entire length of his body. He's much stronger than any other Fell I've fought, and I feel like a butterfly batting against him.

Before I can stop him, he slips his free hand around the clasp holding my facemask and hood in place and wrenches them apart.

Sour air rushes in, and my hair escapes, untwining like a coiled snake across my left shoulder. The angry movement he made ensures that his fingers tangle in my hair, tugging on the white strands while his knife hovers on the other side of my face in a perfect position to cut my cheek.

As my eyes meet his, he sucks in a sudden breath, freezing so completely that his fist clenches painfully against my scalp.

Up close, I can see the flecks in his eyes, dark and inky. The scent of caramel is nearly overwhelming as his body continues to press against mine, covering every inch of me.

I need to scream. I have to call for help now. He's fought me like no other Fell before him.

It's time to admit that I can't fight him alone.

Sound forms in my throat just as a glow brightens the corner of my vision. It's so vivid that I blink rapidly, swallowing my cry, puzzled about where the light's coming from.

It's not coming from him, and it's not a reflection off his blade. It's not even Treble—it's a brighter white than Treble's sapphire lightning and it grows brighter with every tense second that stretches between the Fell and me.

The Fell's gaze flickers from my face to the spot where he fists my hair. He's looking directly into the light, which confuses me because that would mean the light is coming from the spot where he's touching me.

For a second, his grip eases and his fingertips gently brush my scalp. The tense lines of his expression soften, but just as quickly, his lips twist into an angry line, and his forehead creases in a fierce scowl.

He slides his fingers free, splaying them wide as if he's trying not to touch me any more than he has to.

The light fades as he steps away without hurting me, which confuses me even more.

Pacing back from me, he shakes his head, a quick jerk as if he's trying to rid himself of an unwanted thought. His blade arm lowers, and he doesn't reach for the halberd plunged securely into the tree.

His voice grates in the air. "Your beauty is lethal."

I blink at him.

I should be fighting back now that he released me, but... nobody has ever called me beautiful before. My hair is too white —too much like an old fae's—my jaw is too strong, and my eyes are a dull forest green, not bright like other fae's eyes.

What I lack in appearance, I seek to make up for with tenacity.

My people call me fierce. Single-minded. Unapproachable. Cold. Or more simply... *champion.*

"What do your people call you?" I demand to know, wondering if the Fell have names.

He doesn't answer me, his focus suddenly on my lips, but his expression grows more ferocious with every heartbeat.

Suddenly, the fact that he backed off feels like a dangerous thing.

He twists his blade in the air, and my stomach turns with it.

I know without a doubt that he could cause just as much damage with that tiny knife as he could with the heavy halberd he abandoned.

His voice is dangerously soft as he says, "If you want to live, you should scream for your people now."

CHAPTER 2

I won't let him beat me.

I'm the Queen's champion, for star's sake.

What if he'd crept into the Queen's chamber? Could I have stopped him from killing her?

I grit my teeth and narrow my eyes.

Of course I could have.

I just need to remember why I'm here: to kill this Fell.

My legs burst into action and I run straight for him, my hair flying out behind me as I duck, roll, and sail under his swinging knife arm. My hand closes around my dropped dagger, my movements faster than his as I spin, still kneeling, and slash at the back of his calves.

He jumps away from me, avoiding the blow just in time, but before he can turn and retaliate, I plant my free hand on the ground and kick the back of his left knee.

His leg buckles and he drops with a shout.

I leap toward him from behind. My arms sweep around his shoulders and my foot remains pressed against the back of his calf, pinning his knee to the ground while my chest rests against his spine.

My dagger kisses his neck and my free hand tangles in his hair.

A single swipe will kill him.

"Drop your knife!" I order him.

His response is an angry rumble. "No."

I will kill him all the same. "You're braver than most of your kind."

My muscles twitch, ready to sever his neck when he asks, "Am I braver than my mother?"

His mother? I pause, not sure how to respond, my thoughts whirling. Fell must have family, but I never really considered whether or not they have the capacity to love.

Did his mother try to cross our border? Does she lie in a muddy grave beneath the trees where the Border Guards would have buried her?

Did *I* kill her?

My hesitation lasts only a heartbeat, but it's a mistake.

His right hand grabs my knife arm, wrenching it wide as he drops his body and uses the forward momentum to fling me off his back. I land with a crunch, rolling to my feet to see him pitch his knife into the mud.

My eyes fly wide as he raises his fingers to his lips and whistles.

It's the exact whistle I use to call Treble to me when I need him.

The shrill sound cuts the heavy silence around us.

Treble's reaction is like a kneejerk. His glowing form jolts upward in the distance. His lightning spears through the air so brightly that it pierces the fog in all directions, flooding the clearing with light.

Suddenly, everything within fifty feet is visible.

15

His wings rise and fall with a sharp *crack*.

The sound is loud enough to be heard from the sky. Even the distant glitter grass vibrates so hard that its discordant hum scrapes my hearing.

I jump to my feet, my hand shooting toward Treble to stop him from flying to me. I don't know what the Fell is up to and I don't want my thunderbird to be hurt. "Treble! Stay back."

I'm grateful when Treble obeys, but his arched neck and wild eyes tell me he's agitated beyond belief.

I spin to face the Fell.

He gives me a smile that contains no humor, only deadly intent. "I told you to call your people."

I take a step toward him, my blade gripped securely in my hand. "You *want* the Bright Ones to come? Are you mad?"

"Maybe I am," he says. "Losing a loved one makes me do crazy things."

He must be suicidal. He must have come here intending to dig himself a grave.

But why not die by my blade?

His actions don't make sense and that makes him dangerous.

I keep my distance as he steps into the center of the clearing, making himself completely visible.

The cracks of wings and rainbow of lightning filling the sky above us tells me that a squadron of thunderbirds will be upon the Fell in fewer than sixty seconds.

I use my time wisely, slapping my dagger to my hip, where it liquifies and sticks again, then I sprint to the tree where my sword is pinned. I follow a wide arc to avoid the Fell, more confused when his gaze follows me, but he doesn't attempt to stop me.

Nothing this Fell does makes sense.

Wrenching the halberd from the tree, I quickly retrieve my

sword, slap it against my left shoulder, where it liquifies, and decide to take his weapon too since he hasn't stopped me.

I don't have much time to study it, but the curved blade is shiny and etched with a circular symbol I don't recognize. One side is curved like a moon while the other is splayed like the rays of the sun.

This weapon is nothing like the rusty knives the Fell usually carry.

Evander's thunderbird appears above us first, spearing toward the ground a second ahead of the rest of the squadron. Cadence's deep red wings shoot wide, blood-red lightning crackling in the air as she slows her fall a moment before Evander leaps from her back.

He will have assessed the situation from the sky.

Even though he's concealed in armor from head to toe, it's easy to tell it's him since he's the only man in the Border Guard.

He isn't as muscular as the Fell, but Evander is built for speed, his indigo armor sucking at the brightness around us as two daggers solidify in his hands and he runs straight at the Fell.

Behind him, nine more thunderbirds drop into the clearing in rapid succession, their female riders leaping from their backs one by one in a swift beat while the birds rise again. It's an efficient, practiced move that allows each rider to jump to the ground without colliding with the one before it. Treble is the only bird that remains on the ground.

The Fell braces as Evander runs toward him, crouching as if he's about to break into a sprint, but he doesn't try to retrieve his knife.

Instead, he turns his hands palms up and blows softly across his fingertips—an odd move—before he clenches his fists and appears to wait for impact.

I stay well back, holding my breath for the inevitable conclusion to the Border Guard's attack: another dead Fell. My only regret is that I couldn't kill him myself.

At the last possible moment before Evander reaches him, the Fell leaps sideways, launching into a run that allows him to evade Evander's attack. Evander's blade slices across the Fell's bicep, but the cut must not be deep because the Fell keeps running.

My jaw drops as the Fell sprints straight at the landing women, his arms pumping. He leaps toward the first one while she's still reaching for her sword. He opens his fist and shoves his hand against her masked face.

To my shock, she screams, jolts backward, drops her sword, and falls to the ground, convulsing so violently in the mud that sludge splatters up around her. Smoke rises from her mask as it melts off her cheek.

The Fell darts between the next two women, ducking their weapons, shoving them, one on her knee, the other on her thigh. They immediately drop, screaming, their armor melting where he touched them.

What is he doing to them? He didn't hurt me like that when he touched me.

I drop the halberd and break into a run, seconds behind Evander, as the other women converge on the Fell, who continues to dart between them, dodging their blades while succeeding in knocking into them.

Evander spins as I catch up to him. He hooks his arm around my waist and yanks me to a stop so abruptly that he lifts me off my feet.

In the distance, the Fell spins, glancing back, and his eyes narrow as his gaze rakes over Evander and me. In the next second, he's moving again, focusing on the attacking women.

Evander shouts through his facemask. "No, Aura! Stay back. You have to fight tomorrow. You can't get hurt tonight or you'll be weak." He puts me firmly on the ground. "Our people need you. Let me handle this."

His voice holds an accusation and I hear what he's *not* saying: I should have let him handle it from the beginning. I shouldn't have come out to the border, let alone chosen to be the prey tonight.

Regret passes through me. I needed to get away from the palace and all the politics of the Winter Ascending. I needed to stop thinking about tomorrow, so I escaped out here to do what I do best: fight.

It was selfish. A moment of weakness.

Now Evander's worried about me. I'm a distraction he didn't need. No other fae would grab me like he did, but he's behaving like a brother, not a warrior, right now.

Still, I argue with him. "I can help. I can kill him if I use my power."

"Do not! We can't use our power or we'll be contaminated by the creature's darkness," he warns me. "You know the rules. We kill him with our weapons and that's all."

His voice lowers to an angry order. I can practically feel the glare in his eyes. "Now stay here."

I grit my teeth, swallowing my frustration, and give him a curt nod. I've already delayed him from the fight for too long.

Evander doesn't waste another moment, racing after the Fell, who has sent four more women screaming to the ground. They convulse in the mud while only two women remain standing.

I'm torn between needing to watch Evander—and trying to help the women who have fallen.

Trusting that Evander can take care of himself, I break his order to stay exactly where he left me, hurrying to the first woman where she lies in the sludge. She's far enough away from the fight that Evander won't worry that I'm trying to edge my way back into the battle.

Treble shifts to stand beside me, clawing his way through the mud to lower his head to the fallen woman.

I stop him before he can touch her. "No, Treble. We don't know what's wrong with her."

The woman stops trembling just as I drop to my knees beside her.

Her facemask has peeled away from one side of her face. A burn mark the size of my thumb stretches across her exposed cheek, red like berries around the edges but quickly turning black in the middle. It must be some kind of acid. Maybe poison, or some combination of both.

Her eyes are wide open, staring skyward, unseeing. The rise and fall of her chest tells me she isn't dead. She's in some kind of trance.

Careful not to touch her in case the poison passes to me, I hover my hand above her face, cautiously drawing on my power.

My palm warms and a glow emits from my fingertips, the smallest glimmer of starlight.

I have to be very careful. My power can rapidly progress from illuminating to deadly depending on the force with which I call it. Right now, I want to shine a light into the darkness of her mind and calm her.

As the glow from my fingertips lights up her face, her rapid breathing eases and the pained crease in her forehead disappears. My starlight can ease whatever pain she's feeling until we can get her to our healers.

Switching my focus to the other fallen women, I'm startled to see that the remaining two women lie on the ground, and the Fell now holds Evander's sword.

How the stars did he get it?

He beats Evander back through the mud with fierce cuts aimed at Evander's chest and neck.

Evander stumbles.

My eyes widen to see a burned patch of armor across Evander's shoulder, which must mean he was burned when the Fell took his sword.

Evander's still upright. He's fighting the poison, and he still controls his two daggers, but the Fell's attacks are swift and decisive. I've fought enough battles to know lethal intent when I see it.

The Fell may have left the women alive, but he'll kill Evander.

I break into a run just as the Fell stabs Evander's left hand, forcing him to drop one of his daggers. The sword moves in flashes, wrenching from Evander's hand and arching toward his heart.

Evander's other arm swings, sluggish now, but his shorter dagger is aimed at the Fell's heart. He'll take the death blow through his own chest as long as he kills the creature at the same time.

"No!" I launch myself at the Fell, knocking into his side and pushing him off course.

His sword flies wide, missing Evander. Even though I dig in my heels to stop myself falling on him, I'm now dangerously within stabbing distance myself.

From the corner of my eye, Evander drops to the ground with a heavy thud. His eyes are open but unseeing as the poison finally takes control.

I have to help him!

All thoughts of battle strategy fade into the background and survival becomes paramount. I'm surrounded by my fallen people. This Fell is stronger and faster than all of them.

Curse the stars; he's stronger and faster than me.

I'm done following the rules. No matter what poison he was using to defeat my people, he doesn't have my power.

Darkness be damned.

If I don't stop this Fell, he'll find a way into the Queendom and destroy everything I love like his people did before.

Clenching my fists, I take two quick steps into the danger zone right in front of him and allow the light inside me to surge to lethal levels.

Across the way, Treble senses the danger and takes to the sky with a cracking swoosh of his wings, leaving us in foggy darkness once more.

"I am the Queen's champion!" I shout. "I will fight you with my whole heart until one of us is dead!"

The Fell's eyes widen.

His focus shoots to my glowing hand. The color drains from his face, pure shock filling his features.

He drops Evander's sword. His hand flies out in a defensive move.

"No!" he shouts. "Don't do it!"

I'm already leaping toward him.

As my open palm shoots out, so does his.

He touches me a split second before I can touch him.

CHAPTER 3

*H*is hand is like fire.

It lands on my chest right above my heart, the poison melting my armor instantly. But when his palm sinks against my bare skin... it doesn't burn me.

A confusingly blissful, warm sensation spreads across my chest. His palm is calloused and rough, but oddly soothing, even though it grates against me as his entire hand presses against me, skin to skin.

I don't feel the poison, don't feel like I'm losing control.

In fact, it's almost like... I feel more in control in this moment than ever before.

My wide eyes meet his, my reactions to his touch spilling through my body in flashes.

Far too quickly, the warm sensation vanishes and a painful sucking sensation fills my heart, as if my power is being dragged to the surface faster than I was calling it, rushing out of me at full force.

It doesn't hurt.

It feels like I'm breaking free.

Starlight explodes between us, the force pushing outward and upward, flinging us apart and up off the ground.

A scream of fear tears from my chest, my hair and arms splay at my sides, and my back arches.

I'd meant to touch him, spear my power through him and contain it. Now, the explosion crashes across everyone, including my friends.

The clearing lights up around us. Every dark whorl of bark on the tree trunks is illuminated, the struggling leaves glisten and uncurl, the mud turns slick like molten chocolate, and the fog recedes, revealing all the harshness of the barren plain.

The fallen fae are pushed away from me in the force, their bodies rolling through the mud, some of them thudding against the trees.

Opposite me, the Fell is forced up into the air like me. His fists are clenched at his sides and his head is tipped back while droplets of blood lift and suspend at his side where Evander cut his arm.

He lowers his eyes to mine, his dark gaze more piercing than the starlight shimmering around us.

A second later, my power implodes, pulling us back toward each other, dragging me to the earth. I crash onto my knees as the Fell drops to the ground right in front of me.

My power didn't hurt him. It didn't hurt my friends, either, and I don't understand why. I've never used it like that before. I was sure the explosion would kill anyone standing within the blast radius.

The Fell's chest rises and falls rapidly. His fists clench and unclench. A single drop of sweat slides down his face to his jaw.

I can't seem to move my arms and legs, sinking deeper into the mud as I struggle to regain control.

Then I shiver and it seems to break the spell.

"Damn," he whispers.

He gives himself a shake, the same sharp twitch that he made when he seemed to drive back an unwanted thought—except that this time it seems to really worry him.

He drops to the side as if his legs aren't working properly yet, either, clawing at the dirt as he grapples to push himself upward.

As soon as he gets his feet under himself, he stumbles across the distance, grabs Evander's dropped sword, and positions it right over Evander's heart.

From this distance, there's nothing I can do to stop him.

"You have a decision to make, Starlight," he says. "If you want to save your friends, you will do exactly what I tell you to do."

I can't lose Evander. He's my family. Inside my mind, I scream at my legs to move, finally regaining sensation in my arms. I drop forward, digging my fingers into the earth as I try to push myself upward like the Fell did.

Failing dismally, I raise my head. "I will never betray my queen."

"You're saying that because you think you can save him," the Fell replies, inclining his head at Evander. "Even if I stab him through the heart, you believe your healers can bring him back. But he won't survive without his head."

He shifts the sword to point it at Evander's throat. The Fell's muscles bunch. One look at him tells me he's strong enough to drive the weapon all the way through Evander's throat and sever his spine.

"Evander would prefer to die," I scream, thumping my fist into the mud. "I will never do what you want."

The Fell gives me a slow shake of his head, pressing the sword's tip lightly to Evander's throat. My heart stops as a trickle of blood leaks from the cut he makes.

"You're bluffing," the Fell says. "You called him by his name. He means something to you."

Without warning, he raises the sword and rams it downward.

My scream turns into a sob when the weapon thuds into the earth, missing Evander's neck.

Leaving the weapon where it thrums in the ground, the Fell strides over to me, kneels, and holds up his palms.

Each of his fingertips has what looks like a black bubble on it. The bubbles are all burst and black liquid smears his hands.

"The fluid inside these bubbles is poisonous to fae," he says. "There's nothing your healers can do. My hands carry the revenge that is rightfully mine. A spell concealed the poison, which could only be revealed by the breath of the avenger."

The breath of the avenger.

It's old magic. I know hardly anything about the ancient times, but it's the kind of magic that can only be conjured by the most deeply held conviction.

The poisonous bubbles weren't visible on his fingertips when I started fighting him. I thought it was strange when he blew across his hand when Evander first attacked, but that must have been how he revealed the poison.

"That's dark magic," I spit.

His expression turns hard, a muscle in his jaw clenching as he grits his teeth. "Dark magic is the only magic the Bright Ones left the humans."

I glare at the unfamiliar word. "Humans? What is that?"

"Not *what*," he roars, making me jump. "*Who*."

His closed fist thuds against his chest. "You call us fallen ones. The *Fell*. We are humans. You left us in darkness, but we are capable of both darkness and light."

He shoves his hands at me, shifting so close that I could grab him. It's the first recklessly emotional move he's made. "My hands contain both death and life. Beneath these outer bubbles is another layer of spells. I carry the antidote for the poison. I can save your friends... if you do as I ask."

My thoughts churn as I try to think of a way out. Trying to buy time, I ask, "How long do they have?"

"About two hours before they die."

That means time is now my enemy.

I consider the scene around me as the Fell's plan becomes clear. He wanted the squadron to come and help me so he could turn them into leverage. He didn't kill me so that I would become his pawn.

I grit my teeth, testing my legs as sensation returns slowly to them. "What do you want?"

"Simple," he says. "Take me to your Queen."

I stare at him. He must be mad. I laugh. "That is *not* simple."

"All I want is to speak with her."

I scoff. "The Queen will kill you before you say a word."

He shakes his head. "She won't."

What makes him so sure? What could he say that would save his life? Once Evander and the others are healed, this Fell is a dead... *human.*

I struggle to my feet, finally in control of all of my limbs.

I'm not afraid that he will kill me. He needs me as much as I need him, but my heart constricts with fear for other reasons.

I've touched him multiple times, even tried to use my power on him, and I have no idea what the consequences will be.

Luckily, none of the other fae were awake to see me do it or my position as champion would be in question now. It is the nature of my people—the Bright Ones—to fear darkness and I have come closer to it than any of them.

I have risked contamination...

As my heart pounds, I try to rein in my anxiety. "I'll take you to her on one condition."

"Name it," he says.

"You have to come as my prisoner."

He looks up at me, still on his knees. "You mean in chains."

"Yes."

"If that's what it takes." He swiftly stands and holds out his hands, placing his wrists side by side.

I consider him warily. He agreed far too quickly and, despite my demand, I don't have any chains or rope. We never take prisoners, so we never bring bindings.

There's only one way to tie his hands, but it's dangerous…

Making a decision, I give him a clipped order. "Come with me."

He isn't so quick to agree this time. "Where?"

I point. "To the glitter field."

"No." He shakes his head at me, his brown hair slicking to his neck. He gives me a wry laugh. "The most beautiful things in Bright are the most lethal. That includes you and your glitter field. I don't have any choice but to go with you."

He jabs his finger in the direction of the field. "But I will not go near that."

I scowl at him. "If you won't go near it, how do you intend to come with me to the Queen?"

He tips his head at the sky. Above us, Treble's light mingles with the waning moonlight. Sunrise is only an hour away now.

"You'll fly me there," he says.

Of course it's the only way. I didn't expect him to walk through the glitter field, but I also don't want to face the idea of riding so close to him all the way back to the palace.

Luckily, Treble is one of the largest thunderbirds and is strong enough to carry two riders.

Still, I grit my teeth. "I need to gather bindings from the field. If I don't bring you back as my captive, then I'll be branded as a traitor and we'll both be killed on sight."

He studies me for a moment, his forehead creased in disbelief. "Your own people would kill you?"

"The Fell haven't stepped foot in Bright for fifteen years. I'm taking a big risk as it is. My friends' lives are in your hands. Now come with me."

Before I can stalk ahead of him, he narrows his eyes at me, spins, and breaks into a quick stride, clearly not the type to trail after me like a puppy.

I scowl at his broad back.

My scrutiny intensifies when I see that his shoulders at the top of his arms are crisscrossed with scars. They're fine ones. Set apart at precise intervals in a hatched pattern that indicates they were deliberately inflicted.

I catch up to him and keep pace at his side, making sure our arms don't touch. He said we have two hours. It will take a whole hour to make it back to Eteri City and by then, it will be daybreak. If I'm lucky, Queen Imatra will already be awake and eating breakfast in her Inner Sanctuary.

We walk in silence, but the quiet doesn't bother me. The distant hum from the glitter field is soothing on my nerves.

The Fell slows as we near the glitter fronds. "This is as close as I go," he says, his dark scowl daring me to contradict him.

For a moment, I wonder... *who is he?* He didn't tell me his name and I didn't tell him mine. We're strangers and yet... he beat me when nobody ever has. What really gets me is that he beat me without actively trying to kill me.

I take deep breaths to calm my nerves. If I weren't so certain that I needed to chain him, I would never do what I'm about to do.

"Stay here then," I whisper. "Don't make another sound."

When he remains quiet, I tread carefully toward the field. The waist-height glitter fronds sway as I approach them, glowing brightly in the dark.

I take a careful look around, checking the sky in case there are any other fae flying above us. I can't let anyone see what I'm about to do.

The Fell is right about the field. It's lethal to everyone.

What he doesn't know—what nobody knows—is that it isn't lethal to me.

For some reason, the glitter field responds to my needs. I could run toward it and it would part to let me through. Anyone else would be cut to shreds.

It's a secret I've kept since I discovered it when I was a teenager. Not even Evander knows about it.

I take another deep breath before I lower myself carefully to the ground and reach for the nearest stem, gently leveraging it from the earth. Its roots come up easily. As soon as it leaves the earth, the stem transforms from rigid crystal to living material, becoming soft in my hands.

Pulling it close to my body to conceal my actions, I run my hand over the bulb at the top of the stem to remove it, brushing my fingers over the petals as the bulb turns from fragile crystal to soft living material in my fingertips. I quickly slide the removed bulb between two upright stems to hide it on the ground.

The stem I plucked is strong and malleable in my hands. It looks like an ordinary vine now. If someone asks, I can say that I pulled it off one of the trees.

Returning to the Fell, I hold up the vine. "Give me your hands."

He lifts them without a word, casting wary glances at the glitter field.

I hesitate before I reach for him. The poison is still on his fingers. I can only assume that it didn't hurt me before because I released my power when he touched me.

As if he reads my thoughts, he presses his palms inward so there's no chance I'll touch them.

I quickly wrap the vine around his wrists, securing it in a knot, managing to avoid any physical contact while I do it.

His gaze burns me as he watches me work.

I step back, my forehead creased. I sense he could easily slip the knot, but that he won't.

I shouldn't feel intrigued right now, shouldn't care about his motives, but for a warrior like him to agree to be bound proves that he will do whatever it takes to speak with Queen Imatra.

CHAPTER 4

*J*shake off my fears and focus on the task at hand. It's time to hurry home before my time runs out.

I make an arc around the Fell as I stride back to my friends, lifting my fingers to my lips and giving a series of short, sharp whistles.

At my call, all eleven thunderbirds drop from the clouds above us. I sense their agitation. The bond between bird and rider is close. They will be concerned about their riders right now, but they're trained to follow orders.

I give another whistle and Evander's bird lands first, the light from her wings casting a bloody sheen over his body as she leans protectively over him, her eyes following the Fell as he walks more slowly behind me.

I can't help but run the rest of the way to Evander, my heart in my throat.

I'm done putting on an uncaring face for the Fell. I lean over Evander, dragging his torso into my arms before I hover my palm over his face and allow my power to glow across his features.

"Brother," I whisper. "Please be okay."

The agonized crease in Evander's forehead eases as my power soothes his mind. I wish I could see into his thoughts, tell him that I won't let him die.

The only way to get him back to the palace is to lift him onto his bird. Her talons aren't large enough to carry him, but at least she has a saddle that I can strap him into. I'm the only one who shuns the saddle.

Cadence spreads her right wing and extends it toward me. Normally, we either leap onto their backs or run lightly up their strong wing bones, but Evander's heavy, one of the biggest fae.

With great difficulty, I slide my arms under his underarms while facing him and lift him into a sitting position. Then I angle my shoulder under his stomach, gather my legs under myself, and haul him up across my shoulders like a sack of grain.

Rising very slowly, I wobble and strain to stay upright as his full weight settles on me.

The Fell's perplexed voice sounds beside me, closer than I anticipated.

I try to ignore his presence as his caramel scent fills my senses.

"Why don't you use your power to lift him?" he asks.

I huff as I wobble toward the bird's wing, my arms and legs burning with effort as I take the first step upward. "I don't have power over air."

I hear the uncertainty in his voice. "I thought every fae controlled all of the elements."

"You thought wrong," I snap.

"Then explain it to me."

I scowl, trying to concentrate on my task. Somehow, everything the Fell says sounds like an order. He's clearly used to bossing people around.

Still, talking takes my focus off the pain in my screaming muscles as I stumble another step. "Every fae belongs to one of two classes: Sunstream and Eventide. Sunstream fae have powers that reflect the seasons. Frost fae control wind and ice. Solstice fae control heat and fire. Springtime fae help grow crops and Harvest fae... well, you get the picture."

"What about the Eventide fae?" he asks.

I hesitate, since Eventide fae are more rare, and telling him about them means telling him more about myself.

"We control the elements of night and spirit," I say. "The Dusk fae can commune with animals, Dawn fae are healers, and Twilight fae—like me—control starlight."

"There's only one of you, Starlight," he says, sounding more certain than he should be. He shouldn't know anything about me.

He arches his eyebrow at me when I shoot him an angry glare.

I'm not about to confirm his statement.

I need to lean forward so Evander's weight doesn't tip me backward and it's making the muscles in my back and stomach scream.

"I can help you lift him," the Fell says, startling me with his offer.

My gaze snaps to the Fell. "You will not touch Evander again."

The Fell doesn't give up. "You called him 'brother.' He means something to you, Starlight. We need to move. This will go a lot faster if you let me help you."

"Stop calling me 'Starlight'!" I grit my teeth and focus on Evander's weight. "I'm Aura of the Lucidia."

He's quiet. "I know who you are."

I stare at him, my pain forgotten for a second.

How the stars does he know my name?

I snarl at him. "Then tell me your name so we're properly introduced."

His expression doesn't change, unmoved by my order. "Since you don't already know who I am... I can only speak my name to the Queen."

Swallowing my frustration, I finally reach the bird's back, my anger giving me strength to finish my task.

With a scream of effort, I slide Evander onto Cadence's back, gripping him tightly so he doesn't slip right off. I rest for a moment, my chest heaving, dragging air into my lungs, but I don't indulge in rest for long.

Quickly adjusting Evander's torso so he leans over the bird's neck, I maneuver his legs into the saddle and tie the waist strap tightly around him. It will cut into him and leave bruises, but I can't risk him falling off during the flight home.

Satisfied that he's tied on securely, I slide to the ground and give a quiet whistle so Cadence knows to rise into the air and wait for me.

Quickly calling the next bird, I hurry to the first fallen woman, repeating the process for the nine women until I'm covered in sweat.

Halfway through the process, I abandon decorum and peel my armor to my waist, allowing the sallow air to cool my skin. My armor is great for absorbing light and flexible for fighting in, but it's designed for quick aerial battles, not this kind of extended exertion.

Besides, I'm still well covered in a tight waist-length under-garment that covers my breasts completely.

While I work, the Fell picks up his fallen pelt and then his halberd, pulling on the pelt and securing it across his back with disconcerting ease despite his bound hands, before he grips his weapon firmly between his palms.

He takes up position leaning against the tree where he first took a swipe at me.

Every time I lift another fallen woman across my shoulders, he offers to help.

After the fifth one, I'm certain he's doing it to annoy me. He watches my reaction every time, observing my shifts from surprise to irritation.

I've never been good at hiding my emotions, so over the years, I've learned to feel nothing. This Fell is drawing every emotion out of me.

Including emotions I don't like.

He called me 'beautiful' and his genuine expression told me he meant it. Now his gaze follows me even though he remains right where he is and my heartbeat reacts in unwanted ways.

Half an hour later, when the final woman is safely strapped to her bird, my heart is racing for another reason. I've used up too much time.

Maybe I should have accepted his help...

The minute I slide from the bird's back and whistle for her to rise into the air, the Fell strides over to me. The way he grips his weapon despite his chains is incredibly disconcerting. He may as well not be bound.

I take a quick step away from him to keep my distance, but it's a reflexive, learned behavior. There are only two people I allow to come near me these days, both of whom I trust with my life: Evander and the Queen herself. I even keep my distance from Evander's father.

"We need to go," the Fell says.

Before I assume his concern is for my people, he continues. "Others are coming."

His gaze flicks back toward the gloom beyond the nearby trees. "We can't be here when they arrive."

CHAPTER 5

*T*ension sizzles off the Fell, the first real tension I've sensed from him.

Something about the Fell who are coming is putting him seriously on edge.

I'm not afraid of whatever Fell creatures are on their way, but currently, my goals align with his.

I give him a single nod and quickly whistle for Treble, who immediately dives from the clouds above us. The moment he lands, he expands his right wing and tips it to the ground.

"Leave your weapon behind," I order the Fell before I run lightly up Treble's wing and settle onto his back. "Come on."

The Fell shakes his head. "This weapon will save your life."

My life? I scowl at him. He is so full of riddles. Bringing a weapon like that seems like the worst thing he could do, but I don't have time to argue. I can always make him leave it outside the palace when we land.

He eyes Treble's wing before he presses his lips together, uncertainty passing across his face in a moment of brief hesitation. He's definitely psyching himself up right now. I hope it's not because he's afraid of heights.

I arch my eyebrow at him, impatient to be on our way.

He doesn't run like I did, taking careful steps up Treble's wing, his focus on Treble's face.

Treble curves his neck and gives me a perplexed look at the Fell's tiptoeing. It's like watching a dragon trying to creep over eggshells.

"You won't break his wing," I say to the Fell.

"Are you certain?" he asks. "I'm heavier than you."

He seems genuinely worried and I'm surprised by his concern for my thunderbird's welfare.

So is Treble, who can understand everything we say. His luminescent eyes blink softly before he nudges the Fell's back in a gesture that I'm certain is meant to be reassuring but seems to alarm the giant man, who hunches his shoulders over as if he could make himself lighter that way.

"I'm certain." Without thinking about it, I reach down for his bound hands, wrap my fingers around his wrists, and tug him toward me. "You said we have to hurry..."

My voice dies in my throat as white light grows between the back of his hand and my palm, spilling out between my fingers.

What the stars? Is that what happened when he curled his fingers into my hair?

His eyes meet mine. Despite the glow between us, he doesn't seem surprised. "You need to control your power," he says calmly, as if he were my damn mentor. "You've let your light shine many times now."

I jolt back to my seat, dropping his hand to break the contact.

He's wrong that I was controlling my power just now. I don't seem to have any say over what happens when his skin touches mine. I'm certainly not looking forward to what will happen when he's pressed against my back while we're in the air.

I quickly pull my armor back up over my arms to reduce the chances of skin-on-skin contact.

Despite my sudden withdrawal, he retains his balance, climbing the rest of the way and sliding in behind me. His presence at my back is like an enormous shadow dropping over me.

I twist so I can keep an eye on him. With careful movements, he folds his arms up in front of his chest, clutching the halberd between his chest and my back.

I eye the weapon from the corner of my eye. If the damn thing slips downward, it's sharp enough to cut through my armor and slice open my back.

His voice sounds at my ear as he finally settles against me. "I won't let my weapon hurt you."

I find myself relaxing before I remind myself what he is.

I snap at him. "That wasn't your attitude earlier."

I sense a satisfied smile in his voice. "You're strong enough to fight me, Starlight. Even if I wanted to, I couldn't hurt you."

I have no idea how to respond to what sounds like a cautious compliment. Scowling into space, I lean forward and whisper to Treble, "Rise, Treble. Take us safely home—and quickly. The other thunderbirds need to follow us."

It's only as I resume my upright position that I realize the Fell has politely drawn himself back from me.

It takes me a second to picture how close my backside must have been pressing against his groin when I leaned forward. Assuming Fell are anatomically the same as fae, my position would have been provocative to say the least.

A blush burns across my cheeks and I'm glad he can't see it.

Most fae are free with their bodies—even the Queen shares her bed with multiple partners—but the first time I had sex when I was fifteen I passed out afterward. I'd given my consent, but the physical act was like having all of the air sucked out of me and being left with nothing. Not the enjoyable experience I'd heard it could be.

I woke up alone and never tried it again. After that, I threw myself into my work as the Queen's champion, making it my excuse to remove myself from the revelry that other fae frequently indulge in.

I quell my embarrassment as the Fell settles against me again. The cool air eases the burn in my cheeks as we rise into the air.

Treble's wings crack and sizzle. I'm used to the sound—find it comforting—but the Fell flinches, edging closer to me, his muscles tensing as we leave the ground.

I'm honestly not sure that he won't be electrocuted, so I shout into the wind. "Stay close to me. My power will protect you."

I think.

I can't afford for him to die.

"Why don't you use a saddle?" he shouts.

"I don't like it," I murmur, not sure if he can hear me, but I'm done with shouting.

He lowers his voice to a soft rumble in my ear. "Just as well."

As Treble soars into the air, the fog shifts farther to our right.

The Fell was right about expecting company, but whoever's coming isn't close enough to be a problem for us before we're already sailing across the glittering border and up toward the clouds while the other ten thunderbirds stay close around us.

I check their riders carefully, watching for any sign that my friends might slip off, satisfied that they all appear secure.

Without my facemask and hood on, the wind rushes through my hair, whipping it around my face.

The Fell slowly relaxes behind me, the warm wooden weapon nestles against my back, and a few moments later, his fingers curl into my hair, catching the heavy length of it and coiling it at the base of my neck so it doesn't slap me.

I choose to believe that the glow growing at the edges of my vision is caused by Treble's lightning and not the contact between the Fell and me.

He remains silent for the first few minutes, but I sense when he tenses again.

"What is that?" he asks, his lips close to my ear as he curls forward. He can't point now that his hands are tangled in my hair as well as gripping his weapon.

I don't have to look to know what he's talking about.

We just flew past the burn site where my family died.

The dark scar and burned outpost are impossible to miss.

I can't keep the anger from my voice. "That's where your people killed my family."

He's silent and it's impossible to look back to see his expression.

Finally, his voice rumbles in my ear, as angry as mine. "Then it's also where your people betrayed my father."

His hand tugs on my hair, curling tighter and once again I'm reminded of what he is. How vulnerable I am to him right now.

The light around us increases with my sudden fear. I can't spend an hour riding with him like this while he's carrying a weapon at my back. He could double-cross me as soon as we reach the palace parapets where the birds land.

It wouldn't take much for him to kill me, jump to safety, and fight his way inside. He could be lying about carrying the antidote.

He could be lying about all of it.

He could be here to assassinate the Queen and I'm taking him right to her.

With lightning-quick movements, I grab his hands from behind my head and grip the halberd at the same time.

I tuck my knees to my chest, twist, and slide around to face him while holding on to his hands so he doesn't rip my hair out.

He blinks at me in surprise, his hands and weapon now pressing against my left breast, while his fingers remain tangled in my hair.

I need truths from him or I will have to kill him, even if it means killing Evander.

"Who was your father?" I demand to know.

He presses his lips together. Such perfect lips. So fae-like. *Too* fae-like.

I persist. "What is your name and why are you here?"

He narrows his eyes at me and shakes his head.

"Tell me or I'll tip you into the fields!" I threaten, my blood pounding.

My threat simply washes over him. He doesn't budge.

I gasp against the wind as Treble's lightning flickers across the Fell's strong features, casting him into shadow and then light. "Was your father a Bright One?"

Now he startles. "What in the name of the dark stars makes you think that?"

"You don't look like other Fell."

He laughs, a harsh sound. "How would you know what humans look like? You don't bother to look beneath our masks when you kill us."

"You all look like this?"

He leans forward, his dark eyes glittering. "Some human women are more beautiful than Bright Ones."

He's lying. He must be. "If that's true, why do you hide your faces and bodies inside the skin of animals?"

His jaw drops. "You really don't know?"

I give a sharp shake of my head.

My right hand finds my hip where my dagger rests. I'm not afraid to resort to the use of force to make him speak.

His lips twist. I read deeply controlled anger in every angle of his jaw and shoulders. He watches my movements and must know I'm considering using my weapon.

A hint of disappointment appears in his eyes, as if he hoped for more from me.

"The ones who hide their faces are sick," he says. "They're dying. They say goodbye to their families and then they come to the border to face your blades. The Ebon Rot kills them slowly. Your swords are fast."

"Ebon Rot?"

"It's an illness that disfigures and causes excruciating pain. It slowly sucks our lives away."

I can't tear my gaze away from his. "No." I shake my head in denial. "Your people come to attack us..."

"With rusty knives?" His gaze pierces me. "Weapons they can barely hold up because they're so weak?"

I search his eyes, looking for a lie. "They really come to die?"

"The Ebon Rot sets in at around forty years of age. It first appeared fifteen years ago after the final battle between our people. Now nobody escapes it." His lips suddenly twist. "Well, nobody except our King. Somehow he's still alive."

He shrugs, but it's anything but casual. "I have fifteen years before the Rot takes me. I plan on doing something useful with the time I have left."

Sitting back on my heels, I feel sick.

I never looked at the Fell I killed. I was *told* never to look at them. I can't even remember who told me that. Can't remember who told me never to touch the Fell, never look at them, that their darkness would corrupt me.

This Fell... this human... touches me and I...

Glow.

He says nothing. His expression is clear, the dew on his chest evaporated, the pelt he wears tucked neatly around him so it doesn't flap in the wind.

"I'll make you a promise, Starlight," he says, his gaze a heavy weight on me. "There are some things I can't tell you. But what I do tell you will be the truth."

CHAPTER 6

"Why would you promise me anything?" I ask, a bitter taste filling my mouth.

All those Fell I killed... I thought of them as nothing better than mud beneath my feet. But they were sick and dying. They wanted my sword.

"I kill your people," I say. "I would have killed you. Why would you tell me any truths?"

He shakes his head, but it's a slow movement and his voice is barely a murmur. "Too many reasons."

"Pick one."

His voice lowers to a sigh on the wind. "You give them a quick and clean death."

"How do you know? You said they come alone."

His lips press together in a quiet line. "Stories filter back. Sometimes family members follow them. They speak of a single female who rides a blue bird. They say you don't fly with the others and when you kill, your sword is efficient. Not all Bright Ones are so merciful."

I spiral through surprise to indignation. "The Border Guards don't torture—"

"Not anymore." He gives me an acknowledging nod, his gaze switching to Evander's bird. "Not since your brother took over."

I can't shake off my bitterness. "So you'll tell me the truth because I kill your people quickly."

"Not only that…" He shifts closer to me, daring to slide his legs beside mine. A fierce crease appears in his forehead. "Before he died, my father told me—"

A sharp whistle breaks through our conversation.

The Fell's focus snaps to a point behind me.

I twist as the sky above the mountain range lights up like a rainbow. Thunder rumbles across the sky. More thunderbirds!

They soar toward us and I recognize the bird speeding ahead of the others. I know every thunderbird in Bright. This one's wingspan is not as wide as some, but she's fast and nimble. Her feathers are white with burnished orange tips like flames. She was chosen to be part of the Queen's Night Guard because of her speed.

Her rider's hair is as indigo as her armor, tightly braided across her head, the dark blue color making her very pale blue eyes appear bright in comparison as she soars toward us.

She is Mia of the Dusk, the Captain of the Night Guard.

I can't call her my friend. I wish I could, but two years ago she challenged me for the position as Queen's champion and she lost. Since then, our relationship has been strained.

I slip to the side to face her, both of my legs hanging over one side of Treble's body. The Fell releases my hair, edging away from me and gripping his weapon. Whatever he was going to tell me is lost now.

"Commander Lucidia," Mia cries as her bird sweeps around to draw parallel with us. "The Queen needs you!"

My heart kicks inside my chest. I'm not normally away from

the Queen for this long. Not as late as dawn. Her Night Guard surrounds her to keep her safe while she sleeps. Her Day Guard watches over her during the daylight hours. Like the Border Guard, each group has its own captain, but I command all of them.

A quick glance tells me that most of the Night Guards have flown out to find me.

"What's wrong?" I shout.

"She needs your starlight—" Mia's eyes widen as her gaze sweeps across the Fell, her focus quickly darting to the riders lying across their birds.

As a Dusk Fae, she can easily speak with her thunderbird using her mind. I can't hear the command she gives it, but the bird suddenly arcs around while the other thunderbirds and riders from the Night Guard soar around us, each one positioning itself beside a wounded fae.

"What happened here?" Mia demands to know, her gaze landing on the Fell again.

I sense her confusion as well as her interest. Like me, she hasn't immediately identified him as a Fell.

If she had, she would have leaped across the space between us and tried to kill him already.

The only clue about his real identity is his pelt. Fae never kill animals for food or to use their skins.

But Mia's focus isn't on his clothing.

Her gaze follows his face down to his broad shoulders, chiseled chest, narrow waist, and muscular thighs.

Her head tilts, her expression a mix of bewilderment and fascination. Fae don't hide their interest in others. It's only after they commit to another fae at the Spring Pairing that they remain faithful and devoted to one fae for the rest of their lives.

Until then... everyone is fair game.

I glance at the Fell, wishing I knew his name, only to find

that he's glaring back at Mia as if she's the last thing he would ever touch—not that it's dissuading her. Mia is used to playing games to get what she wants.

I demand her attention. "We were attacked by a band of Fell across the border. They used dark magic to cast a spell on the riders. This one carries the antidote. It's the only way to revive the Border Guards."

I emphasize my words as I shout across the distance and level my gaze on her. "He is my prisoner."

As my declaration sinks in, Mia's face pales. "A Fell?" Her gaze darts along the length of his body again. "Surely not."

I grit my teeth and lean out into space, unafraid of the fall as I address her with as much severity as I can. "Captain Mia of the Dusk, you will ensure that the wounded Border Guards are escorted safely to the palace so we can heal them. As soon as we land, I will take the Fell to the Queen, who will decide what to do with him. If she spares his life, then he will heal the Border Guards. Do you understand?"

Mia shakes herself. "Yes, Commander Lucidia."

"Now tell me what the Queen needs," I snap, angry that Mia put her own interests ahead of the Queen's.

Mia focuses fully on me, a sheen of shame crossing her face. Despite the games she plays with male fae, it's unlike her to be so distracted.

She's fully focused again now, drawing herself upright. "A girl is dying."

My heart sinks. "Is she with the Queen?"

"The healers have done everything they can. The Queen has exhausted herself trying to save the child. You're her last hope."

"Then we need to hurry."

"Yes, Commander." Mia turns in the direction of Eteri City.

In response, her bird cracks its wings, spreading a stream of lightning that streaks around the other birds.

It's a silent moment of communication. Mia will tell her bird what to do, and the bird will communicate with the other thunderbirds, who will in turn relay the command to their riders.

For a moment, all of their heads turn toward me, both riders and birds in an unnerving stare.

The message has been received: I have a Fell prisoner.

Seconds later, each Night Guard leaps onto the back of a bird carrying a wounded Border Guard. Mia herself draws alongside Evander and jumps neatly onto his bird, slipping her arms around his waist to make sure he's supported.

With a coordinated crack of their wings, all of the birds burst forward and I breathe a sigh of relief. Now that the wounded are held safely on their backs, the birds will be able to travel at full speed.

The weight of their lives settles on me, heavier than it was before.

I sense the Fell's dark gaze burning my back as I also turn toward our destination.

"A *band* of Fell?" His sarcastic tone makes my heckles rise. I lied to Mia, telling her that we were attacked by many Fell, not just one.

"If they knew you did this on your own, they'd see you as a serious threat and kill you on the spot," I say. "They think our healers can handle it. For now, you're a curiosity."

His cynical response is as sharp as mine. "I could tell."

Before I focus fully on the mountain range ahead of us, I give him one last instruction. "Do *not* touch me again without my permission."

I can't allow him to make me glow in front of my people.

He leans forward and whispers in a very different tone, warm, earthy, making me shiver. "I can't make that promise."

Damn. He said he'd tell me the truth. This time it's a truth I don't want to hear.

I say, "Then know this: If you touch me and make me glow in front of my people, I will have to kill you. Only touch me if it's a matter of life or death."

He's quiet behind me for a long moment. When he speaks, his question sounds confused. "Make you glow?"

I don't answer. I refuse to say anything more about it. He thinks I'm in control of everything, but I'm not. Even so, I refuse to let it scare me.

As the silence stretches between us, filling only with the rush of wind, he shifts away from me, his burned caramel scent receding.

I'm relieved that he listened to me, but at the same time, a small, empty pit opens up in my stomach.

The glow made me warm, a curling, homey warmth I haven't felt before. Now I need to push it away with all of my strength.

Mia's attention may have made the Fell uncomfortable, but he was lucky she was so fascinated by him. His looks will save his life.

I will keep him alive.

Until he saves my friends.

Then I'll kill him.

CHAPTER 7

*W*e soar over the flower fields and then the mountains.

To maintain speed, we take the pass between the peaks, avoiding the highest but most beautiful of the crystal peaks.

The pass appears dark from a distance, but once inside, it glitters with gemstones. The thunderbirds fly single file, dim their lightning, and coast as much as they can, avoiding cracking their wings in case the vibrations causes any rocks to fall.

Treble is the largest thunderbird and finds the confined space unsettling, but I lean over his neck and whisper calming words. The Fell is sitting far enough away from me that I don't feel embarrassed to lean forward now.

When we finally sail through the other side of the pass, the first rays of sunlight gleam over the distant mountain range.

The crystal peaks form a crescent around Eteri City. The peaks in the distance are the home of dragons, including the wise Vanem Dragon. The thunderbirds nest there too, the dragons and birds living symbiotically.

The palace rests on a crest of lower mountains that cuts across the crescent and sits at the heart of the city.

On our way toward it, we pass over snow-covered fields and trees that glisten with frozen dew and finally over the Spinning Lake that rests at the base of the palace. It's safely frozen at this time of the year.

The Frost Fae are in their element right now. While most of our food is grown and harvested in the warmer months, orchards of trees bearing cerulean-blue apples and periwinkle-colored citrus fruits flourish around the smaller villages at the edges of the city.

As soon as the thunderbirds crack their wings, small children run from their homes far beneath us to point and wave. It's not every day that they see two squadrons flying together. It usually only happens during times of celebration.

My heart squeezes at the danger I'm bringing into their lives.

"Fly fast, Treble. Land before the others. We don't have much time left."

Treble responds to my commands, his trust in me complete. His enormous wings carry us high before shooting in a clean arc toward the palace.

The castle is pure white with countless towers, two of the highest towers supporting a landing pad that's wide enough for twenty thunderbirds to land and strong enough to hold the weight of several dragons.

Treble takes us safely to the platform. Normally, I would somersault from his back, but I can't be seen to lose control of my prisoner.

Twisting to face the Fell again, I take hold of the rope and wrap its free end around my wrist, binding us together.

I fold the fingers of my other hand around his weapon.

He doesn't fight me when I tug it from his hold.

"As soon as I speak with the Queen, I'll heal your people," he says.

He'd better be telling the truth.

"Follow me and don't say another word, no matter how I treat you," I say, hoping he's prepared for just how roughly I'll have to deal with him to keep him alive.

The Fell's expression is closed off as Treble lowers his wing for us. Without a word, the Fell follows me to the ground, the rope taut between us.

He watches the other birds land before he studies the doorway into the third tower that rises up beside the landing pad. He's doing what I would do: looking for escape routes and weaknesses in our defenses.

But there's nowhere to go from here but down.

I tug him forward so that every rider can see us. I can already foresee the next few minutes playing out. Mia will call for the healers because she doesn't believe that only the Fell can heal Evander and his squadron. It isn't a bad thing—it will buy me time to take the Fell to the Queen and bring him back. And in the meantime, the healers will keep Evander comfortable.

"Lay the unconscious guards on the platform," I shout as Mia's team lands one by one. Everything inside me screams at me to help Evander, but I can't let go of the Fell now.

Mia descends closest to us. My heart lurches as she slides Evander to the ground. Just as I anticipated, she orders two of the landing guards to fetch the healers.

"Quickly!" she shouts. "They need healers *now!*"

The two women race past me, their indigo armor blurring their silhouettes in the early daylight. At the same time, three women run from the tower entrance behind us, quickly stepping aside to allow the first two women to pass.

The newcomers are dressed in indigo dresses, the uniform that the Queen prefers the Night Guard to wear. It's deceptively feminine. The slits in the skirt and the strapless bodice allow for full body movements, while the fitted corset protects all of our vital organs and provides plenty of places to conceal weapons.

Each of the three women carries liquid daggers concealed across their ribcages.

The three women skid to a stop, surprise shooting across their features when they see the Fell.

The woman leading them is Talsa. Like most of the Night Guards, she's a Dusk fae. She gives a clipped order and the other two step to either side of the Fell, drawing their daggers and taking up defensive poses.

"Commander Lucidia," Talsa says. "Are you safe?" Her coral hair is swept back from her face and cascades down her back. Her pink lips purse in worry and her sky blue eyes cast distrustful glances at the Fell.

It's difficult to form friendships with the guards when any one of them could challenge me for my position, but Talsa's perception and dedication mean that I can trust her.

Unlike Mia, she's immediately on her guard, understanding the danger.

For two years now, I've hoped that she would challenge Mia for the position of Captain of the Night Guard, but to my dismay, Talsa let another Winter Ascending pass her by without making a move.

"I'm safe. The Fell is under my control." I glare at the human. "He won't disobey my orders."

Talsa remains on her guard. "We were sent to bring you to the Queen, but... *Evander!*"

Her gaze darts from the Fell to Evander. Deep worry floods her eyes when she sees him.

She takes an involuntary step toward him before she stops herself. "What happened to him?"

I quickly lay my hand on her arm to calm her. "Evander's

okay. But he's in grave danger. A group of Fell attacked the Border Guards. This Fell has information for the Queen that will help Evander. You must take me to the Queen immediately."

Talsa gives me a quick nod. "The Queen is in the Inner Sanctuary. I'll make sure you reach her without any interference."

She knows as well as I do that the Fell will draw attention. The single vine wound around his wrists won't be enough. We'll have to take the back way instead of walking through the main hall.

As she spins to precede me down the stairs, Talsa murmurs to one of the other women, "Bring more rope. Chains if you can find them."

She throws a glance back at the Fell as we exit the platform through the stone door, her gaze passing over his broad shoulders and strong arms.

"A lot more rope," she calls as the other woman speeds away down the stairs.

Carrying his weapon, I keep the tension on the Fell's bonds without looking back at him. The greater the disdain with which I treat him, the less likely he'll appear to be an immediate threat.

Ten minutes later, we've made it to the bottom of the stairs and twisted our way through quiet hallways toward the entrance to the Inner Sanctuary.

Unfortunately, I have no choice but to pass through a large entrance to get to it and the voices floating from that direction tell me there are already at least twenty fae in the room—most likely the sick child's family and any healers her family called to help her.

We pause as the woman who went to get rope runs up behind us, holding out a bag that clanks as she opens it.

"I brought everything I could get my hands on," she says. "Can you use any of it?"

It's filled with chains, but they're decorative ones. The Fell will pull the links apart in an instant.

Beside them, a long red sash rests, along with more rope. I quickly hand off the halberd to Talsa before looping and securing the sash around the Fell's neck so that it will tighten and loosen at my will.

Then I wrap the rope around his waist and secure it to the vine around his wrists, leaving him with free use only of his legs. The rope will stay where it is until I cut it, but I can still manipulate the sash.

He watches me while I work quickly around him. He wears a wry expression when I go to great lengths not to connect with his skin, but he doesn't try to slip the bindings.

Talsa's forehead is creased with confusion the whole time. "Why isn't he fighting you?" she asks, her forehead creasing. "Is he mute? Or perhaps he's brain damaged?"

The Fell's eyes snap to her, his sharp glare filled with enough anger to make her stumble backward.

"He doesn't fight me because he knows I'll kill him if he makes the wrong move." I yank the sash around his neck tight enough to make him suck in a breath and turn his angry eyes on me instead of Talsa.

Satisfied that I can control the sash, I take back the halberd from Talsa and spin on my heels, dragging the Fell forward.

He catches up to me and leans in. "You're wasting time," he snarls through strangled vocal chords.

I grit my teeth. "You will play this game if you want to live."

CHAPTER 8

*W*hat I really want to do is scream at the Fell. Evander's life is slipping away, but without this show, we'll both be dead.

Especially now that I see whose family stands inside the entrance.

Calida of the Solstice paces at the entrance, surrounded by her mother, three sisters, and four aunts. Their hair is golden like their power that derives from the sun, and their eyes are eerily similar—the color of marigold flecked with ginger.

Calida is the youngest sister, but also the tallest, as tall and lithe as a stem of glitter grass, her mane of dark blonde hair a shining cascade of gold across her bronzed shoulders.

They are one of the most powerful families, their ability to control flame commanding respect and to some degree, fear among other fae.

If they're here, it means the sick child is related to them or someone they care about. If I can't heal her, they will bear a grudge against me for... well, as long as they live.

I tap the halberd on the floor like a drum, hitting the marble with every step as I drag the Fell behind me.

Talsa strides ahead of us, calling out, "Make way for Aura of the Lucidia. The Queen's champion returns..." She glances back at me and raises her voice to a clear shout. "With a tribute for the Queen."

Calida's family parts to allow me through... for all of two seconds.

Calida lurches forward. "What is that?"

She points at the Fell, her dramatic exclamation rising to a shriek.

I draw to a stop, remaining at my full height to stare her down. "A gift for the Queen."

"It's a Fell creature." Her lips curl in disgust as she circles around us.

Suddenly, Mia's reaction to the Fell feels like a gift. If only Calida were as mesmerized.

"We should kill it," she says.

I don't look at the Fell—giving him attention will only make it look like I care—but the slight tug on his restraints tells me he's shifting his weight to defend himself against an attack.

I give Calida an uninterested look. "If you wish to deprive the Queen of her gift and all of the knowledge that comes with it... sure, go ahead. But it will be on your head."

I sense her power growing. She's not as strong at dawn as she will be in the middle of the day when she can draw on the sun's power at its fullest.

Likewise, my own power is fading with the rising sun. Neither one of us is at the height of our power right now.

Firelight pools around her fingers and she drags in a breath that tells me she won't see reason.

For a moment, fear grows at the back of my mind. If it comes to it, I'll have to stop her from killing him and I'm not sure how I can explain my motives without calling my loyalty into question. It doesn't matter that Evander might die. The Queen's safety is paramount.

"Stop." Calida's mother steps up behind her daughter, placing a firm hand on her arm. She is the matriarch of their family, a coldly beautiful woman whose golden eyes are anything but warm. She has no reason to be afraid of Calida's power. She controls the sun's power too and can absorb Calida's rage.

"Why?" Calida snarls at her mother, but the older woman remains as passive as me.

"Because you can't break the rules," she says. "You must not engage Aura Lucidia until you enter the coliseum today."

The older woman watches me as she speaks. She's expecting a reaction from me because of her statement, but I learned long ago to subdue my emotions.

Inside, my stomach sinks. If Calida is going to enter the coliseum... it means she has been chosen as my challenger for Queen's Champion.

I can't think of a worse candidate.

What the stars is the Queen thinking?

Calida is selfish and immature. She's a minor guard in the Day Guard and often shirks her duties and her training, getting others to do her tasks for her.

She's also reckless.

Fire continues to pool in her hands, amber flames licking along her fingertips, her breath dragging in and out of her mouth, increasingly panicky as she stares at the Fell.

I act quickly, tightening the Fell's sash with an abrupt yank of the material. Ignoring his sudden choking and angry eyes, I take a quick, aggressive step toward Calida. "Do it. Kill the creature."

She grits her teeth. "You want me to break the rules and engage you."

"I'll put you on your pretty backside," I say. "No matter where we meet. Here or the coliseum. You should take your chances now rather than wait."

Behind her, her mother gives me a cold stare, but it contains respect.

I've never bowed to anyone or put anyone's commands above the Queen's. I will challenge anyone who gets in my way and Calida's mother has always ensured that her daughters remember that.

Calida's nostrils flare as she inhales. It's a reaction to my threat, but it has another effect.

A curious expression floods her face and her focus shifts back to the Fell. "The creature smells like..."

Thank the stars for caramel.

I take a step away from her as the fire fades from her suddenly loose fingers. She gives herself a shake, not quite relenting in her aggression as she takes another look at him.

He has dropped to all fours on the ground, gasping for breath beneath the pressure of the sash. He thumps the ground as he looks up.

The weak rays of the day's first sunlight hits his back and makes his silhouette glow, highlighting his perfectly masculine shape and the alluring inky flecks in his eyes.

I bend over him, but not for the purpose of releasing him.

Grabbing his hair and pulling his head back, I'm careful not to touch his scalp while making the gesture as dominant as I can.

"He's an unusual specimen," I say, keeping my tone clinical. "I expect the Queen will be quite pleased. She can do whatever she wants with him. But it's *her* choice."

I turn my hard stare away from the glaring Fell to Calida, daring her to contradict me.

"Now," I say. "Let me pass before you kill a dying child."

She startles and shakes herself, this time backing away from me. She's so self-centered she must have completely forgotten about the sick girl.

I don't take any chances that she'll change her mind and make a spontaneous strike.

"Get up!" I snarl at the Fell, yanking the ropes upward and striding forward as he clambers to obey me.

I deftly loosen the binding so he can breathe again but conceal my movements.

The remaining women part to let me through while Talsa quickly follows at the Fell's back. I'm grateful that she inserts herself between the Solstice women and him. I don't trust them not to strike the Fell in the back.

Once I'm inside the room, I nearly stumble.

The Queen weeps beside the fountain in the center of the room, her long silken robes pooling across the floor.

The Inner Sanctuary is filled with flowers, a place of peace where the Queen comes to meditate. Every time she comes here, she fills a flower with some of the essence of her power.

Unlike other Sunstream fae, she controls all of the elements of the seasons, but she doesn't keep her power selfishly to herself.

She gifts the flowers to those who need light in their lives, those who are struggling with some aspect of life. She must have hoped that she could draw on her stored power to heal the girl.

She has sunk to the floor holding the girl, who appears to be about three years old. The child's chest rises and falls, but her breaths are shallow gasps.

Even from a distance, I can see that the girl's arms and legs are twisted in unnatural directions, but they don't flop like they would if they were broken.

I nearly drop the Fell's bindings to run to her.

Hurrying him along as fast as I can, I'm aware of Calida's family gathering behind me, watching me and the Fell with sharp eyes.

The Queen raises her head, her cheeks blotchy. Bright pearls spill across her robes. Her tears… turn to pearls as soon as they drip from her cheeks. She has shed so many of them this morning.

Even when she's crying, she's beautiful. Her lips are perfectly full and ruby red, her eyes are like glittering azure blue gems, and her blood-red hair flows down her back to her waist.

"Aura!" she cries. "I need your help."

CHAPTER 9

*T*he Queen's soft voice wrenches at my heart.

"I'm here." I drop to my knees beside her, still gripping the halberd and pulling the Fell to the floor with me.

For the second time, he lands on his hands and knees beside me, but he seems resigned to being treated like an object now.

Queen Imatra's gaze passes across me to him and her eyes widen in shock.

Her voice is a low whisper. "Aura! What have you done? How could you bring a Fell creature—"

The first full rays of sunlight spear through the glass windows and catch on the halberd's gleaming blade.

The Queen freezes as her focus is pulled to it, the bright gleam reflecting in her eyes. The emblem on the blade blazes in her eyes as if it had come to life.

Her jaw drops and her lips form a perfect circle. "Oh. Dear stars."

The Fell told me that his weapon would save us both.

For some reason, it's had a profound effect on the Queen, and I... well, I have no idea why.

For now, I'll accept that it has caused her to rethink what was no doubt going to be an order to kill him.

Her focus shifts back to the Fell and her demeanor changes from shocked to watchful.

She addresses me carefully. "You've done well to bring him to me, Aura. Whatever you do, do not let go of that rope. You don't know what you're holding on to."

She's right about that. This Fell is a complete mystery to me.

She swallows hard. "First, the child. The healers have tried everything, but her limbs twist farther with every hour that passes. I've drawn on every aspect of my power without success. The darkness is too great…"

The Fell twitches beside me. From the corner of my eye, I see him lean forward, fixated on the child's misshapen legs.

Interjecting myself into the space between them to block his view, I carefully place his weapon on the floor even though I'm reluctant to let it go.

I run my hand lightly over the girl's head, along the damp strands of her golden hair and across her shoulders, resting my palm over the location of her heart.

She's burning up with a fever and her heart is pounding far too fast. Her eyes remain closed, blonde eyelashes heavy across her colorless cheeks. Her lips are rimmed with purple, an unnatural color like a deep bruise.

This isn't the first time I've seen a child inflicted with these symptoms.

"This is the second case this month," I murmur, meeting the Queen's gaze. "What is this illness?"

The Fell's harsh whisper sounds beside me. "Ebon Rot. That's the first stage. But it shouldn't affect children."

The Queen startles and so do I.

Fear fills her eyes and I have no choice but to twist and pull the sash tightly around the Fell's throat. "Do not speak!"

His glare burns me, but I refuse to consider the consequences if he's telling the truth. His people kill themselves once
they are affected. He implied that there is no cure, but... I know
there is.

My power is fading with the rising sun and I need to act
quickly.

I close my eyes and focus on the light inside me. It's a bright
spark that begins as a cold sensation in my mind. Every time I
touch my power, I have the urge to linger in that cold, immense
place.

It's empty somehow but peaceful, a vast expanse of possibili-
ties, as if I'm staring at the night sky filled with stars and each
one could be a version of the future.

I force myself to draw back and pull the power down to my
chest, feeling it flow like a cold stream to my hand, where it
finally becomes warm.

Pressing my palm to the girl's heart, I allow starlight to
trickle across her, sensing her deep inhale. I don't fight the
sucking sensation as she draws on my power.

In this moment, I am giving. There is no take for me.

I open my eyes as soon as her heartbeat slows to normal.

Running my hand down her arms first, and then her legs, I
ease them between my fingers. Slowly, they unfurl beneath the
glow of my fingers like rope uncoiling.

She breathes deeply as I finally sit back. I check the color of
her cheeks—a pale pink again. "She's sleeping now."

A final tear slips down the Queen's cheek. "Your power,
Aura..." She shakes her head, choking up. "It's a blessing
to us."

She raises her eyes to the watching fae with a teary smile.
"Come! Get your kin. She is well again."

Calida hurries forward, skirting wide around the Fell to
gather up the sleeping girl into her arms.

She snarls at me as she draws herself upright. "This doesn't change anything. I'm still challenging you."

I remain impassive. "Of course you are."

Calida backs away with the girl in her arms, but the Queen stops her.

"Wait, Calida," Imatra says. "All of you come forward. You will bear witness now."

To me she says softly, "Rise, Aura."

Somehow, she always manages to give an order without it sounding like a command.

I gather the halberd into my hand and rise to my feet as Calida's family crowds behind us, keeping a safe distance from the Fell.

I sense his gaze on me, a deep burning stare that hasn't stopped since he said the girl was sick. If I look at him, I imagine I will see a thousand stormy thoughts in his eyes.

He just saw me cure the illness that plagues his people and kills them one by one.

The Queen draws herself to her feet, scattering pearls across the floor. They roll into nearby flower bushes as she turns her full attention to the Fell. "State your name."

I loosen the sash around his neck, remaining unemotional despite the marks it leaves on his skin. "Now you may speak."

He clears his expression, rapidly hiding a blaze of emotion as he speaks to the Queen. "You recognize the weapon I brought with me. That means you know who I am."

The Queen allows a small smile to touch her lips. "I recognize the weapon, but that doesn't mean I know the human holding it."

His eyes narrow and his shoulders tense, turning his face fully into the light, demanding that she look at him. "Am I not my father's son?"

She doesn't miss a beat. "You are. But I still wish to know what he called you."

I stare, confused, between them. *Whose son is he?* He said his father was betrayed in the last battle, but he never said who his father was.

A muscle ticks in his jaw, an angry beat. "My name is Nathaniel Shield."

Queen Imatra's lips purse and a look of mild surprise passes across her face. "That's not the name I expected."

Nathaniel... I roll his name around in my mind, wondering why it sits so well with me. But I'm more puzzled by what they're not saying.

The Queen glances at me. "Aura... you are confused?"

I nod. There's no lying to the Queen. "I would like to know why his name is important to you?"

She leaves her position beside the gurgling fountain to circle Nathaniel slowly.

Her gaze runs up and down his body. "We fae take our names from our power. You are Aura of the Lucidia, because Lucidia means *brightest light* in our ancient language. But the Fell take their second name from their occupation, which can change throughout the course of their lives. This Fell... right now..."

She tilts her head, studying him as she returns to a stop in front of us. "He is a Shield. The Fell King's Shield, to be precise."

My forehead creases. He's a... shield? What does that mean?

Nathaniel's stare burns me again and suddenly the breath stops in my chest.

A shield is a defense. An object you hold in front of you to stop the knife aimed at your heart...

The Queen raises her voice and claps her hands with delight. "Today is a day for rejoicing."

Her eyes burn me like Nathaniel's as she continues, jubilant. "*My* champion has captured the Fell King's champion."

CHAPTER 10

"**G**o now," the Queen says to Calida's family. "Spread the news that King Cyrian's champion has been captured."

I half-turn to watch Calida throw her head back unhappily.

She has no choice but to sing my praises, but she will be calculating how to gather our people's support for her challenge now. Beating me in the coliseum is one thing, but the people also need to respect her.

Before she and her family can turn away, Nathaniel raises his voice in a command. "Stop. You will not leave."

Calida whirls back to us with a shriek. "You do not tell me what to do—"

The Queen has also stiffened, an unusual anger flushing her cheeks red. "You will not address my people, Fell."

Nathaniel's response is an angry rumble. "I invoke the Law of Champions."

The Queen freezes like stone. The color drains from her cheeks.

I reach out for her. "My queen?"

She doesn't answer me. Alarmed, I count out the heartbeats while she doesn't move a single muscle.

"That's old law." Her voice squeezes between her bloodless lips. "It no longer applies—"

"The old law is the only law that applies to the Fell. You know that," he answers. "You have no choice but to obey it."

A deathly silence descends on the room. Nobody but the Queen and Nathaniel seem to know what's going on, but the tension between them is strong enough to make me nervous.

Behind us, Calida turns to her family, who are all giving each other confused looks. Even her mother's forehead is creased in bewilderment.

The old laws aren't well known anymore. Only a few fae are aware of them. I've never had reason to study them, let alone understand them.

Imatra's chest rises and falls rapidly as if she's about to panic.

I can't let go of Nathaniel, but it's my job to protect her. Stepping between him and her, I allow her to focus on me, trusting that my calmness will help her.

I keep my voice low and controlled. "Tell me what's going on so I can help you."

She takes a deep breath, her hand fluttering at her chest.

"The Law of Champions is a challenge to the throne," she says, speaking directly to me. "The winner takes all on behalf of their Queen... or King. It exists as a last resort to settle the outcome of war between our races. No monarch has ever invoked it because there's too much to lose: an entire Queen-dom. Do you understand, Aura?"

"You mean our land could fall to the Fell?"

"Yes."

My heart plummets, but I hide it. She needs me to be calm. "What does the challenge involve?"

She swallows visibly, her voice becoming a forced whisper.

"My champion and the Fell King's champion must fight... must fight each other... The winner takes all..."

She squeezes her eyes closed, her eyelashes pressing to her cheeks. "It's a fight to the death, Aura."

A sick feeling rises up inside my stomach and my chest, pressing in on me.

This Fell... who makes me glow... who talks of light and dark and betrayal and loyalty... wants to kill me?

Of course he does. He refrained from killing me at the border because it suited his purpose. He only fought me as hard as he needed to so that he could stand here in front of my Queen and invoke the Law of Champions, to make his challenge for control of our land.

He is a Fell.

He is my enemy.

Now he wants to kill me... despite the fact that he just saw me cure the illness that decimates his people. Surely, any sane person would want to keep me alive, use me somehow to help his people?

More than fear, confusion swamps me now.

Every time I think I have a handle on Nathaniel's motives, he sweeps the foundations out from under me again.

Behind me, Nathaniel remains very still, but I sense his gaze burning into me as Imatra continues speaking.

"Once the Law is invoked," she says, "the champions must be bound, the Law sealed, and the champions must fight within three days. The Law can't be reversed or stopped. If one of the champions refuses to fight, the old magic will take hold and that champion will die at the end of the third day."

As she presses her hand to her heart, my thoughts whirl. "The Fell has invoked the Law," I say. "But you said it has to be sealed too. Whatever sealing involves, I'm sure we can avoid it—"

The Queen shakes her head. "Sealing the Law is a formality. It requires the Vanem Dragon to bind the two champions. The Vanem Dragon can choose when to seal the Law, as long as it is done within the first day."

A hot, boiling mess of emotions rises inside me. I feel like a stone sinking to the bottom of an icy lake.

Thank the stars I'm good at hiding my feelings.

"He won't beat me." I raise my chin and cast a haughty glance back at Nathaniel. My disdain is also for the benefit of Calida's family. I will never show fear in front of them.

"There's only one uncertainty," Imatra says, stepping closer to me. "My champion is yet to be determined."

I blink at her.

Of course… she's right.

Calida might be the one to fight Nathaniel.

I hold in a bitter laugh. She wouldn't have a chance. He'd annihilate her.

Which means it's even more important that I win my fight with her today and retain my position of Queen's Champion.

"I guess we'll find out," I say.

Imatra takes a deep breath, finally regaining her composure. She can't pre-empt the outcome of today's challenge, but the determined gleam in her eyes tells me she needs me to win.

"You must release Nathaniel now, Aura," she says. "He is as bound by the Law as my champion will be. If he hurts any fae from this moment until the fight, the Law will be broken. I'm sure he doesn't want that."

My response is instinctive. My hand opens, allowing the sash to fall, releasing Nathaniel from my grip.

He quickly unravels the sash from around his neck and just as deftly slips the knots I tied around his wrists and waist as if they were nothing.

I'm not surprised by his skill, but Calida lets out a gasp at how fast he undoes his bindings.

"You didn't tie him tightly enough," she accuses.

I arch an eyebrow at her. If she wasn't my challenger, I would be entitled to strike her for insulting me. As it is, I have to make do with a glare. "Nathaniel may be a Fell, but do not underestimate him."

I turn, ignoring the hint of a smile touching Nathaniel's full lips.

How dare he smile at me when he's challenged me to a fight to the death?

It has to be me. I have to fight him. Not Calida. She won't stand a chance.

"There's one last thing before you go, Calida," Queen Imatra says, addressing the tall blonde. "As the challenger, you have the right to choose the environment in which you will fight Aura today. What is your choice?"

CHAPTER 11

a slow, devious smile passes across Calida's mouth. "I choose a desert at high noon."

Calida's shrewd, I'll give her that. She's chosen a desert so that I will struggle against my greatest weakness: *sunlight.*

Like other Eventide fae, I'm at my strongest at night when the moon and stars burn brightly in the sky. It's why the Queen's Night Guard is made up of Eventide fae.

It's also why Imatra has slept soundly for the last seven years, knowing I'm watching over her.

Most Eventide fae sleep during the day and stay awake at night, but I'm not like most. I survive on as little as three hours of sleep in the middle of the day when I'm at my weakest. The rest of the time, I'm devoted to the Queen's protection.

Imatra turns to me. "Aura, as the defending champion, you have the right to choose the weapons with which you will fight. As you know, you will both receive exactly the same weapons. What do you choose?"

I take a moment to consider my choice carefully. Calida had time to plan, but I've only known for a short time that she is my challenger. I can choose as many or as few weapons as I want, but I need to make them count.

When Mia challenged me, I chose the sword because I knew it was her weakest weapon. Calida's weakness is her laziness and her reliance on her power instead of her skills.

"A bow," I say, carefully, thinking it through. "With a single arrow."

Calida casts me a curious look, but I ignore it.

"Very well," Imatra says. "It will be so. Thank you, Calida. You may go now."

As Calida and her family leave the room, Nathaniel's deep voice draws my attention to him.

He says, "I need to heal your friends now."

Imatra gives me a sharp look. "What is he talking about?"

"He poisoned the Border Guards and carries the antidote with him. I didn't tell you because you needed to make your decision unclouded by the fear that the Border Guards might die."

Imatra covers the distance between us, her soft hand brushing my cheek. "You put me first always. That's why I can trust you."

The angle of the sunlight shining through the windows tells me I'm running out of time. "I will take responsibility for Nathaniel Shield while he's here—regardless of which champion he fights."

Talsa steps up behind me, finally able to get close to us now that Calida's family has left. "I will support Aura in that task."

"Thank you both," Imatra says. "Talsa, please take Nathaniel's weapon and prepare a room for him..."

Her brow furrows. I don't envy her decision about where he'll live for the next three days. She can't put him far away from the guards because then we can't keep an eye on him, but closer to her is also a risk.

Her lips purse. "In the room next to Aura's."

I take a deep slow breath to stop the sharp gasp that presses against my chest.

I sleep in a room beside the Queen. That puts Nathaniel on the other side of me and too close to her. I can't hold in my concern. "He shouldn't be anywhere near you!"

My outburst echoes around us, but Imatra remains calm.

"You will be awake to protect me," she says.

"What if Calida succeeds in her challenge? *She* will sleep at night."

Queen Imatra's voice softens. "I said he will sleep in the room next to yours, Aura. Wherever you are, he will be. Wherever *he* is, *you* will be. That's the only way I'll be safe." Sadness dwells in her eyes. "Now, go. Save the others. May the eventide light bless you and keep you safe."

I have no choice but to agree. I give her a quick nod. Then Talsa and I bow deeply before we turn away from her.

"Come with me," I order Nathaniel as I stride away from him.

The moment we exit the room, I pull up sharp as we encounter the Queen's Day Guard—fifteen woman who are all Sunstream fae, their hair and eyes a dazzling rainbow of gold, orange, and even red.

Their captain is Nadina. She's shorter than the average guard, muscled and strong, a straightforward thinker and a fierce fighter.

"Aura Lucidia." She acknowledges me with a respectful bow, but she's immediately on her guard when she sees the Fell.

Her quick, abrupt assessment of him softens as she studies his face and chest. Just like Mia, she appears bemused.

Fae are shallow. They love bright shiny things. Right now Nathaniel is shiny and new. If only he were misshapen and ugly.

I cut her off before she can ask questions. "This Fell is my prisoner."

She gives herself a shake. "A Fell? But he isn't bound."

"The Queen will explain."

Until the Queen makes a public announcement, this won't be the last encounter I have with a fae who wants to know what the stars is going on.

She won't question the Queen's decisions. "Very well," she says.

The Day Guard parts, allowing us to pass from the room even though their collective attention remains on us. Or possibly on Nathaniel's broad shoulders or the way his bare chest glistens or maybe the way he seems to prowl like a ruthless dragon with every step he takes.

Nathaniel catches up to me as I stride away. Somehow, despite my speed, he doesn't seem hurried, but once we enter the maze of corridors, his walking speed increases so that he overtakes me. "Your friends are running out of time."

I glare at him as we turn a corner, passing through a hallway where the walls are covered in silver vines bearing lavender-colored roses.

"*You're* running out of time," I snap. "If you don't heal them, then the Law is broken. What does that mean for you?"

"I'll die," he says.

I jolt to a stop. I can't believe what I heard. "If you hurt a fae before we fight... you'll die?"

He returns my stare. He's unwavering and impossibly calm. "Yes."

"But you already hurt them."

"Before the Law was invoked," he says. "Their deaths are now the trigger point that will break the Law."

"Then... if I stop you from healing my friends, you'll die and this nightmare will be over?"

"Yes."

A bitter laugh pulls from my throat. "You know I won't sacrifice them. You figured that out on the other side of the border. I won't let anything happen to Evander."

"Yes."

"Stop saying 'yes'!" I shout, all of the emotions I've been pushing away crashing into me.

With a single step, I close the gap between us, ending up closer to him that I should be.

I want to thump him. Shove him. I want to draw my sword and fight him right now. I want to drive him to the ground and... inhale the caramel scent of his skin and drown in it.

Damn Fell. He is not shiny and new to me.

I whirl and continue on my way, forcing my anger into the strike of my boots on the stone floor.

I catch Talsa's alarmed look as she hurries after me. "Aura? What really happened at the border?"

Double damn. My emotions got the better of me and I let the truth slip. Never mind. None of it seems to matter now.

"The same thing that happened in the Inner Sanctuary," I say. "This cursed Fell got his way."

CHAPTER 12

*T*he wind rushes around us as we emerge onto the landing platform where Mia and the Night Guards remain watching over the unconscious Border Guards.

A group of healers is scattered among them, some still casting magic into their allotted patient while others sit back on their heels, shaking their heads in defeat.

Talsa left us at the base of the steps, taking Nathaniel's weapon away with her but promising to come back as quickly as she can. He watched her disappear as if he were reluctant to be parted with the halberd.

I thought for a moment he was going to try to stop her, but his jaw clenched and he followed me up the stairs.

Out on the platform, each Night Guard is bleary-eyed, some yawning. It's past their bedtimes, but I have no sympathy for them. If I can operate on minimal sleep, they can too.

I raise my voice, using my full authority as the Queen's champion. "By order of the Queen, all healers will step away from the wounded."

The healers grumble protests and Mia's head snaps up. She

strides over to me, the first signs of real worry making her appear drawn. "What the stars did the Fell do to them? Our magic doesn't work."

"I told you that only the Fell carries the antidote," I say. "Now order the Night Guards to step back so he can cure our people."

Mia's gaze flashes across Nathaniel. Even now, she can't hide the softening of her features as her attention passes from his chest to his stomach and even lower.

Oh, for star's sake.

I step right up to her and into her face. "Get out of the way, Mia, or so help me, I'll throw you off this platform right now."

She lurches backward and hurries away, shouting orders at the other guards, who quickly step to the edge of the platform out of the way.

"Evander first," I say to Nathaniel.

He's already moving toward Evander, who lies on his back several paces away.

I drop to my knees beside Evander and pull his head into my lap. One of the healers must have removed Evander's mask and now his eyes are closed and his breathing is shallow. His arctic-blue hair is braided back from his face, its lengths falling across my knees.

I can't keep the emotion from my voice as Nathaniel kneels beside me. "Heal him. Now!"

Nathaniel raises his right hand to his lips to gently blow across his fingertips.

A golden bubble appears at the end of each of his fingers. Curling the rest of his fingers into a fist, he presses only his forefinger against the blackened wound on Evander's shoulder.

Golden light spills across Evander's skin like water, consuming the angry wound and leaving normal skin behind.

Within seconds, the wound is healed and the golden liquid has vanished.

"Aura?" Evander's blue-gray eyes are like polished stones, but his face is far from angelic. Strong eyebrows draw down into a glare that would peel the skin off any invader. "What happened?"

I lean over him, pressing my hand to his chest to stop him from leaping to his feet. My face is a mere inch from his. "I saved you," I whisper.

"At what cost?" he asks, his voice a mere breath of quiet air that carries as much accusation as a shout.

I have no answer.

Staying close to Evander, I turn my head to snap at Nathaniel. "Heal the others—"

He's already gone. Looking around, I find him kneeling beside a Border Guard several paces away. I guess the threat of death has affected Nathaniel more than he let on.

He moves quickly among the wounded, waking them up. Some of them revive quietly. Others jump to their feet before they wobble and collapse to the platform again.

Evander's expression is unyielding. "Aura—"

"Don't scold me, brother," I whisper, meeting his flinty gaze. "I fought as hard as I could."

His eyes widen. He keeps his voice low. "He beat you?"

My heartrate increases like a thousand drums pounding out of sync. "You fought him too," I say. "You know how strong he is."

Evander's palm presses into my arm. "There's more you're not saying."

So much more. Not only about the Law of Champions, but about what happened at the border, the way Nathaniel survived my power.

"I can't speak here," I whisper. "I have to watch Nathaniel

now, but come and find me once you've recovered. I'll tell you everything."

"Who is Nathaniel?" he asks.

"That's the Fell's name."

Evander nods before he freezes again. "What am I saying? I can't rest today. It's the Winter Ascending. I have to be there when you fight."

"Not if you haven't recovered—"

"Aura." He gives me a firm look. "I'll be there."

I squeeze his shoulder. "Thank you, brother."

I help him get to his feet and call for a healer to take care of him, handing him off to her.

After they walk away, I'm surprised to find Nathaniel standing in the middle of the platform a few paces away.

He's finished.

All of the fallen fae are awake and being escorted from the platform by healers and Night Guards.

Mia is the last to leave. She stops by me, a tension in her posture that wasn't there before. "Who is your challenger today?"

"Calida of the Solstice."

She relaxes. "Hah. She won't last two seconds."

Mia saunters away from me. When she fought me, she fought hard. She wanted my position badly. We both ended up bloody, but I chose to let her live rather than kill her.

My first memories are of death. I refuse to kill one of my people if I can avoid it. But there's some part of me that wonders if she resents me for leaving her alive.

She's not as irresponsible as Calida, but she's far more reckless since that day. Defeat festers. It sits at the back of the mind like a sore. A bit like my own frustration over the fact that Nathaniel manipulated me today.

As soon as Mia's gone, I advance on him. "From now on, you will do everything I tell you *when* I tell you—"

"No, I won't. Other than the rule about not hurting anyone, the Law requires that I remain free to do what I please."

I narrow my eyes at him. "You tricked me. You said you only wanted to speak with the Queen. You omitted to say that your words would seal my fate."

"*My* words?" His eyes darken as if I'm somehow at fault. "Life is nothing but a series of tricks. Fate, destiny—call it what you will —it's waiting to trip you up at every turn and laugh in your face."

My fists clench. "Will you laugh if you kill me?"

The color drains from his face, a confusing vision of shock.

"Never." His hand rises and for a beat, I think he's going to reach for me before he drops it again. "It doesn't have to be you who fights me. The choice is yours."

I recoil from him as his meaning sinks in. "You're suggesting I throw my fight with Calida today. I could let her win. Let her fight you and die instead of me."

"Yes."

"I said *if* you kill me, not *when*, you arrogant pile of goat dung."

I whirl away from him, but he latches on to my hand, deftly lacing his fingers between mine.

Heat spears through my forearm. A bright white glow spreads all the way up to my shoulder, so bright that it shines through my armor, nearly blinding me with its intensity.

I meet Nathaniel's assessing gaze through the glow. His dark eyes are lit up, the stands of his walnut hair cutting across his cheeks.

"I watched you touch your brother—Evander," he says. "Even your Queen. You didn't glow. Why does this happen between us?"

Only the stars know.

"I don't like being grabbed." I thump my free fist toward his throat, but he avoids the thrust with a deft twist without releasing my arm.

He pushes my attacking arm away while he scoops my captured arm against his chest, twisting me so that my back is to him. He wraps his arms around me and holds me tight as if he's giving me a hug. It's weirdly gentle.

"Stop," he whispers into my ear. "We shouldn't fight right now."

"Curse the stars," I cry, wanting to ram my elbow into his ribs and my boot against his shins.

"Tell me why you glow," he demands to know, his voice harsher than I was expecting given how softly he's holding me.

"I'll tell you if you tell me who you really are," I bite back.

I'm bluffing. I have no idea why I glow when he touches me, but I know there's more to him.

If I'm going to fight him, I need to know everything about him. I need to know his motives, his thoughts, his true character. Even now, I'm filing away into my memory the way he defended my attacks so I can learn his moves.

He releases me and jolts away from me. "You already know my name."

I regain my balance, shaking my head as I twist to face him. "Queen Imatra said it wasn't the name she expected. Your name is your occupation. That means she thought you had a different occupation. What is it? Butcher? Criminal? Thief?"

His expression is blank in a way that actually frightens me.

It's the look of a person who has nothing to lose.

I know that look because I see it in the mirror some days. My dark days. When I search my mind for memories of my family and find nothing where my memories should be, only the same empty expanse that I sense when I draw on my power: a deep, dark, cold place.

"My true name was taken away from me fifteen years ago," he says. "I will never get it back. That's all you need to know."

He strides away from me.

I guess he was serious when he claimed that he's free to move around as he wants.

I'm not prepared to let it go. Or let *him* go, for that matter.

I call out to him before he can reach the stone opening in the tower. "Why haven't you asked me about the girl?"

He pulls up abruptly, twisting back to me. "What?"

"The girl I cured. The Ebon Rot. Why haven't you asked me about it?"

Maybe I shouldn't care.

This morning I didn't care.

But that was before Fell creatures had a face—Nathaniel's face—and were capable of emotions. Before the Fell went from being monsters to beings with... *possible*... worth.

His gaze narrows, dark depths reminding me of the same bleak expanse inside my mind. "It wasn't the Rot."

"But you said—"

"I was wrong!" he roars, bleakness consuming his face like a physical force, pushing down on his shoulders so that he hunches.

I take a step toward him.

I don't know why I'm saying what I'm saying. Why I care. Questions spill out of me and I'm not sure why. "What if you're not? Your people don't have to suffer. I could heal the ones who come to the border—"

"No!" His shout echoes around me as he storms toward me.

I backpedal away from him, instinctively reaching for the sword across my shoulder as he descends on me. I'm still wearing my broken armor, but my weapon isn't damaged.

He pulls up sharply a single pace away from me as my sword solidifies in my hands. His dark eyes suck me in and drown me. I try to breathe against the anger, hatred, confusion, and pain I see in him.

"Fate plays tricks," he says, his voice breaking in a way that claws at my heart. "If you can heal them... No." He shakes his head. "Even fate isn't that cruel."

I don't understand him. I don't understand the source of his pain or what he means by cruelty. Maybe it's because I'm the champion he has sworn to kill.

That has to be it.

He's regretting making the challenge because if he wins, he'll give his King control of fae lands, but he'll doom his people to a disease without a cure.

Except that... he chose to invoke the Law *after* he saw me cure the girl.

I swallow a moan of frustration.

He is a deep mystery to me and I'm afraid that the deeper I dig into his motives, the more I'll drown.

CHAPTER 13

"*A*ura!" Talsa sweeps toward us along the platform, rushing to my side as she turns a warning glare on Nathaniel, but her worry is for me. "Are you okay?"

My voice wobbles, but I calm myself quickly. "Yes."

"Then you need to get ready. The fight for your position is in two hours. You need to rest and prepare."

"I can't let Nathaniel out of my sight," I say, unable to keep the strain from my voice. "Until the Queen makes a public announcement, his life is in danger."

Her assessment of him changes. "He could get rid of that pelt. Then he would pass for a fae."

"Except to those who already know who he is," I say, but she's not wrong. If he's willing to give up the fur, then he won't draw as much attention.

I give his perfect form a cursory glance.

Or perhaps he will. But at least, it will be the kind of attention that Mia wants to give him and not the kind that could kill him.

Nathaniel's emotions are hidden again. He's frustratingly

blank. Without me asking, he unclasps the fur and hands it to Talsa.

She recoils from it. "I can't touch that! We don't kill animals." She shudders. "You may as well ask me to bathe in their blood."

Without a word, he holds the fur out to me instead. Goose-bumps rise along his skin as he waits for me to take it. Undoubtedly, the pelt was keeping him warm. My armor is designed to stave off the cold wind—especially at heights like this.

He's only wearing long pants now, which were perfectly fine for the dank, humid woods at the border, but he'll suffer from frost sickness if I don't get him something warmer—and quickly.

I drag the fur into my arms. "Talsa, will you please find Nathaniel a fleece? Preferably one that a Harvest fae would wear, since the color of his hair and eyes most closely matches that class."

"Only if you promise to come down from this tower and prepare for your fight," she says pointedly.

I give her a quick nod, deciding that it's up to Nathaniel whether he chooses to follow me or go on his own way. If he hurts anyone, he'll die. He healed Evander already, so my reason for trying to keep Nathaniel alive is over.

In fact, it might be better if he takes off for the next three days...

No such luck. His heavy footsteps follow me down the stair-case and back toward the Inner Sanctuary.

Talsa quickly deviates in search of a fleece, returning to my side just as we approach the Sanctuary. She hands Nathaniel a warm coat fashioned from sheep's wool, which he takes, again without speaking.

In fact, he hasn't said a word since he spoke about fate, and his silence is beginning to worry me. He's not exactly the talk-ative type, but he usually has something to say.

The fleece is the color of clay and brings out the darkness in his hair and eyes when he pulls it across his shoulders. The thickness of the material makes his shoulders appear wider and his chest broader.

Now he looks like a Harvest fae—or rather, a larger-than-normal Harvest fae.

When he stops shivering, I wonder if his silence was simply an effort to conserve energy.

Shaking off my uncertainty, I veer sharply right to a set of steps beside the Inner Sanctuary, ascending them to the Queen's private tower. The Day Guards step aside at the top of the stairs to let me pass, but they don't look happy about Nathaniel's presence.

They'll just have to live with it.

Many of the rooms in the palace are public spaces. Some are open to the outdoors. Even the Inner Sanctuary can be opened up so that it's possible to walk from the Sanctuary down to the Spinning Lake where Frost fae gather to lend their power to those who want to skate across the lake's icy surface for fun.

But the Queen's Tower is off-limits except to the rare few: me, her guard, and the men she invites to her bed.

Despite its name, the Queen's Tower is wide and squat, making up for its shorter height with three levels of sprawling bedrooms interconnected with stairs.

Passing the guard's barracks on the lower two levels, we ascend onto the upper floor. Here the corridor is wide and beautifully decorated with living plants and intricate tapestries.

I pass multiple rooms before I pause at the first closed door, pushing it open to reveal a small room with a bed, closet, chest of drawers, and small mirror. All of the furniture is the color of gray pebbles.

Nathaniel looms beside me, looking unimpressed, sarcasm dripping from his voice. "You keep a room ready for prisoners. I'm honored."

I cast him a cold, hard stare. "This is *my* room. Yours is the one we just passed."

His eyebrows rise as he takes a second look at my room.

Sure, to an outsider, it probably looks bleak. If he opens the closet and drawers, he'll find more of the same colorless existence. The closet contains indigo armor and weapons. The small chest of drawers contains my underwear and training clothes—mostly black. I don't indulge in frills and trinkets like other fae.

Most fae think it's because I'm cold.

Nathaniel disappears, stops at the open door we just passed, and stares into the room that's going to be his for the next three nights—assuming I win the fight with Calida today.

I pass that room every day, so I know what it looks like inside: distinctly masculine, comfortably furnished, with a very large bed. Every now and then, the Queen's bed partners stay longer than a night, but she has rules—she never falls asleep with them, and I sleep between them and her.

Because their power is weaker than hers, she isn't worried about being alone with them. It's the women she needs protection from.

Even so, she never keeps any man for long. She loves our people, but she has never committed to any particular one of them.

Leaving Nathaniel to ponder his room, I cross my own room to fold up his pelt and deposit it in the bottom of my closet. Then I proceed to the window at the end of my bed, preparing to pull shut the heavy shutters to block out the sun's light.

I sigh when Nathaniel looms in my doorway again.

"Is this by choice?" he asks.

I tug the first shutter closed. "By *this*, I assume you mean my room."

"It's not what I expected."

I shrug. "I don't like clutter. I like simplicity."

"Why?"

I turn to find him leaning up against the wall inside the open door. Coming inside my room is a liberty I wasn't expecting him to take.

I should probably be suspicious of every question he asks me —every move he makes. He'll want to know everything about me so he can defeat me.

"It's the only way I can fall asleep."

"Huh." A slight crease appears in his forehead as he crosses to the window before I can shut it fully.

The Spinning Lake glistens far below us, its surface smoothed out and shining. The city sprawls beyond it, buildings made of earthy stone gleaming in the sunlight.

I'm surprised he hasn't asked me more. My answer wasn't exactly enlightening. The cold expanse that fills my mind when I try to remember my family also fills my mind when I try to sleep. I can't sleep in places that are cluttered with color and objects. Even the cupboards in this room are nearly too much for me.

If I could strip the room down to a soft surface and darkness...

"I can fall asleep anywhere," Nathaniel says, peering through the glass at the frosty expanse outside. "It's being awake that's hard."

Before I can ask him more, he points downward. "What is that?"

"The Spinning Lake."

He makes a face as if it's the most idiotic thing he's ever heard. "It's not spinning."

I roll my eyes. "You can't see it in winter because it's frozen. When it thaws, the water spins gently round and round in the same direction. There's a diamond in the center, far beneath the surface."

"The diamond is hidden, but you know it's there," he says with a smug smile. "A bit like the concealed door in your wall."

Somehow, all of our conversations end with me glaring at him.

The wall between my bedroom and the Queen's is thin enough that I can hear if anything's wrong. There's also a hidden door that allows me to access the Queen's room if she's ever threatened.

Only the champion is supposed to know about it, but Nathaniel identified it in a heartbeat.

He's perceptive, I'll give him that.

Still, it would be nice if a glare could erase him from my life.

"I need to rest," I say firmly. "That fleece you're wearing will only protect you for so long. If you don't want to die, I suggest you stay in your room."

He shrugs his shoulders, reminding me of a careless bear as he lumbers away from me, but he pauses in the doorway. "Why a single arrow?"

I stare at him. "What?"

"You've chosen to fight Calida with a bow and a single arrow. Why?"

I inhale and exhale. The answer to this question could reveal more than I want about how I strategize when I fight. I opt for the truth, but only about Calida. "Because my opponent is lazy and unimaginative."

"That tells me nothing."

"That's the best you're getting."

He shrugs and closes the door behind him.

Finally alone, I sink to my bed. I need a bath—would give

anything to fill the small tub that sits inside the equally small bathroom at the end of my room—but I won't be getting one anytime soon.

Sleep is more important. I've been awake for nearly twenty-four hours and I have less than two hours until I need to get dressed again.

I finish shuttering the windows, dropping myself into darkness before I peel off my damaged armor, strip off my underwear, and slide under the cool sheets completely naked.

Curling my knees to my chest, I try to calm my mind, but the room isn't dark enough. A glow at the edge of my vision forces my eyes open again. There must be a crack between the shutters...

The glow's coming from my chest. Right above my heart.

Right where Nathaniel touched me.

Curse the stars.

I creep across to my drawers, pull out the thickest training shirt I own, wad it up, and press it over my chest, blocking out the light as best I can before I crawl back into bed.

I can't breathe.

A weight presses against my chest and all I can see is darkness. Spinning darkness.

A cold expanse presses in on me, crushing my chest, freezing my heart, and the more I flail and try to get away from it, the harder it squeezes until I'm frozen and falling. Falling through darkness like a stone.

I can't move my arms or legs. Can't breathe. Can't feel...

A scream pierces the air around me and consciousness rushes back in.

I open my eyes to find myself still in my room. It was a

nightmare. Just a nightmare. The freezing pressure is gone. My heart is beating. I can breathe again.

Two new weights press against my shoulders, but these aren't cold.

"Aura!" Nathaniel leans over me, one hand pressed to each of my shoulders. His eyes search mine as he whispers, "Wake up."

I blink up at him.

Light streams around us, but my shutters aren't open. I'm glowing at my shoulders and my heart, casting light and shadow across his face.

I'm not lying in my bed, but beside it on the floor. The sheets are tangled around me.

He's kneeling beside me, his fleece coat draping across my frame as he leans over me.

The most shocking part isn't that I'm naked beneath the sheets but that I don't feel a shred of fear that he found me like this.

I try to clear my head. "What happened?"

"You must have fallen out of bed. I heard the thump from the corridor," he says.

I stare up at him, wishing I could see beyond the strands of his hair that fall across his face and obscure his expression. "I've never fallen out of bed before."

He shrugs, a hint of a smile playing with his mouth. "It's not something anyone plans to do."

"Right." I tug at the sheets, checking to make sure they're covering all my important bits. Luckily, they're charcoal gray. White sheets wouldn't hide much at all.

He releases my shoulders and the light recedes, fading from my skin.

"You don't have to tell me why this happens," he says, leaning forward again and running his finger across the top of my shoulder, making light play across his hand. "But I know it shouldn't."

I shiver, suddenly focused on his lips. They make such perfect sounds. Like his chest. When he speaks it's a rumbling sound that reminds me of a dragon that's carefully controlling its strength and power.

His entire palm presses against the side of my neck beneath my left ear. His fingers curl into my loose hair while his thumb strokes across my jawline, his gaze following the soft white glow that forms and fades as he moves.

"Don't die today," he whispers.

CHAPTER 14

I blink at Nathaniel in surprise. *Why would he care?* "Calida isn't strong enough to kill me."

He presses his lips together in a firm line as his eyes meet mine. "Desperation makes people dangerous."

I narrow my eyes at him. "She's ambitious, not desperate—"

"I know darkness when I see it."

My lips part. A stubborn denial rises inside me, but I push it away. The coliseum is the only place where fae are allowed to fight to the death. In any other circumstance, killing is only permitted by order of the Queen.

I challenge him. "Do you see darkness in me?"

A suddenly broad smile breaks across his face. He shakes his head at me, a slow side-to-side motion, a laugh in his voice. "None at all."

If I didn't know better, I'd think he was teasing me.

His smile fades, becoming serious, as if he were suddenly reminded of something. Or as if he'd given himself a mental slap. His eyes are deadly serious as he says, "Even at your worst, there's no darkness in you."

At my worst? What does he know of my worst? He must be thinking about how we fought each other this morning. After all, I did hold a knife to his neck and would have slit his throat if he hadn't spoken about his mother.

I want to ask him about her, but he straightens and leans back on his heels.

"The Day Guards will gather outside at any minute," he says, rising to his feet. "I heard Talsa say she was getting armor for your fight and then she'd wake you up. That's why I came out of my room. I'll open the windows."

Sitting up, I press the sheet to my chest, watching him as he strides to the window and opens the shutters.

"It's better if I'm not here when she gets here," he says.

He's gone within seconds.

I rise to my feet, still pressing the sheet across my body.

Before I can process our interaction, Talsa slips inside the room. She stops when she sees the open window.

"You're awake. Just as well. I let you sleep as long as possible, so you'll need to hurry."

Her hands are laden with clothing and she's also juggling a flask of sugar water, which she slides onto the top of the drawers before she lays out the clothing on the bed.

There's not much to the armor. Straps to cover my breasts. A pair of very tight, very short shorts to cover my pelvis.

I won't be able to wear any sort of heavy armor in the desert environment that Calida has chosen or heat sickness will knock me out.

What takes up the most space in Talsa's arms is a snowy-white fleece that will keep me warm on the walk to the coliseum.

"Thank you," I murmur. She doesn't have to take care of me. I usually do all of this by myself.

She pauses in the middle of my room. "I know that one

day... I might want to challenge you. But that doesn't mean we have to be enemies." She smooths down the front of her indigo dress. She's been awake as long as I have and the strain is starting to show around her eyes. "I sure as stars don't want Calida to win today."

She gives me a smile and I return it, saying, "You should be asleep already. Nadina and the Day Guards will take care of the Queen now. I appreciate all you've done for me this morning, but it's time for you to get some rest."

She shakes her head. "There's no way I'm going to miss the fight. I'll be standing behind the Queen's podium. Evander will be there too."

He should be resting, but he's never missed any of my challenges.

"How is he?" I ask.

She smiles. "Much better. All of the affected Border Guards are recovering well in the infirmary."

"I'm glad to hear it." I clear my throat. "Okay, well, please keep an eye out for Nathaniel then. I won't be able to watch him while I'm fighting."

"You don't have to worry about drama. The Queen made an announcement while you slept," she says. "Nathaniel is not to be harmed. She's seating him alongside her on her podium."

"Really? That's unexpected."

"Nadina doesn't like it, either," she says.

I try to shake off my misgivings. It's not my place to question the Queen's decisions. "Thank you, Talsa. I'll look for you in the crowd."

After she leaves, I dress quickly, braid my hair, drink as much water as I can, and cast a critical eye over myself in the mirror.

My hair is such a pale shade of blonde that it looks white. I'm not sure if it was ever lustrous. The ends are so dull these days that I try to keep it tied into tight braids to hide it.

Dark rings have formed beneath my eyes, stealing away the deep forest green of my irises and leaving them hollow-looking.

I scowl at my image before I pull on the fleece and my boots and stride from the room.

The Day Guards have gathered in the wide corridor outside with Nadina at their head. She waits at the Queen's door. It's my job to escort the Queen from her room to her podium at the coliseum. Once she's safely seated, I'll return to the preparation rooms under the coliseum to wait for the fight.

Nadina opens the Queen's door as soon as I approach—and promptly closes it behind me once I pass through.

Inside, Imatra sits at the enormous mirrors on the opposite side of the room.

Her room is a massive bedroom decorated in silver and gold, with its own sitting area. She places a poppy in her hair. The diamond crown she wears on her head catches the soft winter sunlight, matching the stones that drip down the front of her pearly white dress.

I can see myself in the mirror's reflection as she rises to her feet and turns to me. She is grace and beauty, a luminous image next to my washed-out form.

"Aura," she says, holding out her hands for me. "Come here."

Ever since I became her champion, she has treated me more like a daughter than a warrior.

"Today is about you," she says. "I'm not allowed to wish you luck, but if I could, I'd tell you that you don't need it. You are the strongest champion I've ever had."

"I live only to serve," I say, bowing to her.

"I know you do." She dips her hand beneath my chin so that I raise my eyes to her. Her lustrous gaze is filled with worry. "But remember that the walls between our rooms are thin."

I blink at her for a moment before her meaning sinks in.

My stomach drops to the floor.

She heard Nathaniel come into my room—probably each time before and after I slept.

But how much of our conversation did she hear? And what did she think of it?

She clasps my hands in hers. "Nathaniel is powerful and alluring. He's... *magnetic*. It's in his bloodline. But you must remember—*please* remember—that the Fell are wicked. The most wicked of all creatures to walk this Earth. He wants to destroy you and then destroy my Queendom. Our lives. Our peace."

I grip her hands. "My queen... you know me. You pulled me from the building that the Fell burned to ash. I owe you my life. I will never betray you."

She hurries to press her hand to my cheek. "I trust you, Aura. More than anyone. Never fear that I don't. I'm only worried for your safety."

The concern I see in her eyes goes beyond her worry about Nathaniel.

She doesn't want me to fail today. She doesn't want to go back to sleepless nights, waking with night terrors like she used to. If anyone can defend her, it's me. If anyone can stop the Fell slaughtering our people like they once did... it's me.

"The Fell creatures killed my family," I say. "The fire that was lit in my heart that night will never die. If I speak with Nathaniel, it's only to gather as much information as I can. I need to know his weaknesses so I can exploit them."

Her eyebrows rise. A relieved smile relaxes her lips and the tension leaves her eyes. "Of course. I should have known. You have always excelled at battle strategy. If only you were my champion when the Fell attacked us all those years ago."

I give her a small smile. "I'm not sure that I would have been much use at seven years of age."

With a sad laugh, she presses a kiss to my cheek. "Please be safe today, Aura."

I step back. "Are you ready, my queen?"

She gives me a nod.

I stride ahead of her and open the door with a command, "Prepare for the Queen!"

The Day Guards have already formed two rows between which the Queen will walk. They're dressed in ceremonial armor that glints in the light, their hair loose in honor of the occasion.

I'm surprised to see Nathaniel standing at the back of the line, boxed in on each side by a Day Guard. I guess this is the safest way to escort him to the coliseum. They're certainly serious about guarding him.

I lead the procession with the Queen walking behind me as we make our way down the stairs and through to one of the external wings.

The coliseum is located on the side of the palace opposite to the Spinning Lake, but it's a longer walk away. It takes us twenty minutes to pass through the city streets to the enormous structure.

The streets along the way are mostly empty. Everyone will have gathered in the coliseum already. They don't want to miss a minute of the events today.

As the giant stone structure rises above us, the din of voices increases.

I stride toward the private door at the side, which is guarded by more Day Guards. "Open for the Queen!"

They allow us through and we ascend the stairs to the Queen's podium. It's placed higher than the other seating areas with a view of the entire coliseum.

As soon as I appear on the podium, a deafening roar rises from the crowd. Many of them chant my name.

Aura Lucidia. Aura, Aura, Aura.

Thousands of fae fill the vast arena, overflowing into the aisles and up behind the seats in the elevated viewing area.

It looks like nearly every fae in the Bright Queendom has come to watch me defend my title. They're packed in so tightly that many have removed their fleece coats despite the winter chill—a chill that won't reach me in the wide coliseum below.

Sunstream fae have already created the desert environment in which I'll fight, and the glare off the sand below chills my heart.

"Aura." Evander never has to shout for me to hear his voice. It helps that as a Frost fae, he can control the wind, carrying his voice directly to me.

He stands with Talsa and a group of Night Guards who have stayed awake for the event. They fill the seats behind and slightly below the podium.

"I'm glad you're here," I whisper. The wind he sent to me catches my speech. It will carry my words back to him. "Are you okay?"

"I'm fine, but I'm worried about what the Fell will do. Please be careful."

"I will."

That's all I have time for before the Queen enters the podium under my watchful eye, taking her seat at the front while Nadina and the guards form a barrier at her back.

Nathaniel passes me next, followed by the same group of guards who surrounded him on the walk here.

He catches my eye, but that's all before they show him his seat on the far right-hand side of the podium and take up position around him.

Calida's family also sits on that side of the podium, in the seats below it, surrounded by other Solstice fae. I already feel the burn of their stares. They will be praying for me to make a mistake today.

The Queen inclines her head at me. "Thank you, Aura. I will watch you fight."

It's all she's allowed to say. I've heard her say it six times now. Six times I've defended my position since I fought and gained the role when I was only fifteen years old.

I bow low to her, turn, and stride back down the stairs.

There's no pomp and circumstance for me, not like there will be for Calida. She will prepare in one of the rooms beneath the coliseum with an entourage of helpers, but I shunned all of that during my first year as champion.

Reaching the lower corridor—also lined with guards—I enter my preparation room, remove my fleece and boots, drink another flask of water, and take a deep breath.

A bow and arrow wait for me on the table in the center of the room. I grip them in my hands, test their weight and strength, and then I exit the room into the underpass leading out into the arena.

It's time to fight.

CHAPTER 15

*S*unlight beats down on my shoulders and back as I exit to the crowd's jubilant roar.

The heat within the sealed but transparent combat area hits me immediately.

Magically-enhanced sand scorches my toes and burns the soles of my feet. The sand dunes stretch from one side of the arena to the other, fine grains shifting with my smallest movement, making my footing uncertain.

Sweat trickles down my face and between my shoulder blades as I make my way to the center of the arena, but I refuse to reveal how weak the heat makes me.

Calida enters the arena a moment later, taking up position opposite me, planting her bare feet confidently on the uneven ground.

Like me, she's wearing the barest armor—straps across her breasts, thighs, and groin—but unlike me, she's enjoying the heat.

I turn to face the Queen's podium high above us as I remind myself why I'm here.

Protecting the Queen is my life. I've given up everything—friends, the possibility of love—so that I am single-minded in my task.

If Calida wants my job, then she'd better be stronger and faster than me, because she'll need to be if she thinks she can fight Nathaniel.

The crowd's roar is insatiable as I take a knee on the sand, but this time I'm not bowing to the Queen. I'm not required to pay respect to Calida, but it's become my practice to give my opponent one last chance to back out.

The roaring fades as the watching fae lean forward to hear the words I repeat each year, a promise I make to all of my opponents.

When the silence is deathly, expectant, I look up to meet Calida's sharp gaze.

"My name is Aura of the Lucidia," I say, using a spark of my power to allow my voice to carry beyond the combat area. "If you do not yield, I will kill you."

Her fist closes tightly around the bow and arrow she's holding. It's identical to mine: One sturdy bow. One arrow. No more, no less.

"You overestimate your strength, Aura Lucidia. You've exhausted your usefulness. The Queen deserves a new champion." Calida tips her chin, looking down her nose at me.

Behind her haughty façade, I recognize the hunger in her eyes. She not only wants to stand at the Queen's right hand. She wants to defeat *me*, Aura Lucidia, the undefeated champion.

She's only sixteen. She was only a baby when the Fell attacked and doesn't realize that we're not fighting for glamor or glory, but the strength of our defenses.

To challenge me is to declare that I'm not fit to protect the Queen, an accusation that I will not tolerate. My position has taught me that the minute I doubt my own abilities, it's my duty to step down.

That time is not today.

"Very well." Lightly gripping my arrow in my left hand and my bow in my right hand, I return to a standing position and walk thirty paces away from her.

The crowd's roar rises again as I turn to acknowledge the Queen. Eyes lowered, I press both the bow and arrow lightly to my forehead before extending my arms toward Imatra in a gesture of fealty.

My strength, weapons, and life are hers.

When I stand, she rises from her seat to address the crowd. As soon as she moves, silence falls over the coliseum as quickly as if she'd shouted for it.

"My people," she says, her voice carrying across the distance. The way she uses her power to be heard is effortless. "The Winter Ascending is a time of aspiration. With my permission, anyone may compete for a higher position in our society, whether it is as Captain of the Harvest or to take charge of the precious books in the royal library. But while it is a time of ascending, it is also a time of moving on. There is no defeat, only change. Through order and acceptance, we remain peaceful."

She pauses with a smile. "And always bright."

The onlookers break into a cheer. The Queen demands order and obedience in our society, but she is fair, and her decisions are always just.

She continues as soon as the cheering dies down. "Today, on the last day of the Winter Ascending, we are gathered to witness a challenge for the highest position in Bright: the position of my champion. The winner will stand above all others. She will have power to command the Captains of my Day and Night Guards, as well as power over the Border Guards. She will stand at my side as my most trusted protector against the Fell creatures whose wickedness destroys everything they touch."

She turns to cast a glare at Nathaniel and the hush that has fallen over the crowd takes on a new edge of tension.

I force myself to remain where I am. It's the first reckless action Imatra has taken around Nathaniel. If she's trying to incite violence against him, she won't have to say much more to cause a riot.

The podium is too far away to read facial expressions, but Nathaniel remains seated and completely still. He faces forward, not toward the Queen, but in my direction.

Is he watching me when he should be watching her?

It will only make her more angry to be ignored.

Imatra's voice rises with an edge of fury. "The Fell creatures have challenged us. They seek to destroy everything we are. But we will not let them. We will follow the Law with care and attention. We will allow this Fell creature to walk among us. We will not break the Law by shedding a single drop of his blood until the fight between champions. We will not kill him like he wants to kill us. We are bright! And we will never succumb to darkness!"

She lifts her right arm in my direction, the sleeve of her thick fleece coat falling away from her porcelain white wrist.

She shouts, "May the winner be the brightest of all!"

When she drops her arm, my fight will begin.

I exhale as the moment stretches out, my focus becoming sharp, every grain of sand suddenly visible to me, glittering like tiny stars.

I have to do this fast.

For a moment, I imagine it's the middle of the night and I'm at my strongest...

The Queen's arm drops.

So do I.

My bow hits the ground with a whisper as my right hand dives into the sand, scooping up a handful of grit as I break into a sprint, my arrow still clutched in my left hand, my bow left behind.

Calida has already notched her arrow and pulled her bow string taut, trying to follow my movements. She has two seconds to fire a clean shot.

She doesn't have to kill me to win, but she's aiming for my heart. Nathaniel said she would take her shot and he was right. If she didn't intend to kill me, she would have dropped her bow like I did.

I run in a zigzag, making it difficult for her to hit me, but I keep to a predictable enough pattern for her to anticipate my intended path.

My heartbeat slows as the muscles in her forearm tense. Her right hand twitches, the fletching feather at the end of the arrow catches the light, and she looses the arrow—

Energy bursts through my legs as the arrow spins in a perfect curve toward me.

At the last possible moment, I leap out of its path.

The bolt flies to my left, its sharp arrowhead cutting across my bicep before I dive toward the fiery ground, plant my left fist in the sand still clutching the arrow, and flip through the air. I land close enough to Calida that I can see the sudden fear in her eyes.

She's fired her only arrow.

Now she drops her bow.

Her arms fly up to defend herself, sunlight spearing across her head and shoulders as she prepares to harness her power.

Her strength lies in raging heat and flames. She's strong enough to burn me to ash.

If she were smart, she would have started with her magic instead of wasting time trying to use the weapon. She's lost precious seconds and I don't intend to give her time to harness her energy to its fullest. My own energy will be sapped soon.

My right hand opens, pitching the full handful of sand into her eyes. She screams and flails, clutching at her face as the sunlight she was calling to herself vanishes.

Not giving her time to recover, I leap forward and spin to gain momentum.

My foot connects with her chest so hard that she flies backward, landing with a thud three paces away. Unlike her, I've trained in combat every day since I was ten years old.

I don't need magic to fight my battles.

Now that my right hand is free, I snap my arrow in half, drop the blunt end, and leap into the air, the sharp end of the arrow gripped like a dagger.

Crashing onto her before she can get up, I plant one knee on the sand to take the full force of my fall so I don't break her ribs, while my other knee pins her chest.

Her thrashing stops. She opens her streaming, red eyes just in time to see me.

With a fierce scream, I drive the arrowhead at her right eye.

CHAPTER 16

*T*he entire arena is deathly quiet as my weapon hovers a scant hairsbreadth away from Calida's face.

If I wanted to, I could have killed her.

She freezes. A scream dies in her throat. Tears flood her face and drip down her cheeks. I sense her wild heartbeat beneath my knee. She knows I didn't have to stop.

My gaze hardens. She's barely more than a child. I was younger than her when I fought in this coliseum, but I'd lived the life of an adult for several years before then.

She can try to harness her magic now, but I will kill her before she can gather enough daylight to fight me.

My glare is hotter than our surroundings, sweat dripping from my face as I shout. "Do you yield?"

Her lips press together before an angry, childish shriek emits from her mouth. "You blinded me. That wasn't fair!"

"Do you think that the Fell creatures will fight fair?" I thump my free hand against her shoulder and raise my voice to a roar. "Do you yield? Or will you lose an eye?"

Hatred fills her face and it makes me want to rage at her.

Does she think I wanted this life? Does she think I wanted my family to die so that I would become this way?

I have nothing but my job as a protector. I'm doing her a favor.

Her lips quiver. Her pride must be fighting her logic right now.

"I yield," she finally shouts.

I immediately pitch the arrow into the sand several paces away and rise off her. I give her a short acknowledging nod after she clambers to her feet.

The arena remains quiet as my feet crunch through the sand.

Returning to my dropped bow, I stoop to pick it up. The onlookers won't make a sound until the Queen announces the winner.

I want nothing more than to run out of here and into the winter chill, but I need the outcome to be official first. Our normal summers never affect me this badly because they're abated by cool breezes and crisp nights; the environment in the coliseum is like an oven.

A glance back at Calida tells me she's still standing where I left her, her eyes filled with daggers, but there's nothing she can do now. She lost—and far too fast.

No other challenger has been subdued so quickly. I annihilated her reputation, but at least I left her alive.

I turn away from her to take another knee, this time to honor the Queen.

A second after I touch the ground, the rapidly approaching sound of crunching sand fills my hearing. At the same time, a shout from the podium makes my head snap up.

Nathaniel is on his feet. "Aura!" he shouts, pointing behind me.

Surely, Calida wouldn't—?

I twist, my eyes shooting wide as she leaps at me, the broken arrowhead gripped in her hand.

I drop and roll to the side, narrowly avoiding the fatal stabbing blow she aims at the back of my neck. A coward's attack.

Missing her target, she lurches forward, landing on her hands and knees before she attempts to jump away from me, but my battle instincts are in full swing.

Sand sparkles around us, flying into the air with my movement as the handle of my sturdy bow crashes against her throat.

I hurl us forward, driving her into the sand as she chokes against the force across her neck. My left hand snaps out to grab her wrist and stop her from stabbing me in the side.

I have a split second to make a decision.

I should kill her. She's proven that she'll fight dishonorably. She has chosen to become my enemy.

All it would take to end her now is for me to drop my knees on either side of the bow. The pressure would break her neck.

But... *damn the stars*... Nathaniel shouted a warning to me.

If I kill her, it will look like he influenced my decision.

I can already hear the whispers that will start... I haven't killed an opponent since I became champion. They will say that the Fell's wickedness made me more violent... made me darker... made me kill her. Then they'll ask if I'm still loyal.

I have only one choice.

My right palm flattens, pressing to either side of the bow rammed against her throat.

I draw on the tiniest spark of starlight power left inside of me, the smallest shot of light.

The bright spark shoots from my fingers into her body and she can't do more than gasp before she goes limp beneath me, her unconscious eyes closing.

I struggle to breathe, my chest heaving.

That was the last of my strength.

Blood drips from the cut across my bicep. Until the Queen breaks the desert spell over the arena, I'm in danger of collapsing, which will make the outcome unclear.

I have to remain upright.

I release the bow and shuffle off Calida, staying on my knees as I turn to face the Queen again. A drop of sweat falls from my forehead, sizzling on the scorching sand as I bow my head over my raised knee.

Lifting my face, I wait for her verdict.

The silence around the coliseum feels like glass. Not only did Calida try to stab me in the back after she yielded, but Nathaniel warned me about it.

A fae tried to kill me.

A Fell tried to help me.

It's hard enough for me to process what happened, let alone for the watching fae.

Up on the podium, Imatra rises to her feet. Even from this distance, she looks very pale. Her hand might be shaking as she lifts it, but I'm not sure.

The desert scene vanishes from the coliseum, and the heat breaks, a soft carpet of grass appearing beneath my feet. I inhale my first clear breath since entering the arena.

Fresh air. Thank the stars. My energy returns. Not much, but enough to keep me alert.

I breathe deeply, remaining on one knee as a strong wind grows nearby, swooshing around Calida's unconscious body and lifting her into the air before gliding her toward the underpass and out of sight.

It's the Queen's magic. She will place Calida in her preparation room where the healers are waiting. Then Calida's family will come to collect her.

After that... who knows what will happen to her after what she attempted to do to me.

As for me, as soon as the Queen announces me as the official winner, I will return to my room, pick up my fleece, and... *not* go on with my life.

Unlike every other battle to defend my position, my next fight is far more terrifying.

The Queen's verdict begins as a soft murmur. "The fight is over. The winner is clear. My champion is..."

Her voice swells as she speaks, growing in volume, until it cracks across the arena, a violent shout not like her at all. My eyes widen as the sound washes toward me in an unexpected wave. This has never happened before. *Is she angry?*

"Aura of the Lucidia!" she screams. She grips the railing as if she's not in control, her pale face turned toward the distant mountains.

She screams my name again, but it's like the scream is being ripped out of her. "Aura Lucidia is my champion!"

Lightning spears across the far mountains and a hundred distant dots rise into the air, cracking wings casting sharp electricity across the mountain peaks.

More thunderbirds than I've ever seen rise at the same time.

From the middle of them, a much larger form shoots into the air, its enormous wings sweeping the creature high above the others.

At the same time, a violent wind grows around me, plucking at my body and flinging me to the grass.

I don't have the strength left to fight it.

"Aura!" the Queen screams, reaching out across the railing as if she wants to fly to me. "Prepare yourself. The Vanem Dragon comes to seal the Law."

CHAPTER 17

J attempt to push myself up with my arms, but the wind presses down on me, forcing me to faceplant into the grass.

Oomph.

I hate how powerless I feel right now. *I should be stronger than this!* Normally, I would be, but my strength is sapped.

Up on the podium, the Day Guards have quickly moved into a protective formation around the Queen, drawing her away from the railing, while the frightened fae around the arena cower and cling to each other in the increasingly freezing wind.

It's like my dream.

Freezing air spins around me, playing havoc with my balance, squeezing the breath from my chest.

"Aura!" Evander's voice reaches me on the wind, but I can't pinpoint where he is. "It's old magic," he shouts. "We're trying to control it. If you can hear me, stay close to the ground!"

It's not like I can do anything else. Managing only to raise my head, I finally locate Evander and a group of other Frost fae who stand with their arms outstretched beside the podium.

They've worked their way toward the front and must be trying to tame the wind, but the way their arms are buffeted around tells me it's no use.

If it's old magic... well, who knows how old magic works?

Another shout reaches me and at first I think it's Evander, but it's a deeper roar. I squint through the wind and the now swirling dust and snow—an odd combination of sand and ice.

I gasp as Nathaniel darts between the guards. They try to grab him, but he leaps right off the podium into the swirling wind.

He soars downward and lands safely on both feet with a thud that vibrates through the ground beneath my prone body.

He said that old magic was the only magic that applied to the Fell. Somehow, it's not affecting him the way it's affecting everyone else. In fact, he looks... stronger.

He runs toward me at a speed that takes my breath away. If that's how fast he can move...

Well, I wanted to discover his weaknesses. I guess it's just as important to discover his strengths.

"Aura." He pushes through the wind and debris to crouch at my side. He exhales with what sounds like relief as he focuses on me. "You're okay."

He actually sounds worried. He reaches for me as if he's going to help me up, but I recoil from him, afraid of the inevitable glow when we touch. Especially in front of thousands of watching fae. "Don't touch me!"

He jolts to a stop, retracts his hands, and lays himself carefully down on the ground so he's facing me.

My teeth are chattering now because of the cold, my jaw practically bouncing on the ground, and I hate how vulnerable I must look.

"You're afraid of glowing," he says, "but nobody can see you right now. The space around you went dark. That's why the

Queen was screaming for you. Evander's going crazy trying to stop the wind."

He glances back at them. "You can see out, but we can't see in."

I force sound through my chattering teeth. "If you touch me and I glow, they might see through the dark."

He considers me for a moment. "I see your point. If that happens, they'll jump to conclusions and think you're attacking me—or that I'm hurting you."

His muscles flex as he sits up and slips off his fleece coat. It's the only thing keeping him warm. He might be resistant to old magic, but he's not immune to the cold. Goosebumps rise and his muscles shiver beneath his skin as soon as he takes it off.

He wraps the fleece around me and tugs me into his arms, lifting me back to my feet.

It's warm inside the coat. Even warmer inside the circle of his arms. I tip my head back to see him, knowing I'll have to give the fleece back soon.

His dark eyes meet mine. "Keep it on," he says, rubbing my arms through the thick material as if reading my mind. "The wind will stop soon enough."

"Will we be visible again when it does?"

He shrugs. "Probably."

"Then I need to give it back before that happens. Imagine the uproar if they saw us like this."

His chest vibrates with laughter as he breaks into a smile. "Drama."

My smile fades. He doesn't look at me as if he hates me.

In fact, if I think back to the moment he stepped out of the mist this morning, even then he didn't look at me with loathing. My first impression was bravery. Determination. He had a plan and he was resolute about carrying through with it.

And just now... he jumped off a platform and raced into darkness to find out if I was okay.

I'm filled with intense confusion. It's impossible to figure him out, to understand his motives. He chose a path that could lead to my death, but now he's looking at me as if he's worried about my safety.

"Why do you want to kill me?" I whisper.

The laughter in his eyes disappears. "Maybe I don't."

"But you invoked the Law—"

Lightning cracks overhead, drowning out my voice as it strikes the ground only a few paces away.

Nathaniel flinches and pulls me closer to his chest, but I struggle against him with a sharp rebuke. "Thunderbird lightning can break through any darkness!"

He jolts away from me, immediately placing distance between us.

I don't have time to give back his coat, but at least I'm not standing in his arms anymore.

Seven thunderbirds circle overhead, including Treble, whose blue-gray feathers are lit up with lightning that crackles across the stadium.

A deep thudding sound reaches me through the howling wind and a new shadow looms over us.

The Vanem Dragon dwarfs the thunderbirds circling around him. His ruby red wings extend half of the width of the combat area, his powerful legs and claws thumping onto the grass as he lands with a roar. "The old magic is awake!"

Fire smolders inside his mouth as he throws back his head, the light in his eyes more alive than a flame. His brown eyes latch on to me as he folds away his wings, a creature of pure power and wisdom.

He thuds toward me, an enormous, scaly, breathtaking beast.

CHAPTER 18

*I*t isn't the first time I've encountered the Vanem Dragon but each time he seems more regal and powerful than the last.

Breathe, Aura.

With every step he takes, the fire smoking around his mouth and nostrils calms and the wind dies down around us until it's nothing more than a whisper.

At the same time, a sort of cocoon forms around us. The tunnel of wind merely expands so that it swirls farther out, raging even faster around the combat area. The fae in the stadium cling to each other while we are left in the quiet center.

Stopping directly in front of me, the dragon's shadow drops me into darkness. Lowering his head, he says, "Rise, Bright One."

I stare at him in confusion. I'm already standing.

The dragon swings his head across to Nathaniel, who has taken a knee, his head bowed.

My eyes widen in surprise as the Vanem Dragon nudges

Nathaniel's shoulder with the tip of his enormous snout and speaks again, softly. "Rise, Bright Heart."

I'm in shock. The Vanem Dragon is calling a Fell *bright*.

As Nathaniel rises to his feet, finally lifting his head, the Vanem Dragon considers him carefully and calmly. "You have your father's courage, Nathaniel Shield."

Nathaniel remains silent, more subdued than I've ever seen him.

"You can speak freely," the dragon says, his eyes glowing again. "We can't be heard over the wind."

Nathaniel meets the dragon's gaze. "You told my father to seek peace."

The dragon nods. "I did."

"Instead, he found death."

I gape from Nathaniel to the dragon, my surprise deepening, but at the same time, my chest hurts right around my heart.

Nathaniel told me that his father died in the final battle between our two races and now it sounds like the dragon was involved in that.

I've never heard of any instance where a dragon deigned to speak with a Fell, but then... I don't suppose my people would admit it—assuming they knew. The dragon is *our* wise one, not the Fell's.

A deep sadness fills the dragon's eyes, the kind of sadness that makes me feel like a hole just opened inside myself.

"You think I betrayed your father," the dragon says to Nathaniel.

"Did you?"

The dragon shakes his head. "Your father summoned me to the Spire on the border between Bright and Fell. He asked me if peace would ever be possible between the fae and the humans. I told him that only great courage would bring an end to war. I thought he could be the one to create that peace."

"He rode out at the head of the human army that night," Nathaniel says, his lips turning down at the corners, his voice bleak. "His horse dragged his body back... in time for him to gasp his last words."

Nathaniel meets the dragon's eyes, his own filled with greater fire than the dragon's. "What happened in the fight? I have a right to know."

"You need answers, but I have none." The Dragon hangs his head. "My sight was dark that night. From the moment the sun sank behind the horizon, I couldn't see anything. I couldn't lift my wings, couldn't move. All of the dragons and thunderbirds on the mountain were grounded and sightless. A dark magic took hold of us and didn't release us until an explosion of light split the horizon—the brightest light I've ever seen...

"By the time I flew to the border, Queen Imatra sat weeping in the middle of the glitter fields—glitter fields that weren't there before that night. She was surrounded by hundreds of humans and a squadron of fae, all dead. She was in shock and wouldn't speak about what had happened.

"Days after, she told me that the Fell—the humans—tried to use dark magic to kill her. They created an explosion that filled the horizon with fire. She fought back by creating the glitter field and it cut down the human army."

The dragon sighs. "I'm sorry. That's all I know."

Nathaniel shakes his head in denial. "My father never used dark magic. There has to be another explanation."

"I'm sorry, Nathaniel—"

"That's not all," I whisper. "Not entirely."

My heart is bleeding. Everything I've heard has struck through me with painful stabs. Nathaniel's father followed the Vanem Dragon's advice only to die because of it.

Now Nathaniel needs answers about his father the same way I need answers about my own parents.

Nathaniel turns sharply to me. The dragon's eyes glow with a sad fire as it swivels to face me.

"Aura…" the dragon begins. "You don't have to relive it."

"Queen Imatra was holding me," I say to Nathaniel before I can't get the words out. "She was holding me in the middle of the glitter fields. I survived too."

When the dragon nudges forward as if it's going to try to soothe me, I step back.

"I can't relive what I don't remember," I say. "I have nothing before that moment. All I know is what I was told: My mother was leading the squadron of Border Guards who were killed. My father and I were inside the outpost that burned to ash in the explosion. Whatever the explosion was… it left me alive to crawl…"

I close my eyes and force myself to breathe. "To crawl through the ash to the Queen."

I try to see the dragon through the hot tears burning at the back of my eyes. I've pushed away my emotions for so long. I want to believe that I can handle anything, but it turns out I have a breaking point.

I'm tired. I've fought two battles today that have left me drained. Nathaniel and I don't have much in common, but we've both lost family to the war between our people.

I let the tears fall because I can't stop them and I've given up trying. "I remember seeing you fly toward us, Vanem Dragon," I say. "You wanted to land, but the Queen screamed at you that the glitter field would hurt you too, so you flew away. I don't know anything else—even though I wish I did. I don't even remember my mother."

When I look at him, Nathaniel is quiet. He nods slowly. "We've both had people we loved taken from us."

"We both want answers," I whisper.

"Aura." The dragon's suddenly sharp command makes me

jolt upright. He towers over me, his expression a stern mix of fire and steam. "You must take Nathaniel to the burn site. Perhaps you will find answers there."

A bleak laugh leaves my lips. I've been back to the burn site before and I've come away no wiser. "If there were answers in that place, I would have found them already."

The dragon lowers his head. His eyes up close are like endless pools of fire. "You have nothing to lose and everything to gain."

My forehead creases as he pulls away from me.

"And now," the dragon says. "I must do what I came here to do. Beware. When the wind drops, you will be seen and heard once more."

He inhales slowly, the scales along his neck burning brighter, fire glowing in his throat as it builds inside his mouth.

Heat increases around us and the Vanem Dragon's eyes crinkle with a smile before he lowers his head and begins to walk, carefully blowing a plume of fire at the edge of the circling wind.

He strides through his own fire until he has created a wall of flames circling inside the wind that rises up around us.

"The fire will eat the wind," he says with a wink. "And then I will swallow both."

With an earsplitting roar, he exhales again and this time when he inhales, he pulls the flame and wind toward him. It rushes in a stream of ruby and white as he drags fire and air into his body, his chest puffing up with the force of nature he swallowed.

Silence grows around us as the howling wind streams into the dragon's body.

Up in the stalls, the watching fae cling to each other, but they slowly open their eyes, their hair and clothing mussed up and wild after the raging storm that ripped through the stadium.

Up on the podium, the Queen grips the white railing, her dress settling against her body as the wind dies. The poppies she'd placed so carefully in her hair have scattered, her tresses a wild mess around her face.

She grips a handful of poppies in her hand against the railing, sending a thick stream of crimson sap down the white barrier. Even from this distance, I can see that her chest is heaving and her eyes are wide, but she doesn't speak.

Around her, a group of Frost fae, including Evander, lower their arms. Evander looks for me first, his shoulders relaxing when he sees me.

"Aura, please tell me that you're okay?" he whispers on the wind.

"I'm okay, but please stay back." His magic catches my words and whisks them away.

The Queen leans toward him and he speaks to her for a moment, no doubt telling her what I said.

The dragon throws back his head with a grin, demanding my attention as a shiver runs the length of his body from his head to the sharp tip of his tail. "Ah, the old magic tastes sweet."

His voice grows in volume, telling me that the magic he swallowed is giving him more power.

"The Law of Champions has been invoked," he roars. "I have come to bind the champions and seal the Law." He lowers his head to us. "Aura and Nathaniel, face each other and clasp each other's forearms. As soon as you touch, you will be bound and then I will seal the Law."

I swallow my fear. If I glow, the watching fae will think it's part of the ritual, a consequence of the old magic, not some weird reaction I can't control. Well, not that I can control anything to do with the old magic.

The air is warm around the dragon and Nathaniel stopped shivering as soon as he arrived. I slip off the fleece, placing it carefully on the ground before I turn to face Nathaniel and step up to close the gap.

He holds out his hand, turning his palm up, waiting for me to take his hand.

I reach out. My fingertips slide along his skin before I curve my palm around his forearm. His fingers close around my arm, anchoring me as we stand face to face.

The glow from our connected arms is gentle. White. The same as it has been all day.

The watching fae lean forward in the stalls, a thousand pairs of eyes on us, a murmur building among them.

It's an intense relief not to have to hide this glow anymore. What a strange feeling. I should be anxious right now, but just like Nathaniel is a contradiction of mysteries to me, I find myself relaxing in the glow, my lips rising into a small smile as I meet his eyes.

The deep, dark of his gaze draws me in, his hand gentle around my arm, his calloused palm making me feel alert. It's like drowning except that I'm not fighting it.

The dragon leans toward me. "Aura?"

I raise my eyes to his. "Yes?"

Ferocity grows in his eyes and his voice lowers so much that I have trouble hearing him. "This shouldn't be possible. The Law must be satisfied in the right order, but…"

"What is it?" I whisper.

The glow in the dragon's eyes deepens and I have trouble deciphering his expression.

Is he afraid? He can't be. Surely. The Vanem Dragon is never afraid.

He growls. "You and Nathaniel were already bound."

CHAPTER 19

J try not to react, but it's impossible to stay still.
My eyes widen and I nearly let go of Nathaniel's arm, but he holds on.

"How?" I demand to know.

The dragon glances from Nathaniel to me—and back again.

Nathaniel has become my focus too. What shocks me most is that he doesn't look surprised by this news.

"You knew," I whisper as a gentle breeze brushes my face. I've gone from boiling to freezing and back to hot, but this time the heat is born from panic.

The breeze at my face is seeking, telling me that Frost fae all around the arena are pulling at my words, listening to everything we say no matter how softly we speak.

"It's okay," Nathaniel says. His thumb brushes across my arm as if he's trying to soothe me. "It happened this morning. When we fought at the border and you…"

He pauses. It's a long pause, long enough to tell me he's skipping over describing the events.

The strong snatch of wind around us tells me that our conversation is being carried all the way back to the podium.

This time, the way the Queen's hands move across the railing tells me that she has chosen to use her own power to hear us. Her frost power isn't quite as strong as her other powers, but she won't want to miss any of the details in translation.

I squeeze my eyes shut.

I remember what I screamed at Nathaniel before I used my power on him: *I am the Queen's champion. I will fight you with my whole heart until one of us is dead.*

"You invoked the Law without knowing what you were doing," he says. "I tried to stop you, but it was too late."

I remember his hand landing on my chest, the way he'd tried to push me away a split second before I touched him and let my power loose.

I'd used my power and bound us to my words.

"You invoked the Law and bound us," he says. "After that, I had to carry through. I had to come here. You'd already sealed our fates."

I'm not sure what I'm supposed to feel. I'm numb mostly. Incapable of reacting. "I did this. Not you. *Me.*"

I asked him why he wanted to kill me. He told me he didn't. Before that… I'd asked him why he'd been ignoring the way I healed that little girl.

He told me that fate couldn't be that cruel.

I might have the power to heal the illness that plagues his people, but I've forced us into a fight to the death.

If he trusted me to help them… If he thought I might get past all the history between our people and help the humans… then he might choose to die so that I can live…

He's right: Fate is too cruel. But it's a fate of my own creation.

"Very well," the Vanem Dragon says. "The Law has been invoked. The champions have been bound."

He lowers his head with a glint in his eyes. "Don't react. You won't be burned, but I must seal the Law now."

Fire builds in his mouth as he opens his jaws above our arms.

Burning isn't all I'm afraid of. It looks like he's going to bite our arms right off.

I grip Nathaniel's arm tighter, satisfied to see that he also appears alarmed. He drops his weight as if he's going to pull us both away from the dragon if he has to.

The dragon purses his lips and the air around his mouth turns crimson. A soft tentacle of ruby-red smoke drifts from his mouth and wafts toward our connected arms to form a circle around them.

"The Law was invoked at dawn this morning," the dragon says. "It is now sealed. The Law must be satisfied before dawn on the third day."

He lowers his head to murmur, "You have nearly used up a day. That leaves you three full nights and two full days before you must fight. Use your time wisely."

He raises his head with another roar, towering over us again, but this time, he appears like a guard, a sentinel daring anyone to disobey him.

"The rules of the Law are clear: First, no fae may spill a drop of Nathaniel's blood. Likewise, no Fell may spill Aura's blood. Second, Nathaniel may not harm another fae, just as Aura may not harm a Fell. Contravening either of those rules will lead to the offender's immediate death.

"From now on, Aura and Nathaniel will walk side by side, never out of each other's sight. They will eat, sleep, and breathe together. Aura will teach Nathaniel about the fae. Nathaniel will teach Aura about the humans. By the time they fight, they will have walked a thousand miles in each other's shoes. They will understand each other's hearts. They will know the other better than they know themselves. *That* is the curse of the Law of Champions."

He lowers his head one last time while the air continues to pluck around us.

Many fae are listening to every word we say now. All of the Frost fae scattered through the stadium are pulling our words through the air and feeding them back to those who aren't close enough to hear.

Evander will have heard everything, but he doesn't send any messages back to me.

What was said here will be repeated over and over among the fae, spreading like a vine. It will either carry seeds of new understanding or grow thorns of resentment and anger.

Only the next two days will reveal how my people will react.

"You chose a difficult path when you engaged each other in battle this morning," the dragon says, backing away from us. "By the time you're forced to fight again... neither of you will want to."

With a sweep of his wings, he takes to the sky, a magnificent blood-red beast.

The thunderbirds crack their wings, spearing the air with lightning as they soar upward with him. Treble drops lower, circling around us twice before following the other birds. He knows I'll call him when I need him.

The stadium is silent.

My people aren't cheering my name now.

I did this. I risked the entire Queendom.

I look to the Queen, waiting for her verdict, bracing for her reaction. I promised her that I would never betray her.

My only purpose is to protect her, but now I've risked everything...

She grips the railing, speaking softly. "My people. We have faced revelations today. Events we never expected. But the unexpected can only make us stronger."

She breaks into a confident smile. Broken poppies rise from the seats around her, reforming into perfect flowers as she lifts her arms.

"Aura captured the Fell champion," she says, her voice swelling. "She already fought him and beat him. In three nights she will fight again. She will win!"

The sky opens up as her power streaks from her fingertips. Frosty winter air sweeps across the combat area and snowflakes begin to fall around us. Perfect. Silver. Glittering.

The mood within the arena changes. The tension eases, the wary looks stop.

The fae focus on their Queen, who calls out, "My people! Rise up and celebrate! We have never had this chance before. Aura has given us what we need. We are the brightest to walk this earth and soon we will control Fell country. We will drive away the darkness that sickens the land and put an end to their wickedness and destruction."

She tips her head back and shouts, "Aura will win and we will prevail!"

The arena erupts. Fae jump to their feet. My name is screamed so loudly by so many voices that my ears hurt.

Imatra could have crucified me. Instead, she has given me a very clear order: I will win. At all costs. After that, the Fell will be annihilated.

Nathaniel's hand slips from mine. He remains standing tall, his shoulders back, steady in the face of so many fae screaming for his blood. Snowflakes land on his naked shoulders, melting against his chest.

The sounds of the roaring fae fade into the background. They aren't cheering for me. They're cheering for what they think I am.

A killer of humans.

CHAPTER 20

I don't wait for the cheering to die down.

I move past Nathaniel, slowing to brush my arm against his.

I'm finished with ordering him around, but I need him to know it's time for us to leave. The Queen will want all eyes on her when she descends from the podium. The longer we stay, the more attention we take from her.

Talsa and Evander wait for us at the entrance to the underpass. Talsa is juggling both our fleece coats and a flask of water, but Evander steps between us before she can pass them to us.

"Aura," he says, striding toward me. "This is my fault. If I'd protected you this morning, you wouldn't have had to—"

"It was my responsibility," I say, stopping him. "I invoked the Law without knowing what I was doing, but it was my choice, not yours. It wasn't your fault."

My brother exhales, his chest deflating, his fists clenching, but the look he gives Nathaniel could flay the skin off him. "I guess I know what you needed to tell me."

He squeezes my shoulder and I read into the gesture everything he's not saying aloud. He already lost his mother. He doesn't want to lose me too.

At the same time... he's angry with me because I created this situation.

"Be careful, Aura," he says, drawing upright to cover his emotions. "Your life is about to get very complicated, but above all, do not die on me. Promise me."

I can't promise him. Can't voice what I know could be a lie, but I nod, unable to speak.

Evander swings away from me, but he pauses beside Talsa, dragging her into his arms, flask and fleece and all.

She tips her head back, murmuring quietly and nodding before he presses a kiss against her temple and walks away.

I'm left surprised. My brother is an intensely private person, but the affection he just showed Talsa speaks to a connection that must have been growing for a while.

I want to ask her about it, but I hold my tongue as she passes us the coats. I have to trust her to talk to me when she's ready.

She ushers us into my preparation room. It's cold and silent inside—both of which I welcome after the panicky heat and deafening noise of the arena.

Nathaniel pulls on his coat and takes up position leaning against the wall on the left-hand side of the room while I slump into one of the chairs at the table.

Talsa hands me the flask, but I push it gently away. "Nathaniel first."

Her brow furrows. "You're dehydrated—"

"So is he." I drop my head into my hands, rubbing my forehead, my mood swinging like a stone tied to a string.

The truth is I don't think I can swallow anything without throwing it right back up. It's better to appear grumpy than sick to my stomach. The first can be confused with strength; the second will look like weakness.

Nathaniel speaks from the side of the room, directing his question at Talsa. "What should I call you?"

Talsa stiffens, still gripping the flask. "You may address me as 'Talsa of the Dusk.'"

He peels himself off the wall and closes the gap, reaching for the flask. "May I? Talsa of the Dusk?"

With a huff, she hands over the jug and relocates to the side of the room.

He pulls up the other chair and takes a seat opposite me. Then he sets the flask quietly onto the table and nudges it toward me.

"Small sips," he says. "Or you'll bring it back up."

I stop rubbing my forehead to glare at him, but he returns my scowl with an unwavering stare.

"Okay, then," he says when I don't reply. "We'll go one for one. I'll start. That way I'll throw up first. Deal?"

I blow out an exhale. "Fine."

He takes a small drink from the flask before he pushes it across the table.

The aftereffects of fighting are kicking in and my hands shake as I raise the flask to my lips, sloshing water across my mouth. I manage to swallow a tiny amount.

Pushing the bottle back to him, I say, "Explain something to me: you can't hurt a fae. That means you can't hurt them in *any* way, doesn't it?"

His eyebrows draw down in a wary-looking furrow. "It's possible that even bruising a fae could be fatal for me. I'm not completely sure about that, but I'm not about to test it."

"But a fae can hurt you—as long as they don't spill your blood or kill you, is that correct?"

He sighs. "It is."

I shake my head in disbelief. "That doesn't seem fair."

He wraps his fingers around the bottle, but his focus

remains on me. "The Law of Champions is old law. *Nothing* in the old law is fair. It's designed to make the next three days the hardest we've ever faced. A champion who wants to win a country for their monarch has to live long enough to fight the final battle."

I squeeze my eyes shut for a moment. I had no intention of conquering Fell country when I fought Nathaniel this morning. "What now?"

"Now, we rest," he says. "We both need sleep this afternoon. You're normally awake at night, yes?"

I nod.

"Then I'll follow your routine."

I snort. "My routine involves a few hours of sleep and many hours watching the Queen."

He grimaces. "She's going to love having me around." Then he gives me a quizzical look. "What exactly are you guarding her from? I didn't see angry mobs at the palace gates."

I sigh. "Civil unrest among my people is far from obvious."

I'm not afraid of talking like this in front of Talsa. I trust her not to repeat our conversation.

"Fae are quiet about their intentions," I say. "The Queen has been challenged on a political level more times than I can count. Most challenges come from the Solstice fae. Calida's family is always stirring up some kind of trouble, but as long as the Queen controls an army of guards—and has me—all they do is talk."

"I wouldn't have guessed. It all seems so peaceful."

"Don't judge by appearances," I say, arching an eyebrow at him. I reach for the flask and take a longer sip. The liquid slides down my throat and soothes my nerves. I take another long drink before I return the remaining half to him. "The rest is yours."

As soon as he finishes the bottle, he stands and hands it back to Talsa. She gives him a scowl, but her glare comes slower this time.

By the time we leave the room, the roar of the crowd has abated. The Queen will have left and every other fae will be returning to their homes.

I spin as a figure moves in the darkness of the corridor.

I'm immediately on my guard until I recognize the woman who strides toward us through the shadows.

Serena was the Queen's champion before me—a Solstice fae like Calida but with a very different temperament. The color of her hair and eyes are identical shades of amber streaked through with gold.

She started training me when I was only ten, but I didn't know she was grooming me to take her place until she asked me to challenge her. Well, *asked* is a gentle way of putting it.

My fight with her was fierce. Neither of us would yield, but I held back. I didn't want to hurt her.

I still remember the way she screamed at me during the fight. *Is this how you would protect the Queen?*

After that, I nearly killed her.

Now the pinch of her bronzed lips tells me she's intensely unhappy. "You should have killed Calida."

Well, at least her anger isn't about Nathaniel.

"Hello, Serena," I say. "It's been a while."

"Don't play niceties with me," she snaps.

As she steps fully into the light, the scar I gave her becomes visible across the side of her slender neck. Our most talented healers worked over Serena for hours to save her life, but no magic could erase the burst of my starlight that cut across her neck that day.

Now the anger on her face is startling. "Calida's family has been causing trouble for the Queen for years. Calida tried to stab you in the back. She dishonored every fae—even her own family."

"Then her family will deal with her."

"Don't be naïve. If she was willing to dishonor herself in front of a thousand fae, consider what she'll do in the shadows."

"It's not my job to kill my people," I snarl, anger rising inside me. "I'm here to protect the Queen."

She casts a pointed glance at Nathaniel. "Well, you're certainly doing a great job of that."

Power sparks between my fingertips as my anger rises. "If you want another scar to match the one you already have, keep talking."

She tips her chin at me. "Next time you face Calida, bring that anger."

Her long coat slides across the pearly stone walkway as she spins on her heel and strides away from me.

Her gold-tipped boots smack the ground as she throws back at me, "You'll need it."

CHAPTER 21

*T*he power fades from my fingertips.

I wish Serena wasn't right.

Talsa edges up behind me. "Ignore that witch."

My eyes widen in surprise. Talsa is reliable, steadfast, and dependable. It's rare for her to curse anyone.

Her coral hair swirls across the collar of her coat. "She's right, of course. You should have killed Calida when you had the chance. But even so, it's not her place to make it sound like it was an easy choice. None of your choices have been easy today."

I stare at her, pretty sure my mouth is gaping. As rare as Talsa's anger is, it's rarer that anyone speaks in my defense.

Warmth fills my heart, but then it fades. What I said to Nathaniel is true—fae are subversive. They always have an ulterior motive. And it's always the ones closest to you whose betrayal you don't see until it's too late.

My voice quiets and my eyes narrow. "Why are you helping me today? The Queen's champion has no friends. Only challengers."

"But you do have family." She shifts a little before she glances along the underpass.

The only other person here is Nathaniel, who has stepped back into the shadows at the side of the corridor.

Talsa clears her throat. "You risked everything to bring Evander home and save him. You treat him like your blood brother and he loves you like his blood sister."

"I'm not sure how that obligates you—"

Oh.

The kiss Evander dropped to her forehead.

She's trying to tell me they're together. I suddenly think back to the moment when I arrived with Evander from the border this morning. Talsa had frozen in shock and worry. At the time, I thought it was because of all the potential casualties, but her focus was purely on Evander.

"Are you and Evander...?" I dare to ask.

Talsa's sky-blue eyes light up with her smile. "We'll ask the Queen for permission to be married at the next Spring Pairing."

I can't stop the smile breaking across my face. "That's wonderful. You don't need my approval, but I'm glad."

"I know you thought I should challenge Mia as Captain of the Night Guard," she says. "But I want children. I want to be a mother. If I take on the role of a captain, I won't be able to have a family until someone challenges me. *This...*" She gestures at the indigo uniform peeking from under her coat. "It can't be my life."

"I understand." I bite my lip. "You both hid it so well."

She grimaces. "We had to. There are a lot of rumors about Evander. We had to be careful."

I press my lips together in distaste. "I've heard the whispers." *Even if nobody dares say them to my face.*

"What whispers?" Nathaniel asks, breaking into our conversation.

When I glare at him, he shrugs. "Just curious."

"*Curiosity* is the problem," I snap. "You may have noticed that under the Queen's matriarchy, the majority of command positions are held by women."

"It's a little obvious."

"Well, Evander is one of the few men to hold a senior position. You see, male fae are physically larger and stronger than women, but their magic is much weaker. Evander is one of the rare men whose power is as bright as any woman's. It's one of the reasons the Queen placed me with his family. We were both *curiosities*. Things for people to stare at and whisper about. Sometimes the whispers are tolerable. Mostly, they aren't."

I'm not about to repeat the rumors, but Talsa interrupts me with a blunt: "They say he's not actually strong, but he sleeps with high-ranking women to gain their favor and steal their powers. There's even a nasty rumor that he slept with Aura and somehow siphoned off her power so he was strong enough to win his fight to become the Border Guard Captain."

That rumor was particularly sickening. Evander has always looked out for me. I've always had his back. Even if we weren't born from the same parents, he's my brother. My love for him is as a sister.

I give Nathaniel a bitter smile. "Lies, of course. My world is only pretty on the surface."

"I'm beginning to see that." His gaze suddenly flicks past me toward the end of the underpass that leads out to the city.

A breeze wafts through the corridor, cooling my cheeks as shadows move in the distance.

Nathaniel prowls past me. "It's time for us to move."

When we exit the underpass, I'm not surprised to find Nadina and half a dozen Day Guards waiting for us, but I am surprised when she approaches me with her hand on her hip where her weapon rests, as if she thinks she'll need it.

The other guards are doing the same.

"The Queen has ordered us to escort you to the palace," Nadina says. "She wishes for you to rest. I will continue to watch over her today. Mia will guard her tonight. The Queen will call you when she wants to speak with you."

My stomach sinks. It's a veiled order to stay away from the Queen until she's calmed down. Imatra may not have publicly criticized me, but she's definitely upset.

I don't react.

"Very well," I say.

I start to walk past Nadina, but I freeze when the guards quickly surround me—front, sides, and back.

Normally, I would walk at the front, leading the others. Now I face a Day Guard's back while Nadina takes up position on my right-hand side. The other Day Guards step up to surround Nathaniel and even Talsa. Their hands rest on their hips, where their weapons are concealed.

Nadina faces forward, but her head is turned to study me, a hard stare.

She's waiting for me to retaliate against their aggressive move.

My jaw clenches, but I swallow my anger. The Queen has ordered this. If I hit back, it will be like a strike against the Queen.

I hear Evander's voice in my head, the way he used to calm me as a child: *Stay frosty, Aura.*

I sense Nathaniel's gaze burning my back as we're escorted back to the Inner Sanctuary. He's perceptive enough to sense the changed mood and the way I'm suddenly being treated as a threat.

Many fae fill the streets now and the two Day Guards walking ahead of us nearly lose their voices shouting for people to clear the way.

The fact that I'm being escorted won't go unnoticed, but I hold my head high.

Nothing has been easy today, but I've got through it so far.

I can get through this too.

CHAPTER 22

*W*hen we finally arrive at the bottom of the stairs to the Queen's Tower, Talsa breaks off from us with a pointed stare at the Day Guards blocking her way until the women step aside to allow her to leave.

She swings back with an overly cheery and equally pointed declaration. "I'll see you at the Ball tonight, Aura. Since you're still the reigning champion, you'll need to be there."

The Winter Ascending always ends with a city-wide celebration.

The Queen opens the palace to the most powerful fae while there are smaller celebrations hosted throughout the city for everyone else.

The party starts at midnight and goes until dawn. Sunstream fae hate that it happens at night when they would normally be asleep, but they can catch a half night's sleep before it begins and then see in the new day when the sun rises.

I turn to face Nadina. "Thank you for your assistance. I can take the Fell creature from here."

She opens her mouth, as if to object, but Talsa's loud reminder mustn't have slipped completely over her head.

I'm still the champion. The Queen's mood will pass and then Nadina will be beholden to me again. She has been the Captain of the Day Guard for longer than I've been champion. Her respect for me has always been unwillingly given, but she understands the hierarchy.

"Very well," she says. "We will follow."

I exhale my first clear breath since we left the coliseum.

Making it to the top of the staircase and to Nathaniel's door, I spin to him with a command. "I will come for you at sunset. Make sure you close your door. The Day Guard will stand guard outside it."

"Aura." There's a warning in his voice as he stops at the door to his room, practically dwarfing the open doorway in his thick coat.

The Day Guards gather behind him, scowling at him because he isn't entering his room like I told him to.

"Never out of each other's sight," he says, his dark eyes refusing to let me go.

"What?"

He sighs. "Try stepping into your room. You'll see."

I scowl at him before I stride toward my own door.

He remains in his doorway watching me.

I step into my room. At least I try.

Oomph.

It's like hitting a wall.

Rubbing my chest, I step back from the doorway, glaring at the open space that I can't seem to move through.

Nathaniel takes careful steps toward me.

It's like watching a bull trying to tiptoe.

"I was hoping I was wrong," he says. "But the dragon was

clear: *From now on, you will walk side by side, never out of each other's sight. You will eat, sleep, and breathe together.*"

"That was a metaphor," I say, a deep, unhappy denial. I shake my head violently. "He didn't mean it literally. He couldn't have."

"We could separate before the Law was sealed, but not now."

He actually sounds sorry. I guess the idea of sleeping near each other is as repugnant to him as it should be to me.

I find myself gripping the doorway as the full impact of the Law starts to sink in. "Well... what about when we need to bathe?"

He leans in close. "That's a conversation we need to have *not* in front of witnesses."

Dear stars.

I try to ignore all of the staring guards. I can't even...

"Your room is larger. It has a couch," I say loudly, striding back to his room. "You will be sleeping on it."

I throw my head back with a haughty stare at the guards as Nathaniel steps inside.

I close the door firmly behind myself, shutting out all of the prying eyes in the corridor, including Nadina, who stands with one hand on her hip and both eyebrows raised.

Nathaniel perches on the edge of the couch.

The room is unlike mine in so many ways. Not only are the walls soundproof, but the decor is pure luxury. The walls are painted a pale blue interlaid with silver filigree.

A massive four-poster bed rests on the right-hand side covered in a blanket made from the softest wool. The pillows and sheets are spun from the smoothest silk and the drapes hanging around the bed are transparent. They're deliberately designed that way so that silhouettes are easily visible through them.

The left side of the room has a plush couch with intricately carved wooden legs and so many pillows that Nathaniel has already knocked two of them onto the floor.

Massive closet, massive bathroom, massive mirror on the wall deliberately placed to reflect everything that could possibly happen in that bed.

Massive great damn mistake.

"You said you can't sleep in cluttered spaces," Nathaniel says, resting his hands on his knees.

I'm surprised by his concern, but he's right. I really didn't think this through. "I'll make it work."

I throw off my coat, slinging it over the carved wooden chair beside the door as I head to the bathroom. Of course, it doesn't have a door.

This room was built with only one purpose in mind. The Queen may appear demurely beautiful in public, but like every other powerful fae, she doesn't deprive herself of whatever she wants.

Sometimes I think I was born into entirely the wrong race. Thank the stars for Evander and his father, who both believe in hard work and trust above gaining power.

A deep clawfoot bath sits at the far side of the bathroom, along with shower facilities, two snowy-white sinks, and yet another very large mirror.

I splash my face with water and wipe away the dust, gripping the edge of the sink and leaning over it for a moment.

The battle comes back to me in flashes, worse than my fight with Nathaniel this morning. I didn't have time to process that fight afterward. I had to keep going, but now...

Splashes of sand. Golden and glittering.

Calida's scream of rage.

The *snap* as I broke my arrow.

Heatwaves shimmering across my vision.

The crunching sand beneath my feet as I ran straight at her arrow.

Dammit.

I process my traumas far better in my own empty room.

All the bright, shiny things I'm surrounded with right now glint everywhere I look. Even the soap sparkles.

A hand on my shoulder snaps me back to the present.

Nathaniel stands beside me. The room is warm and he left his coat behind. It bothers me that I was so affected by the fight that I didn't hear him approach me.

His deep brown eyes meet mine in the mirror. "Maybe we should relocate to your room," he says softly. "I can sleep anywhere. The floor will be fine."

I don't like the way the dark rings under my eyes look worse in the harsh lighting as I look back at him.

"I said I'll make it work," I snap, irritated at how thoughtful he's being.

Despite my attempt to wrench out of his hold, he doesn't let me go. "Stop," he says. "You're hurt."

I edge away from him, but his hand deftly strokes down my shoulder to the cut across my bicep where Calida's arrow sliced across my arm.

I shiver at the unexpected warmth from his touch and the soft glow rising from my skin that makes the rest of the room dim in comparison.

"You need a healer," he says. "Or at least a bandage."

"So do you," I shoot back at him.

He glances at his own arm, where Evander's blade cut him this morning. The blood has clotted, a jagged line of crimson across his skin.

His eyes darken for a moment, the tension around his mouth increasing.

Before I know what he's doing, he spins me so that my back is pressed against his chest.

His right arm slides around my stomach, dragging me so close that I can feel all the muscles of his thighs, stomach, and chest. I shiver at the glow between us, the way it brightens and wanes in time with my rapidly increasing heartbeat.

"Look," he orders, before I can lift my boot and kick his shin to make him let me go. "In the mirror."

Standing like this, our left arms are positioned side by side.

Our cuts are nearly identical.

He sustained his wound fighting Evander. I got mine fighting Calida. We both darted right to avoid a killing blow and ended up with cuts across our left biceps.

"We have the same wound," I breathe. "What does it mean?"

His cheek presses to the side of my head. His right arm softens around my waist, his hand curling around the top of my opposite hip.

He seems distracted, but he focuses on our wounds in the mirror again. "Probably nothing. Maybe something. I don't know."

Remaining pressed against him, I turn my head away from the mirror, facing the bathroom wall. "I glow because we're bound together, don't I?"

"No," he whispers. "I don't think so."

My forehead creases but I don't pull away. "But the Vanem Dragon saw me glow and he said that we were already—"

"Binding is darkness, Aura. We're bound to kill each other. The energy around us is the darkest possible magic—the very opposite of light. *That's* what the dragon sensed." His voice lowers. "I think you glow because..."

He slowly shakes his head and falls silent.

"Because why?" I ask.

He dips his head and turns me very carefully to face him.

While one hand wraps around my hip, his other travels up my side and across my shoulder blades to release my braids, his fingertips easing my hair loose.

He's so intent about it, his focus completely on my hair, that I don't pull away.

I know I can. Any second now... I will.

"Look," he whispers, turning me to face the mirror. Every movement he makes is precise and cautious. The way he touches me... it's like he's handling porcelain.

My forehead creases as I consider my reflection. Even with the glow between his chest and my shoulder and hip, I look tired and drawn.

Then his hand sweeps up my neck in his first rapid movement to tangle in my hair and rest beneath my ear, triggering shivers that run to my toes.

In the mirror, my eyes light up.

The dull forest green disappears. Glowing emerald color splashes through my eyes. My cheeks blush pink as if the sun has kissed me. My lips fill with healthy color, parting in shock.

The woman glowing at me in the mirror is alive, full of strength.

Who is that person?

She has never been me.

I try to breathe, near panic as Nathaniel carefully slides his hand away from my neck. As he moves away, the color fades from my cheeks, the light dies in my eyes, and my lips press together.

I feel like I've lost something and I want it back.

CHAPTER 23

"No." I grab Nathaniel's hand and press his palm to my cheek, watching the lights dance across my face again.

The warmth in his hand is like stepping into a dark expanse, but it's not empty. It's perfect and whole.

I try to breathe. "Is this what you saw when you took off my mask this morning?"

This morning, he told me that my beauty is lethal. I didn't know what he was talking about. That woman in the mirror—she is certainly something. Lethal? Beautiful? Maybe. *Alive.* Definitely.

Possibly even... *powerful.*

More powerful than I ever looked before.

"Why?" I ask, turning my wide eyes to him. "What is this?"

I grip his hand to my cheek, even though he's poised beside me as if he's on the brink of pulling away.

His gaze travels from my face all the way down to my boots. I'm still dressed in my battle clothing, which is to say that I'm not wearing much at all. My feet are more fully covered than any other part of my body.

"I thought maybe you knew, but now I see that you don't." He very firmly pulls his hand away, leaving me to return to the dull skin that I'm used to living in.

I close my eyes and turn away from who I really am.

I should be shocked that I want his touch back, but I miss that *me*. I want her back. I want to feel the way she feels... *whole*.

"We need to rest now." Nathaniel clears his throat and backs away from me. "I'll use the bathroom after you're done. If I stand against the back wall around the corner, I can't see in."

I feel empty as I say, "Do you think that will work?"

He growls as he rapidly turns and strides away as if he really needs to be somewhere else. "It had better or I won't be responsible..."

He disappears around the corner.

"Damn!" He jolts back into view, rubbing his forehead. A string of curse words flies from his mouth before he takes a deep breath. "Of all the..." Another string of curse words flies at the invisible barrier he must have stepped into.

His cursing finally stops.

He takes a deep breath, turns to face me, and says, "So it looks like we can't allow a solid object to block our view of each other. Which means neither of us gets any privacy."

I guess not.

I could try to cover up with a towel. Maybe even try to wash with a cloth slung around me, but it seems a bit pointless.

It's the curse of the Law of the Champions.

"Eat, sleep, and breathe," I say. "We are to be stripped bare in front of each other. All of our flaws and weaknesses revealed."

Casting a regretful glance at the mirror and the me I can't be without his touch, I turn my back on him, slip off my boots, and unwind the strapping from around my chest.

My fingertips rest for a moment on the scar at the top of my left breast—a small crescent shape I've had for my whole remembered life. It reminds me of the crisscross of scars across Nathaniel's shoulder blades, but now is not the time to ask him about them.

I shimmy out of my shorts and cross to the shower, turning it on and stepping under the steady flow. Closing my eyes, I yank the water pressure up to its fullest so it crashes around me, splashing across my head and shoulders.

Now at last, the glittery room around me fades into nothing. The wash of water is like a downpour of rain that blocks it all out. Sand and grit rinse from my hair and gather on the bottom of the shower to scratch my toes. A crimson line flows from my wounded bicep down my arm and turns the water weakly red.

I wish I could stay here forever, but I force myself to reach for the faucet to turn the shower off. Quickly squeezing the water from my hair, I cross one arm across my breasts—as if I haven't already given Nathaniel an eyeful—and grab a towel from beside the shower to wrap it around myself.

When I look up, I find Nathaniel leaning with his back against the left side of the doorway, his gaze firmly fixed on the upper door frame.

I guess he's not ready for all of my flaws.

As I grab a second towel for my hair, he asks, "How did you get that scar?"

I pause. It's a small scar. The kind he wouldn't see if he hadn't looked.

"How did you get yours?" I challenge.

He hunches his right shoulder forward. "I asked a witch to make the cuts—one for every person I've lost. I went back to her many times."

I hadn't expected him to answer me, let alone so fully. "You've lost a lot of people."

He shrugs. "It was her idea to turn the scars into a lattice. She said I was making a prison of death for myself, so I may as well wear the bars in plain sight. She didn't exactly approve of the path I chose for myself."

"What path is that?"

When he doesn't answer, I try a different question. "Is she the one who created the spells on your hands?"

"She is."

"Do you have many witches in Fell country?"

"Only one. She's as powerful as your Queen. But she lives in darkness instead of light." Without pause, he asks me again, "How did you get your scar?"

I shiver. His honesty demands honesty in return, but my scar is another big unknown. Droplets of water gather as my hair continues to drip across my shoulders, the second towel feeling heavy in my hands.

"I don't know," I say. "The Queen said it must have been from flying debris during the explosion. I guess I'm lucky to be alive since it could have cut through my heart, not just my skin."

He nods and crosses to the pile of towels beside the sink, getting a new one. "Here," he says. "Let me."

He drapes the towel across my head, lining it up with my forehead before twisting it gently around my hair and stepping back again.

I scowl at him before I pat the perfectly-positioned neat twist. "I can dry my own hair."

"I know you can," he says, giving me a faint smile that quickly fades away. "But... I needed to do that for someone who isn't sick."

I'm confused by the emotion in his voice and what is clearly an important gesture for him.

Clearing his throat, he points to the door where he was

leaning before. "The mirror doesn't help. But you can focus upward if you wish."

Of course. No matter which direction I face, I'll either see Nathaniel or his reflection.

Somehow I don't think he'll have any flaws.

I focus on the wooden door frame as hard as I can, aware of his movements, finding my gaze lowering when the water turns on.

No flaws at all. Every muscle is in exactly the right place. The water flows down his perfect back and thighs. Even his shoulder scars look like they belong.

The rushing water is a soft lull and I realize how bone-deep tired I am. It's already been a long day. I allow my eyelids to lower. Only for a second.

"Aura."

I jolt upright.

Nathaniel stands beside me with a towel slung low around his hips.

My heart thuds too loudly in my chest. How could I fall asleep like that? How *did* I fall asleep when I normally can't sleep in cluttered spaces?

I should have stayed awake and on my guard. I definitely don't like being taken unawares.

Nathaniel gives me a smile as if he's trying not to laugh. "Should I be offended that you fell asleep when I took off my clothes?"

Is he... teasing me?

My cheeks burn as his laughing gaze dances across my face.

I try to swallow my embarrassment. "There are clothes in the cupboard that should fit you. Assuming you want them."

I move out of the way so he can leave the bathroom to rummage around inside the closet. The Queen keeps clothing for herself and her male visitors in this closet. The men's clothing is in random sizes but I'm hoping Nathaniel will find something wearable.

He discards the less-than-practical clothing into the bottom of the cupboard before pulling out a soft white shirt and navy blue shorts. I avert my eyes again as he drops the towel to pull them on.

Then he gives me a quizzical look. "What about you?"

I shrug, feigning nonchalance. "I don't like sleeping in clothes." *Can't* sleep in clothes. But I don't tell him that. Sheets are as much as I can stand against my skin while I sink into cold oblivion.

He arches an eyebrow at me, but I hold my head high.

"Couch," I say, pointing as I stride past it.

When I glance back at him, he's grinning at me as if he doesn't mind me bossing him around. I'm not really sure what to make of this lighter side of him. He seems to have left his serious side in the bathroom with his clothes.

I plant my hands on my hips at him and demand an answer. "What?"

His smile softens. "You fell asleep while I stood five paces away from you. You wouldn't do that if you didn't trust me. Even if just a little."

"And that makes you happy?"

"Very."

I swallow hard. In the fae world, trust is barely existent. Maybe between married couples, but other than that, even a lover is likely to maneuver around you for some personal gain. It's accepted and expected, so nobody's feelings get hurt.

Until couples are paired together, love is a commodity. So is trust.

But apparently not to Nathaniel.

"You tried to stop me," I whisper. "This morning when I invoked the Law, you told me to stop."

His smile fades. His dark eyes are serious again.

He gives me a single nod.

I ask my question carefully because I *need* the answer. "If you didn't come here to invoke the Law, why did you fight me this morning?"

CHAPTER 24

*N*athaniel takes a deep breath. Inhales. Exhales. He's quiet for so long that the sound of his breathing is the only answer I get.

I persist. "You were prepared. You had the spells ready on your hands. What was your real plan?"

His smile is long gone now. "I told you this morning that there are some things I can't tell you, but I will always tell you the truth." He takes a small step back. The distance between us suddenly feels unsurmountable. "I'll give you answers tomorrow morning."

"Why not tonight?"

"Because you don't trust me that much yet."

"Can a night really make a difference?" I ask.

He smiles at me. It softens the determined edge in his expression, his dark eyes, the strands of wet hair falling across his face, the droplets of water on his shoulders soaking into his shirt.

Maybe. Just maybe it can.

I force myself to turn away. I crawl onto the bed before I

lower the sheer curtains on every side and slide under the sheets. Once there, I discard the towel from around my body and the other from around my head, dropping both outside of the curtains.

Too late, I realize that I didn't close the shutters over the windows, but Nathaniel's silhouette moves beyond the curtains, drawing the blinds closed and dropping us into darkness.

I wait a moment to find out if the way the Law works will stop us from sleeping separately, but I guess the curtain between us is sheer enough not to break the rules since I can make out his shape on the couch.

It's not as dark as I need it to be—sunlight creeps through the cracks, far too bright.

With a groan, I grab a pillow and pull it over my head. I sense Nathaniel pause before I hear the soft sounds of couch cushions being rearranged.

I didn't think it would be possible, but I'm so tired that I'm soon asleep and the nightmare I'm in fades into oblivion.

The moon's rising wakes me as it always does.

I sense her light ascend high in the sky, even though I can't see her.

In the space between awake and asleep, I'm surrounded by a dark oblivion that I can't quite touch, the cold seep of nothingness that I crave in the daytime.

Then my starlight power trickles through me, icy and crisp, calling me to shine... and wake up.

My eyes open to the gentle sound of a soft inhale.

For a second, I'm confused. It was like the night sky was breathing with me, but now I stare upward into the dim darkness and the unfamiliar ceiling, trying to place my location—the wrong bedroom. Wrong sheets. Wrong pillows. The pillow I pulled across my eyes has slipped to the side, but I'm still gripping it.

I remember that Nathaniel sleeps only a few paces away.

I remember that I'm caught in a nightmare and if I stop and think about it for more than two seconds, I'll end up screaming my lungs out.

I listen for his breathing, wondering if he's awake yet.

Eat, sleep, *breathe.*

It feels like breathing will be the easy part. Everything else is hard.

I'm about to slide from the bed when I hear a soft *swish.* Then an exhale. The sounds are out of time with Nathaniel's deep breathing.

Fear rakes through me and my instincts scream. A friendly visitor would have knocked, waited for us to wake up—would not be creeping through a dark bedroom.

Is the intruder here for Nathaniel or me?

Any movement will alert them that I'm awake, even a whisper-quiet one.

I stare hard into the darkness, making out the female silhouette creeping across the room at the base of my bed. She must be dressed in tight body armor because her silhouette is clean, her hair tucked up.

She passes by the bed and heads for the couch.

I told everyone Nathaniel would sleep there.

She raises her arms above her head and the gathering darkness around her hands tells me she's carrying a weapon that absorbs light.

I take my last deep breath, but I'm no longer afraid. I'm a twilight fae. I'm at my strongest now at the rising of the moon when the first stars sparkle in the night sky.

Energy spears through me, speeding my movements to an

impossible velocity. I slip from the sheets, roll beneath the curtains, and leap with all my strength.

She grunts as I knock into her and force her to the floor. Despite landing hard, she keeps hold of her weapon, jabbing it at me with quick, quiet thrusts.

I dodge left and right before I leap off her, flipping and landing in a crouch with one hand planted on the floor.

She hesitates, the dagger gripped in her hand.

At the same time, Nathaniel rises up behind her, a looming shadow.

She spins and jabs the knife at his chest. He darts to the side just in time, but he doesn't retaliate like I thought he would, bouncing backward on the balls of his feet instead, dodging the blows.

Her attacks are rapid and quiet, but his evasive moves are faster. He's strong enough to disarm her—easily. He disarmed me this morning.

"Fight back," I whisper.

But as I look up from the floor I remember... he can't.

The damn Law. He can't hurt her or he'll break the Law and die anyway.

A low hum of anger grows in my throat.

He may not be allowed to hurt her, but I can.

I leap upward again, following her movements in split-second time, and grab her hand as she retracts it. I yank with all my strength, pulling her back so hard that she flips in the air and makes a graceless landing.

The dagger is now mine. What's more, I'm now standing between her and Nathaniel. Right where I should be.

"You want him, you go through me," I say.

"Traitor!" she hisses.

I let the accusation wash off me. I was hoping I'd recognize her voice, but she kept it low. She has to be Calida. Serena warned me that Calida would strike in the shadows.

Slashing at her chest, arms, and neck as she struggles to evade the blows, I drive her toward the window.

She tries to disarm me and fails.

She tries to hit me and fails.

I will make sure she fails at every attempt to hurt Nathaniel.

She backs into the shutters but spins and flings them open, leaping nimbly onto the windowsill just as I thrust the dagger at her ribs. I graze her side, the knife sliding harmlessly across her armor.

Her hand flies out as she falls through the opening.

A blast of sunlight streaks from her palm, searing the space beside me as it cuts across the room.

I struggle to register the sound her power makes. The sickening snarl of flames that burn and consume.

Her black-clad form falls through the air into darkness below.

She's gone, but the burning scent in the room is now my nightmare.

CHAPTER 25

*N*athaniel slides to the floor, his back to the wall beside the door as I run to him.

His clothing is on fire. I can't imagine what the flames are doing to his skin.

I snatch up the woolen blanket from the bed as I race toward him, throwing the blanket across his burning shoulder and pressing it to extinguish the flames.

Panic fills my chest, squeezing my lungs. More panic than I thought I would feel for him, but I can't second-guess my feelings right now.

Kneeling beside his legs, I carefully peel back the blanket to check the damage. His right sleeve has burned away, the material still glowing. I swallow a scream at the mess of his shoulder and collarbone on his right side.

"Nathaniel!"

He sways forward and drops against me as I struggle to grab his waist and support his head without touching the wounds.

His skin lights up where we touch, bright enough that I can see that the blood has drained from his face.

He's barely conscious.

"Damn," he whispers, his eyes closed, his head dropping against my shoulder. "That hurts."

"You need Frost magic," I say, not wanting to touch the wound in case I make it worse. "The sunlight will keep burning until we counteract it."

But how to help him? There isn't a single Frost fae who will touch him... except maybe... Evander... whom Nathaniel tried to kill...

A groan of frustration builds and my stomach drops a thousand miles. Evander has always been protective of me, loved me, but he's even more stubborn than I am. He might blame me a little for invoking the Law, but he blames Nathaniel more.

"Not a drop of blood." Nathaniel groans.

"What?"

"Can't spill my blood... The fire cauterized the wound. No blood. She didn't break the Law."

That's how she got away with hurting him. But if she'd succeeded in killing him, she would have died too. She's a suicidal assassin. Which makes her even more dangerous.

His head sinks all the way onto my shoulder, his forehead pressed to the curve of my neck, facing me.

I'm frozen as I try to think of the quickest way to contact Evander. At this time of the evening, Evander would normally be up on the platform, preparing to fly out to the Border. In fact, he'd usually be gone by now, but after the events of the day, he might have delayed his departure—if we're lucky.

"Aura," Nathaniel whispers against my neck, breaking into my thoughts. "You're naked."

The flurry of my thoughts stops.

So I am. The blanket I used to put out the flames rests across my lap, but I'm completely bare from the waist up and my chest is pressed against the ragged edges of his burned shirt.

"Shh. I need to get help." I need to figure out how to get him to Evander. The platform is too far away and Nathaniel's too heavy for me to carry him there. Evander has to come to me— but how to call him? *Dear stars, how?*

Nathaniel's right hand shakes violently, filled with tremors, his wounded arm unsteady as he raises his fingertips to my face. The space between us lights up and I remember what I looked like in the mirror when he touched me.

"So damn beautiful," he says.

His hand falls away, shivers running through his chest.

He's going into shock. He'll be unconscious soon.

I try to swallow my panic, the panic that I didn't expect to feel. "Nathaniel?"

He doesn't respond and the room is quiet again.

Somehow, the silence clears my head. No matter how much hatred my people have for the Fell, I'm bound to Nathaniel. I bound myself to him. Sure, I did it without knowing what I was doing—I didn't do it on purpose, but I did it *with* purpose. I swore that one of us would die by the other's hand.

He will not die except at the end of my blade. *Mine.*

Accepting this rationalization of my feelings, I think fast.

Treble will be waiting on the platform right now too, ready for me to come out and take my evening ride. If I were a Dusk fae, I could communicate with him from a distance, but I'll have to hope that a whistle will work.

Easing Nathaniel's heavy body onto the floor beside the wall, I turn him onto his left side so that his wounded arm doesn't touch anything. The damaged blanket falls away from me as I run to the window, my fingers already to my lips.

I whistle as loudly as I can, sending prayers to the stars that Treble will hear me. He's trained to distinguish my whistle from other sounds, but I've never called him from this far away before.

I whistle again, growing more desperate, trying to get moisture back to my dry lips.

If he hears me, he will be here in seconds—

The crackle of lightning and Treble's thudding wings fill me with relief. A sob rises into my chest. That damn panic again.

I don't think I've ever seen such a beautiful sight as when he drops to the window, arching his wings to slow his descent. Blue-gray lightning streaks around him and lights up the darkening night sky.

"Treble! I need your help!" I call across to him, trusting him to understand me. "Please call Cadence. Tell her I need Evander to come to me right away."

Treble's wild eyes swivel to the room behind me. His eyesight is incredibly strong, so it will only take him seconds to see Nathaniel's burns. Not to mention, the smell of burning flesh fills the air around us and it's hard to ignore.

With an answering shriek, he banks away from the side of the tower so he can crack his wings—a double-crack that indicates an emergency. For a moment after that, he becomes quiet, coasting as he communicates with Cadence.

I take advantage of the moments before Cadence arrives to run to the closet and pull out an oversized shirt to cover my nakedness before I race back to the window.

Seconds later, Cadence appears in the distance. She spears toward the tower at full speed as if she's going to hurtle right into it. Her wine-colored wings are alight with crimson electricity. At the last possible moment, she swoops to the right.

Evander leaps from her back, diving through the air and the open window. His flight is perfect. The wind he controls catches his body and slows his descent, allowing him to hit the floor on his hands, somersault, and land on his feet. He's dressed in full armor but hasn't put on his facemask yet.

"Aura! What's wrong?" His gaze immediately lands on

Nathaniel. He jolts to a stop and takes a firm step backward. "What happened?"

"We were attacked by a Solstice fae. She burned Nathaniel—"

"And you want me to stop the burn." His clipped response tells me I'll have a fight on my hands.

"I need your help, Evander."

He whirls on me. "Why?" he demands to know. "That creature tried to kill me."

"No, he didn't!" I grab Evander's arm, refusing to let go even when his eyebrows draw down in a threatening scowl and the air around me freezes so cold, it would make any fae cower.

Despite what Nathaniel said about Evander stopping any torture of the Fell creatures, Evander isn't known for his mercy. He's had to fight very hard for respect—and he still doesn't have it.

"If Nathaniel wanted to kill you, he would have slit your throat while you lay helpless on the ground," I say, anger growing in my voice, and my power rising to brighten the space around us. "You know it's true."

Despite my statement, there's no give in Evander's expression, no softening. "He attacked us, Aura. He had a plan to hurt us."

"What about our plan?" I throw my head back, daring him to contradict me. "We planned to kill *him*. Him and all of his people. One by one until they're all dead. Isn't that our plan?"

I glare into Evander's face, searching for an unstiffening of his jaw, a hint of understanding. Anything that tells me he's hearing me right now.

Deep anger grows inside me when I don't see it.

Evander takes a step back and shakes his head. "I won't help him."

CHAPTER 26

*E*vander pulls away from me, but I refuse let him go.

"No!" I cry. "You don't get to walk away from me right now. I don't know what Nathaniel was planning to do this morning—what he really planned—but this path we're on now... this is *my* doing. I made this happen, not him. If you don't stop the burn, then by the time I meet him in the combat area, he'll be half-dead."

I allow my power to trickle through my hand into Evander's stiff arm, a cold, angry burn. I haven't thought of Nathaniel as a creature for hours, long enough that I hate using that description, but nothing less will convince Evander.

"Fighting such a pathetic creature while he's dying will be a dishonor to me," I snarl. "Is that what you want, Evander? For me to dishonor myself and our family this way?"

He stares down at Nathaniel with an angry twist on his lips. He looks at me again and his chest deflates. "No. I don't want that for you. I'll stop the burn. But I'm doing it for you. Not for him. His people killed my mother. I won't ever forget that."

I know his pain. I've felt it all my life. But Nathaniel wasn't the one who lit our lives on fire. I want to tell Evander that I don't give a damn who he does it for, but I hold my tongue and release his arm, watching carefully as he kneels beside Nathaniel.

Evander draws on the cold around us, the frosty breeze wafting through the open window, to build a stream of icy air beneath his palms.

Frost particles land on Nathaniel's arm and shoulder, his collarbone, neck, and chest where the burn is spreading, the cold temperature slowing the angry damage, counteracting it, until the redness fades and the burning stops.

I drop to my knees beside Evander as he finishes his work.

"I've stopped the burn," he says. "But his skin is badly damaged. You need a healer for that."

I resist the urge to gather Nathaniel's hand into mine. I can't do anything in front of Evander that suggests my motives are anything other than strategic. Not that I really understand my motives right now, but I know I need courage and Nathaniel has more bravery than I've ever seen.

I bite my lip, knowing what I have to do to help him. "I have to go home, don't I?"

Evander's expression softens for the first time. "Only if you want the Fell creature to be whole and healthy when you fight him."

I squeeze my eyes shut. "I was so angry when I left..."

"Then don't go back. It's up to you."

He rises to his feet, towering over me for a moment before he offers his hand, a peace offering of sorts. "You have to go back eventually."

"Crispin won't help me. He hates the Fell."

Evander makes a sound in the back of his throat that reminds me of the disapproving noises Nathaniel makes. "He's your only option."

I nod, knowing Evander's right. Then I swallow hard. "The Law stops me from leaving Nathaniel's side, but I need clothes. Can you bring me boots and armor from my room?"

Evander's unhappy hum grows louder. "Need underwear too?"

I grimace a 'yes' at him. Thank the stars he's my brother and has a very practical approach to life.

He's gone before I can say another word, returning quickly with a full suit of armor, a new pair of boots, and some under-clothes. I guess it doesn't take long to choose my clothing when the only items hanging in my closet are suits of armor.

"Make it quick," he says, handing me everything before he turns his back and fixes his gaze out of the window at Cadence, who coasts next to Treble. "The Queen's ordered reinforce-ments to the border in case the Fell creatures try to attack. I'm due at the border already."

I don't waste a moment, hurrying to change. "How many reinforcements?" I ask as I dress.

"Everyone she can spare. She's having dinner right now with her most senior Night Guards. All of the minor guards are being sent to patrol the border. I need to get out there before it turns into chaos."

"What about the Ball? Is that cancelled?"

"Hah! And stir up unrest? No. She's keeping this all quiet. Don't be surprised if I'm not there though. Talsa is coming with me to the border too."

When he speaks Talsa's name, his voice softens for the first time since he arrived. It's not exactly the right time to congratu-late him, but I don't know when I'll get another chance.

"I'm happy for you, brother," I say.

His expression softens even more as I do up the final clasp on my armor. Encased in the sleek material, I feel in control again.

A cold sense of determination fills me.

I know who I am in these clothes. I know what I'm capable of. I am still the Queen's champion. I am still the commander of her guards.

I twist my hair into a quick bun at the nape of my neck, pulling up my hood, but I don't worry about a facemask. "I'm done."

Evander gives me a quick half smile and then a firm nod as he turns back to me.

I return the nod before I focus on Nathaniel again. "Before you go, you will help me get Nathaniel onto Treble's back. After that, you can go."

Evander does a double-take, meeting my commanding eyes.

I'm no longer asking. I'm telling.

A smile grows on his face. "Welcome back, sister. I was worried the Fell had already broken you."

I snap back at him. "Don't insult me, Evander."

His smile grows broader.

He reaches out and wraps his arms around me. His hug is warm, but his voice is tense. "I'm afraid for you, Aura."

I squeeze my eyes closed against his chest. Our relationship has changed since we were children growing up in the Grove. Life has become complicated with rules, hierarchies, and power plays.

The bond of brother and sister has been challenged, now more than ever.

"You've always been a good brother to me, Evander," I say, pulling back. "I don't know if I ever told you that, but I mean it."

He drops a kiss to my forehead. "I'm glad you came into my life, Aura."

Stern again, he clears his throat and steps back from me.

A gust of wind rushes through the open window as he calls

the air around us, gathering it beneath Nathaniel's unconscious body.

I sense the force build inside the room, swooshing around my legs and chest as Nathaniel rises into the air, the air becoming a visible white stream circling his body.

Striding to the window, I whistle for Treble, who flies as close as possible to the tower. Evander twists his hands, directing the flow of air to turn Nathaniel's body and take him out across open air.

I ignore the prickle of fear at the back of my mind as Nathaniel floats beyond the windowsill with nothing below him but the surface of the Spinning Lake far beneath.

I would like to think that his would-be killer lies dead on the lake's surface, but she wouldn't have jumped from the window if she didn't have a plan of safe descent.

As soon as Nathaniel's body is clear of the window, I jump onto the windowsill, gather my legs under me, and leap out into the air. Treble tips to the side and catches me on his back.

We rise up level with Nathaniel's floating body and I take hold of his feet, drawing him toward me while Evander eases him across. The safest place for him is in front of me, so I wrap my arms firmly around his waist before leveraging his torso back to lean against me.

As soon as Evander releases him from the air tunnel, Nathaniel's full weight falls against me, pushing me backward, but I remain steady. If I let him go, he'll fall to his death.

As Treble rises into the air, Evander leaps from the window onto Cadence's back. He gives me a quick wave before he speeds away.

I'm on my own.

"Treble," I call across the wind. "Take me west to the Grove."

Back to the home I left behind.

❄

The dark forest spreads for a hundred miles beneath us, covering the western peaks of the mountains and far beyond, all the way out to the ocean.

The palace is now a distant blob behind us, the landscape beneath us passing from city to villages, and then trees. A controlled wilderness.

The silver lining of the boundaries that the Queen has placed between herself and me is that it leaves me freer than I've been for years to do what I want. Nobody will notice that I'm gone in the time it should take me to heal Nathaniel and get back to the palace.

My destination is the heart of the forest at the top of the mountain, the place we call the Grove. This is where trees are grown and felled, where the Queen's furniture is crafted, and the lumber cut for new homes.

It isn't as high as the peaks in the north of Bright where the dragons and thunderbirds live, so it isn't quite as cold. Even so, I shiver as we soar higher, approaching the humble cabin that rests in a clearing ahead. It's not the only one of its kind—other cabins dot the mountain at intervals—but it was built on one of the highest spots.

It's ironic in some ways that I grew up with a view of the sparkling city, living at the same height as the Queen in her palace.

We land in the clearing outside the cabin. The building is dark, and there are no lamps lit along the porch.

All healers are Dawn fae, part of the Eventide class like me, but Crispin always kept odd hours—awake half the day and half the night. His healing powers are as strong as any woman's. Like Evander, that means he's treated very differently by other fae.

The ground is covered in leaves and dusted with snow.

Settling down onto it, Treble lowers his wing and angles it toward the ground, but I already know I'm going to struggle to pull Nathaniel from his back. Nathaniel's so heavy and I'm afraid of hurting his injured shoulder. I can't anchor my arms beneath his shoulders, but dragging him by the waist will be much harder.

I'm not about to go to the trouble of pulling him to the ground if nobody's home.

"Crispin?" I call into the darkness, gripping Nathaniel while I remain on Treble's back. "Crispin?"

My voice falls into silence. The breeze whispers around me and the trees creak and groan.

I swallow my pride and try again. "Dad?"

Nothing.

Oh, and just wonderful, my arms are finally going numb from holding on to Nathaniel for so long.

I drop my head to his shoulder, trying to decide if we should take to the air again. Crispin could be anywhere in these woods. I'm not giving up, but I might have to search for him.

I'm surprised when Nathaniel stirs, trying to turn his head to see me. "Aura?"

"It's okay. I'm getting help." *Trying to.*

I sense the wariness in his voice. "Where are we—"

Oomph.

I scream as a hard object hits me from behind, smashing me off Treble's back.

CHAPTER 27

*M*y arms fly wide but not fast enough.

I yank Nathaniel with me and we both crash across the clearing, landing hard.

I bounce multiple times, kicking up snow as Nathaniel rolls away from me. I land closer to the tree line while he stops farther inside the clearing.

This time, the ground thuds as a large creature pounds toward me. I sense the air shift above me. Twisting onto my back, I look up just in time to see a living tree branch crash down toward me.

Holy stars.

An entire tree is attacking me; uprooted, its roots dragging across the ground. Granted, it's a small one, but its branches are as thick as Nathaniel's thighs.

I roll out of the way just in time to scream at Treble. "Fly! Hide in the clouds!"

The last thing I want is for Treble to get hurt—especially if his wings were crushed.

I recover from my shock fast enough to roll out of the way of another branch—this one aimed at my legs.

A second branch swings at my head as I try to roll to my feet. It narrowly misses me and hits a nearby tree instead.

An angry hum meets my ears. Ducking between thudding branches I make out the shape of a humblebee hive hanging from the tree that was hit. The hive is a large silver cone that matches the color of the silver stripes on the humblebees' bodies.

Oh, dear stars. Humblebees are peaceful creatures—unless their hive is attacked. Then they retaliate with swift ferocity and their stings burn like dragon's fire.

The last thing I need right now is a swarm of humblebees ganging up on me with this damn tree. It will only take one more unwanted bump on the hive for the bees to swarm. The tree's branches have already bruised my ribs, maybe broken a couple. I'm not about to let it pound me into the ground while the bees sting me.

Dodging another swipe and descending into a defensive crouch, my hands shoot upward, starlight shrieking through my arms and up into the attacking branch.

With a *crack*, the wood splits and shatters, showering me with debris. The tree gives a final groan and its roots burrow into the earth again.

As soon as it stops moving, I wait a beat to listen to the silence around me, breathing a sigh of relief that the bees' angry humming has stopped along with the tree's attack.

I jump to my feet, running to Nathaniel to check that he's okay.

He's unconscious again. Dirt and leaves stick to his wounds and now the chances of infection are a thousand times higher.

I scream out my anger as I rise to my feet, my fists clenched, and stand at his side, ready to protect him from the next attack.

"Aura?"

It's a voice I haven't heard for many years. Deep, fatherly. The closest to a father I ever knew.

Evander's dad emerges from the tree line. Like Evander, he has strong eyebrows that draw down with a ferocity that would make anyone run for the hills, but his hair is ash-gray like his eyes. Evander inherited his mother's Frost power as well as her arctic-blue hair color and her more slender physique. Crispin is bulkier, and somehow even broader and more muscular than I remember.

I guess seven years changes people.

"Nice welcome," I say, calling across the clearing since he hasn't come closer. "I take it you're still mad at me."

"Not as much as you might think."

He doesn't have power over nature—only Springtime fae could have controlled the tree just now, so I call out a challenge. "Tell your friends to show themselves or I'll cast light into their hiding places and make it very uncomfortable for them."

Five men, equally muscular, emerge from the trees. Judging by the size of their arms and chests, they're woodcutters. Each of them has dark brown hair shot through with forest-green highlights, a trait that belongs to Springtime fae.

Five men to control one tree.

They've learned to combine their power to achieve the strength of one woman. But I won't belittle their efforts. They've figured out how to work together, not against each other, a quality that Crispin tried to teach me. It only made me feel more alone.

My power couldn't be combined with anyone else's.

My starlight kills new plants, burns dead ones, cuts fae instead of healing them, and fails in sunlight.

I had no place here in this timber community, but I couldn't make him understand that.

"Why are you here?" Crispin demands to know.

"I need your help."

"What makes you think I'll give it?"

No reason. Not a damn one that will make up for me walking out on him seven years ago.

"Because I'm asking," I say.

He hesitates before he strides toward me, his anger growing. "Who's asking? The Queen's Champion? The Twilight fae? The girl who turned her back on her community? Or the daughter I raised to know better?"

He stops within the circle of twilight that I'm sending through the dark, his anger rapidly fading as he peers at me.

I struggled to answer his first question. Silence is the only answer to this one.

My hair is already pulling from its bun, my hood askance, so I pull both free as I stand my ground and return his silent stare.

"I was wrong," he murmurs. "Here stands before me a woman I haven't met before."

His gaze drops to the ground—to the person I'm protecting —as if he's seeing Nathaniel for the first time, but I know he's been aware of Nathaniel the whole time. Nothing escapes Crispin's sharp gaze.

"You brought a Fell creature to my door," Crispin says, his eyes narrowed to gray slits.

"I need you to heal him."

He peers at me again. "Why does a bright, courageous woman need a dark creature healed?"

"Because he's the reason I'm bright." My answer slips from my mouth before I stop it. Too much truth. Without enough explanation.

I brace for Crispin's response, but he simply nods. "Better not say any more about that."

He turns to the watching men. "Bring the creature inside. Do it quietly. We've already made enough noise."

I remain close to Nathaniel as four of the men stride toward us and pick him up, two at his shoulders and two at his feet, lifting him as easily as the timber logs they're used to carrying.

The fifth man draws level with me. He's older than the others and I find myself gaping up at him. "Gehrig?"

"Little Aura," he says, a warm smile growing on his face. "I used to carry you on my shoulders through the trees."

"I remember. Those are good memories."

He gives me a slow nod. "Better to keep the good memories and discard the bad. I apologize for your reception just now."

I shrug. "I didn't expect a warm welcome."

"It's not that." He places a hand on my shoulder, firm enough to make me pause. "We thought you were someone else."

My forehead creases, but he moves on, entering the room ahead of me. I consider what he could possibly mean. I'm dressed in the same armor as the Queen's guard. Both Night and Border Guards wear this armor when they ride out on their thunderbirds. Who did they think I was? And why would they attack that person?

Inside, the cabin feels larger than it looks from the outside. The bedrooms are upstairs. Downstairs is divided into two areas: living area and kitchen.

Crispin directs the men to lay Nathaniel on the rug in front of the cold fireplace before he kneels at Nathaniel's side. "I need the fireplace lit, a bucket of water to clean his wounds, and a knife to cut off his shirt."

Several of the men set about lighting the fire while Gehrig heads to the kitchen for water. I pull my dagger from my armor, handing it to Crispin as I kneel on Nathaniel's other side.

Crispin quickly rips through the burned material and carefully peels it from Nathaniel's chest before rolling him onto his uninjured side to inspect his back. He pauses there, staring at Nathaniel's back for long enough to frustrate me.

"What are you waiting for?"

He leans on his heels. "I need to be careful. This is not an ordinary Fell."

"Why do you say that?"

Crispin points to the scars on Nathaniel's shoulders. "Do you see the mark?"

I know what Nathaniel's back looks like. "I see scars."

Crispin leans forward. "Beneath the scars."

I relocate to Crispin's side and lean closer, studying the crisscross of cuts across Nathaniel's shoulders.

Nathaniel said he had a cut for every person he's lost, that a witch crossed them over each other like the prison bars Nathaniel had created for his life.

If I squint hard enough, *maybe* I can also make out an image beneath them, a series of crescents and straight lines inked into his skin.

No amount of squinting is going to tell me what the mark used to be. The scars have obliterated its true form. "I can't make it out."

"I would have guessed it was a mark of ownership," Crispin says, "but this creature is nobody's slave. He's well fed, strong, and healthy. What do you know about him?"

"His name is Nathaniel Shield. He's the Fell King's champion."

"So I heard," Crispin says. "What else, Aura?" Crispin tips his head. "Not his name. Not his occupation. *Who* is he?"

"I don't know. Not really." My frustration grows stronger. "Are you going to heal him or not?"

"Of course I will. But if you don't know who he really is, then you don't know what you're asking me to do."

"I know that I'm supposed to face him in the arena at the end of the third day," I say, knowing that Crispin will have already heard about it. Even out here in the mountains, news from the city travels fast. "I know that he lost his mother and that she was sick before she died. I know that he's a fierce fighter and he..." *Could kill me.*

I swallow. "What I know most of all is that if you don't heal him, it will destroy every good memory I have of you as the fair and honorable man I know you are."

Crispin presses his lips together as if he's holding his tongue.

He turns Nathaniel onto his back again and begins at the heart of the wound—the burn strike from which the flame spread. He reaches for the water and cloth that Gehrig left beside him while we were talking, beginning the task of cleaning out the debris from Nathaniel's fall.

After he puts aside the cloth, a dark glow begins beneath Crispin's palms. It's a deep ebony, much darker than any healing power I've ever seen. Much darker than Crispin's power usually is.

Alarmed, I grab his arm before he can release the power into Nathaniel. "What are you doing?"

He casts a glance at me. His eyes are filled with ebony power, overflowing with darkness. "The sunlight that struck him was created with malice, Aura. Darkness attracts darkness. I must suck out the malice before I can heal him."

A shiver runs down my spine. "Darkness attracts darkness. Do you really believe that?"

"It's the nature of the old magic. It's filled with all the nuances of the human heart: both light and dark, happiness and sadness, anger and love. The new magic we know is made only from light." He focuses fully on me for a moment. "His attacker drew on malice to make the fire burn more fiercely. She drew on old magic. Maybe without knowing it."

I release his arm. He's Nathaniel's only chance. I have no choice but to trust him.

CHAPTER 28

*A*s soon as the dark light touches Nathaniel's chest, he trembles, shivers racking his body.

I nearly reach out to stop Crispin again. How do I know he isn't killing Nathaniel quietly? Crispin lost his wife in the last battle with the Fell. It was one of the reasons why I was placed with him.

"Trust me, Aura," Crispin whispers, casting another glance at the hand I'm reaching toward him, ready to pull him away from Nathaniel. "He may be a Fell, but I won't hurt him."

My heart remains in my throat until the dark light beneath Crispin's palm finally changes, becoming golden like it should be.

Then new skin begins to grow across Nathaniel's chest and shoulder, extending down his arm. Nathaniel's breathing deepens, his features relax, and the color returns to his cheeks.

I can breathe again.

"Thank you," I say quietly.

Crispin leans back with a tired exhale. "He'll sleep now, but you shouldn't leave his side. He could wake up at any time and he might not react well to his unfamiliar surroundings. Especially if he thinks we've hurt you."

I nod. "I'll stay right here where he can see me."

Crispin pauses in the act of rising, staring down at me. His voice takes on a stern tone, as if he's shaking his head at me. "Aura."

I don't take my eyes off Nathaniel. "Crispin?"

"You didn't contradict me."

I turn to look up at him, finding his expression as stern as his voice. "What would I contradict?"

He arches an eyebrow at me. "Think about it."

Without giving me time to demand answers, he gestures to the watching men. "We're good here. You can all go home."

"Are you sure?" Gehrig asks, his thick arms folded across his chest.

"I'm sure." A broad grin breaks through Crispin's scowl. "If the Fell tries anything, Aura will protect me. If I try anything, Aura will protect the Fell. I'm sure we'll all get along."

One by one, the men quietly leave the cabin, slinking out onto the porch and away into the woods. I watch them disappear through the open door until Gehrig closes it behind him with a final smile at me—still warm.

Crispin sets about cleaning up while I relocate to the well-worn armchair near the fire. Curling my legs to my chest, I rest my head back and sink into the familiar leather, inhaling the scents of my childhood.

How is it that a scent can take me back so swiftly?

An unwanted burn of tears builds behind my eyes as I remember sitting in front of this fire on many cold winter evenings. Evander loved to leave the doors open and let the frost in, reveling in the crisp air that made him feel alive, while I would huddle in blankets, gazing through the frosty windows at the stars that glittered in the winter sky.

Sometimes—often, actually—I'd follow Evander outside and we'd climb the peaks behind the cabin and compete with each other about whose power could make the sky sparkle brighter—snowflakes or starlight.

When Crispin reappears beside me, I smile up into his grumpy face.

"That's my chair," he says.

I don't move. "That's why I'm sitting in it."

With a huff, he sinks onto the nearby couch. It's not quite as well-worn, but it's still scuffed. It has a couple of frost burns where Evander scorched it before he could control his magic. Or so I was told. That was before I came to live with them.

"I didn't belong here." I chew my lip as I stare into the fire.

Crispin sighs out an exhale. "You don't belong to her, either."

He means the Queen.

I take a deep breath because I've had this conversation with him before. It didn't end well the first time and it probably won't end well now. At least neither of us can storm out this time. Well, maybe he can. I can't leave Nathaniel behind.

"She pulled me out of that explosion, Crispin. I owe her my life. I've always owed her."

He leans toward me with pure vengeance in his eyes, his voice as sharp as claws. "When will you consider your debt paid? When you're dead?"

I can't face the certainty in his gaze that he's right. Will my loyalty to the Queen get me killed? If I weren't so loyal to her, would I have reacted differently to Nathaniel this morning? Am I already reacting differently to him? And does that mean I'm already less loyal?

Scary thoughts. I don't want to face them. Not yet.

I say, "If that's what it takes."

"No!" He thumps his knee so violently that it makes me

jump. He lurches to his feet and paces around the room, skirting a path wide of Nathaniel and all the way around the back of me.

Crispin wears the floor down twice—and I don't try to stop him—before he finally drops back onto the couch, his shoulders hunched over.

He seems to have left all of his anger behind on his path because now he only sounds defeated. "I've kept a lie for fifteen years," he says. "A lie I thought would spare you, but now I realize it only made you a slave. You deserve the truth."

A chill passes down my spine, making me snappish. "What truth?"

He meets my eyes. "Didn't you think it was strange that the Queen chose to place you with a widower and his son? A home with only men in it? When there are so many other families to choose from?"

I consider him carefully. "You lost your wife to the Fell. Evander lost his mother. Imatra knew you'd understand what I was going through. She was looking out for my heart—"

"Your heart!" He scoffs. "She has no care for your heart, Aura." He closes his eyes and takes a deep breath. "When she came back from the battlefield, she sent out word to every powerful family in Bright. She asked who would volunteer to take you into their home and raise you."

The crease of denial in my forehead is deep now. "That's not what happened. She said she chose you—"

"Nobody wanted you."

His statement drops onto me like a block of ice.

I freeze where I sit. Tightness spreads across my chest. My back is stiff, my jaw hurts where my teeth are clenched, and my breathing is shallow.

I force myself to operate outside of my feelings, to ask for answers without showing my emotions. "Why?"

"Because nobody knew you existed before that night."

My demand is short and sharp. "How is that possible?"

"Your parents kept you a secret. Nobody knew they'd had a child, let alone that you had the rarest of all powers. Our first Twilight fae."

I swallow. Take a breath. Hold my head high. "Okay, so I was a surprise," I say, trying to rationalize it all. "Why hate me for that?"

"You lived on the border miles away from our civilization, hidden from the rest of us. All it took was one Solstice fae to suggest that you might be the child of a Fell creature. Your parents weren't alive to deny it or explain why they'd kept you a secret and... well... you know how whispers grow poisonous in Bright."

I turn away from Crispin to stare into the flames. A log crackles and drops. I taste ash in my mouth.

Unable to look at him, I ask, "How did I end up here then? Did she make you take me?"

"I asked to raise you."

Now I search his gray eyes. Is he telling me more lies to spare my feelings?

"Evander and I heard about you," he says, his gaze compelling me to believe him. "We understood what it meant to be different, and we were hurting after our loss. Evander especially... He was only a boy, but he already understood very clearly that we were different than other male fae. His mother had been a shield for him against the world, but she was gone."

Crispin clears his throat. He never cried in front of me, always a rock of endurance. "We went to the city to find you. We knew from the moment we saw you that we had to take you away from that place. You were standing in the middle of the Inner Sanctuary with your little hands clenched as if you were daring the whole world to fight you. Your cheeks were pale and all the light was gone from your eyes... Only the stars know what you saw that night to steal the light from your heart..."

He clears his throat again. "Imatra was more than happy to send you as far away from herself as possible—all the way into the mountains, where she didn't have to deal with you again."

I'd stayed with Crispin for three years before Imatra had come into my life again. "If she wanted me gone, why did she send Serena to train me?"

Crispin exhales and it sounds careful, as if he's measuring his breaths against the tension between us. "The winter you turned ten years old, you and Evander started playing a game at night where you would stand together on the peaks up behind the cabin. Do you remember? He would fill the sky with snow and you would strike through every damn snowflake with starlight. You turned the sky above the mountain so bright, they could see it from the city."

He gives me a wry smile. "The Queen couldn't ignore your power after that. Nobody could."

"Why are you telling me this now?"

His scowl returns. "Because you don't owe her anything, Aura. You don't know what happened the night your parents died. Maybe she pulled you from the explosion. Maybe she didn't. All you have is her word, and she's lied to you before."

I'm silent. Struggling to process. If she lied to me about placing me with Crispin... What else did she lie about?

"You were the only other survivor, Aura," Crispin says. "If only you could remember the events of that night for yourself."

"The Vanem Dragon told me to go back to the burn site," I say. He told me to take Nathaniel with me, that we both need answers. Now more than ever. "Maybe I'll remember something this time." Something more than darkness.

Crispin doesn't reply. Maybe he hopes I'm right. Maybe he knows it's unlikely.

Crispin has said more to me in the last ten minutes than he's ever said before. Even when I lived with him, he was stoic, providing food and shelter, a broad shoulder to lay my head on when I needed a father, kind words when I needed encouragement, but he was never emotional like he is tonight.

"I'm sorry I left," I say into the quiet.

"I'm sorry I didn't tell you the truth," he answers.

"You did the right thing." I tip my face away from him, curling deeper into the chair.

The Queen kept me secluded from everyone in the days after the explosion—before Crispin came for me.

I was surrounded by flowers and pretty baubles and sweet treats, none of which healed any part of my damaged heart. If I'd known that the entire fae community had rejected me outright, anger would have festered inside me.

I've never attempted to discover the limit of my power, never used it to its fullest, but if my anger had turned to vengeance, I might have tried to hurt them.

The couch creaks as Crispin rises, murmuring, "Goodnight," but I have one more question for him. "Who did you think I was when I came here tonight?"

"Ah." He scratches his chin, a wary light entering his eyes. "That's complicated—"

A soft crackle reaches my ears, the low *snap* of lightning in the distant sky that only thunderbirds can make. My forehead creases because I'm sure that Treble wouldn't fly down out of the clouds unless I called him.

I hold up my finger for silence, halting whatever Crispin was about to say.

He eyes me. He won't be able to sense the disturbance in the air like I can. Years of being around thunderbirds, combined with my power, have made me more sensitive to the sound.

"Three thunderbirds," I say. "Approaching from the east."

The color drains from Crispin's face and his eyes flood with unusual fear. "That's who I was expecting."

CHAPTER 29

*C*rispin launches into action, grabbing my arms and squeezing so tightly, it makes me wince. "I was foolish to send Gehrig and the others home, but I can't change that now. Don't come outside, Aura. No matter what you see or hear. Promise me."

My eyes narrow at him. "If you're in trouble, I can help you. Whichever fae are coming here, they're under my command—"

"Are they?" He points at Nathaniel. "Was the fae who tried to kill that man under your command?"

"I—" *Damn.* The fear in Crispin's eyes tells me he truly believes I can't help him. Something has him completely spooked.

"If they see you, the situation will escalate," he says. "I can handle it. *Don't show yourself.* Stay with Nathaniel."

Crispin throws the bucket of water over the fire, dousing the light inside the living area until the embers leave a mere glow.

Then he strides to the door, sidling through it as he steps outside into the moonlight and pulls it closed behind him.

It's not in my nature to hide in the shadows. I've always

stepped out into the light, made myself a target, trusting in my strength to defend myself. Curled my fingers into fists at the world.

I slink across to the window and ease the curtain aside the merest sliver of a crack so I can see out without being seen.

Three thunderbirds circle overhead before landing in the clearing. Their riders leap from their backs as soon as they touch ground.

The woman leading them is Nadina. The other two are minor Day Guards.

Flames lick around Nadina's fingers as bright as if the sun shone high in the sky above her.

My forehead creases with confusion. Her power comes from the sun—it should be completely diminished at night.

She flicks her hair back, the flames gliding across her neck without hurting her. Her action reveals a golden rose pinned to her armor at her collarbone.

My eyes widen in surprise at the flames glowing around the rose.

It's one of the Queen's flowers. The kind she grows in the Inner Sanctuary. A repository of her power. But why has she given the power of the sun to Nadina to come here with her hands alight?

"Crispin of the Dawn," Nadina shouts as she takes up position in front of her thunderbird. "Come out from the shadows."

Crispin steps down from the porch into the circle of light provided by Nadina's flames.

"Why have you come to my home, Nadina of the Solstice?"

Nadina's features twist, her lips forming a cruel line. "You continue to cause trouble for the Queen and you have the insolence to pretend you don't know why I'm here."

"You're here to make me stop."

Nadina smiles, her teeth yellow in the golden light. "Not so stupid after all."

She gestures to the two women standing beside her. They're each wearing a golden rose, flames licking along their arms.

Nadina points at the cabin. "Burn it down."

Anger rises inside me as the women stride toward my childhood home, the fire growing brighter around their hands.

There's wood everywhere. Dry wood. Their fire will incinerate my home. The only real home I remember having.

My lips press together in a determined line. I can cut them both down before they even get close.

I prepare to take hold of the door handle when Crispin shouts, "It won't make me stop! Children are dying and the Queen turns a blind eye. I won't stay silent."

His shout doesn't stop the two women, who keep coming until he roars, "Burn the whole forest! When the city fae don't have wood for their fires, they'll ask questions."

Nadina holds her hand up for the two women to wait.

"*Boys* are dying," she spits. "The children of woodcutters who will never amount to anything more than laborers. Why should the Queen exhaust herself trying to save those who aren't worth saving?"

"Every fae is worth saving," Crispin says. "Even the smallest, most vulnerable fae can become the most powerful."

Nadina's eyes are narrowed now. A snarl rests on her lips. "You're referring to Aura."

"You started the rumor that she was part Fell."

Nadina throws back her head and laughs. "Oh, you simple man. The *Queen* started that rumor. I just helped her spread it."

I can't see Crispin's face, can only imagine his anger as his entire body tenses the same way mine has.

"Why would she do that?" he asks.

"Who knows?" Nadina shrugs it off. "Her reasons are her own."

"What did you get in return?"

She laughs again. "Look where I am. The Queen rewards those who obey her." Her smile fades. "She destroys those who defy her. What will you choose, Crispin? Silence or destruction?"

Crispin's hands clench into fists. His power is in healing. His only ability to defend himself lies in his physical strength, but he can't make a move against Nadina. The minute he threatens her, she'll burn him like Nathaniel was burned.

Slowly, his fingers uncurl and his shoulders slump. "The Queen really won't help us." He takes a step back, his head bowed low. "I won't cause any more trouble."

Nadina looks surprised at his sudden lack of resistance. Then her eyes narrow with suspicion.

She strides up to Crispin, extinguishing the flame from her hand before she grabs his chin, wrenching his face up to study him. She's a little shorter than me, but she has twice the strength of any male fae.

She must be convinced he's telling the truth because she spits into the snow at their feet. "Pitiful. No fight at all. I thought the man who raised Aura would have a spine, but I guess not."

She shoves him away from her and calls the other women to come back before she snarls at Crispin. "We're leaving. Don't give me a reason to come back or your home won't be the only thing I turn to ash."

The three women leap onto their birds, landing neatly in the saddles before they rise into the air and disappear into the night sky again.

My teeth are clenched so hard, they might crack.

I stand back as Crispin closes the door behind him, leaning against it.

It's dark with the fireplace doused, but my starlight is already glowing around my hands, casting light and shadow across the space between us.

I could ask him about the Queen. Or about Nadina. Or about the past. But it's easier to play the role of the champion than to face what all of this means for me personally.

I break the silence. "Tell me about the sick children."

"Boys are dying," he says. "Sons of Harvest fae—woodcutters. I've never seen an illness like it before and I can't cure it. I've tried everything."

"What does it look like?" I ask, even though I know the answer.

"Twisted arms and legs. Ashy lesions all over their bodies. They burn with fever and even Frost magic can't cool them. Five have died so far."

The Ebon Rot. It has to be.

I can't control the rage and distress rising inside me. "I could have helped you. I've healed other children."

"I know," he says quietly. "That's what started all this. I heard that you'd cured several girls with the same illness so I sent a message to the Queen asking her to send you to us. She refused. She said she couldn't spare you."

I suddenly feel sick. "When was this?"

"Five weeks ago. I thought maybe she didn't understand how urgent it was, so I traveled into the city myself. She refused to see me. I wasn't even allowed to speak with Evander. Instead, Nadina grilled me about our timber operations. She claimed we were behind in delivering the new furniture for the palace.

"I came back here and told everyone what happened. As you would expect, the men were upset—both Springtime and Harvest. A group of them went to the city and were turned away. They didn't leave quietly. Two weeks later, a squadron of Day Guards arrived to inspect the timber mill. They set fire to one of the storage huts and then told us we'd have to work twice as hard to meet our deadlines now that we'd lost the timber that was in the hut. Then, a week ago, this arrived."

He treads carefully to the mantelpiece over the fire, navigating through the dark, and returns carrying a small wooden box. The Queen's symbol—a stylized rose—is etched into the side.

He doesn't hand it over, tipping it instead, so I can see inside.

Through the glass lid, my starlight allows me to see a violet rose sitting on plush velvet material. The flower's petals are exquisitely formed, deepening to purple in the center.

"It's poisonous," Crispin says. "I was lucky that Gehrig was with me. He sensed the danger and stopped me from touching it. It's a clear message to stop asking questions. The whole timber community has been living on a knife's edge ever since."

My hands glow with power, but my fingers are bloodless from pressing them into tight fists.

I try to focus on the immediate danger. "Don't engage the Queen or her guards again. She obviously won't help you and you'll only endanger yourselves."

"But—"

"I can help you." My eyes bore into his, asking him to trust me. "Is anyone sick right now?"

He shakes his head. "The last boy died four days ago."

Only four days. I press my fist to my stomach as pain billows inside me. Somebody's son. A brother.

I lift my head and focus on the way forward. "Do you still have flares?"

He gives me a questioning look. "Yes, why?"

"If another child gets sick, send up a flare at night. I'll see it and come to you."

"Are you sure? It's a long way to see... let alone to come..."

"I sense everything that happens in the sky. Especially at night. I won't miss it. And I won't ignore it." I curl over my fist for a moment, unable to ease the pain in my chest. "I wish I'd known."

I don't have the heart to tell him that I might not be alive in two days and his worries will be so much worse if the Fell King lays claim to Bright. But for now, I have to do what I can.

He studies me. "The girl who left this house would never have gone against her Queen."

"I'm not that girl anymore. I haven't been her for..."

Has it only been a day? Not even twenty-four hours since Nathaniel strode out of the mist swinging his blade and started cutting through the lies in my life.

"For long enough," I finish.

"I hope I can trust you."

"Trust is earned," I say, suddenly realizing how dangerously loyal I've been to the Queen without proof that my faith in her was deserved. "I'll earn yours."

With a careful glance at Nathaniel, who remains asleep on the floor, Crispin gives me a firm nod of agreement. "He'll need clothes. You can take whatever fits him from Evander's room. Good night, Aura. It's good to have you home."

As he heads toward the stairs, I call out to him. "I can't be here when you wake up."

He doesn't look back. "I know."

That's all he says before he climbs the stairs more slowly than he used to. Seven years has worn him down in ways I never expected.

As soon as he's gone, I shut off my power, leaving myself in darkness. Before I know it, I've dropped to my knees and I'm crawling across the floor to Nathaniel's side.

I curl up against his chest, his legs, his arms, pressing my face to his shoulder as I fail to stop the burn of tears.

I'm far more emotional than I have been for... years. But in a single day, the foundations of my world have started cracking beneath my feet.

The person I trust most in the world—my beautiful Queen—isn't who I thought she was. I'm facing death, facing new truths and old lies, and I'm tired of shutting out my emotions.

I tell myself it's okay.

I can cry as much as I need to. Nathaniel is unconscious. He'll never know that I needed his comforting scent and the warmth of his skin. He'll never know that I cried against his shoulder.

By the time he wakes up, I'll be myself.

He will be a Fell, and I will be a fae, and we'll be enemies again.

CHAPTER 30

I'm numb when Nathaniel finally stirs.

I stretch out my aching arms and legs, my armor pulling against my body like an unwanted second skin.

It's nearly midnight—the time when my power is at its peak —but I contain the starlight, only allowing the smallest glow to shine between us.

I'm prepared for him to wake up angry, ready to fight anything that moves, but instead, he's quiet, lying on his back, staring at the ceiling with a faint crease in his forehead. "Where am I?"

"The home of a healer," I say. "He helped us. You're not hurt anymore. We're safe here."

I only realize what a lie that is once I say it. Only two hours ago, Nadina threatened to burn this place down.

"We're as safe as we can be," I say.

A deep crease forms in Nathaniel's forehead. He turns his head, casting a gaze across me as I push myself into a sitting position. His focus stops on my face and I retract my power, turning away before he can study me too carefully.

I should have washed my face. The tear tracks will be too obvious.

"You look different," he says.

"It's midnight. My power's strong right now." I clamber to my feet, deflecting the conversation. "So is my hunger."

I hold my glowing hand up to peer through the side door to the kitchen before I point in that direction. "Food. Now."

He sits up, leaning back on his hands. "There are plenty of seats."

It's an odd comment. I have no idea what he's getting at. I arch my eyebrows at him, jabbing my glowing fist in the direction of the kitchen so my impatience will be unmissable.

"Food," I say again, emphasizing the word.

He clambers to his feet. He's only wearing sleeping shorts, slung low over his hips, and he definitely needs more clothing. "You were lying on the floor with me, but there are plenty of seats."

With a cranky hum in the back of my throat, I advance on him. "And you think... what? That I was worried about you? That I couldn't leave your side? That I couldn't breathe in case you died? Is that it?"

Before I know what he's doing, he crosses toward me as fast as I'm advancing on him, forcing me to stop and backpedal rapidly.

Not fast enough.

His fingers curl around my bicep, his other arm circles my waist, and he pulls me close, as close as I lay to him when I was crying.

I stiffen in his arms as he raises his hand to trace the treacherous tear tracks down my cheeks.

"Something happened," he says, a quiet but certain statement. "It must have been bad if you needed comfort from a Fell."

I chew my lip, my gaze falling to focus on a spot on his jaw, unable to handle the genuine concern in his eyes. "A lot can change in a day."

I try to breathe in the circle of his arms, finding it much harder than I expected. The way he's stroking my back should be calming, but somehow it's irritating in the way that touch is frustration when it's not enough, when it needs to be more.

My armor is an immovable barrier between his apparently soothing intentions and my starving skin. "Will you... please... not ask me anything more about it?"

I want to tell him about the sick children, but it will only bring up the subject of *fate* again.

I can't tell him that the Queen I loved started whispers about me that could have caused me to be homeless and hated. Or that she refuses to save dying children and sends her guards to threaten anyone who speaks out about it.

I won't tell him that I was worried he might die.

Forcing myself to meet his eyes, I realize that I'm glowing around his fingertips splayed across my cheek. The slow graze of his thumb across my jaw makes me shiver.

"So long as you're okay," he says, his voice low and soft like a wolf's growl.

I force a nod. "As okay as I can be."

Despite my assertion, he doesn't open his arms. "Thank you for healing me."

"It wasn't me. I didn't... I mean... I brought you here, but I couldn't help you. I couldn't stop you hurting." I purse my lips against all of the awkward words.

A glimmer of a smile lifts the corners of his lips before he hides it. His fingers glide from my cheek to my hair. "I think *this* is my magic power," he says, his hand sliding through the white strands.

"What is?"

"Loosening your hair ties."

My lips part in surprise as he casts me a challenging look that dares me to contradict him. Somehow, he's right. I've braided or tied my hair a thousand times today, only to have it come undone every time he's around me.

"Why is it this color?" he asks. "I've never seen hair like this."

"Except on old women," I reply dryly. "It's always been this way." I shrug my shoulders with an exaggeratedly provocative tilt. "I think it's trying to look like twilight." *And failing miserably.*

"It does when I do *this.*"

His other hand sweeps up my neck to my cheek, making me gasp as heat rushes through me.

Oh, dear stars. What is this excruciating warmth that makes my toes curl and my body ache in unfamiliar places?

He tilts his head to mine, his lips only an inch away. My breathing increases as he pauses there, so close to me that I can inhale the same air as him, so close that my focus becomes pinpoint.

His lips. The perfect dip in the center of his top lip that I want to explore. The growing intensity in his eyes.

"If only you were human," he whispers.

The press of his hands across my neck and cheeks isn't enough. I sway just a little closer, closing my eyes as I tip my head.

I'm close enough for our lips to touch. The barest, lightest contact—so light, it could be mistaken for a whispered breath between us.

Heat and shivers strike through me at the contact, a soft inhale dragging at my chest as I pull at all the needy sensations that rampage through my body to my core.

This... the barest touch... fills the space between us with impossible wishes. What if I pulled him closer? What if—?

His hands clamp around my face, not hard, but firm enough to keep me where I am, to stop me.

His voice is a husky rumble. Forced. Determined. "If only I weren't hungry."

I open my eyes.

His jaw clenches as he pulls away, as if he's shutting down whatever impulse caused him to touch me to begin with, his hands falling away from my face and arms.

I'm forced to accept his deflection to food.

I take a deep breath and turn toward the kitchen before he can see the confusion of emotions that must be flooding my face.

I nearly kissed him. I think I did kiss him. Maybe. For a second.

It was the lightest touch, but my body's aching all the way from my heated cheeks to low in my abdomen.

I give myself a mental slap.

I'm relieved. Of course I'm relieved that he didn't kiss me back. I don't know what would have happened if he had.

We're destined to stand across from each other in the arena in a little over two days. One of us will destroy the other. I can't keep closing the gap between us like I just did. Or he just did. I'm not sure now who reached for whom first.

Unable to trust my voice, I walk swiftly to the kitchen and scavenge in the pantry for bread and cheese, grabbing up a couple of apples from the fruit basket on my way back to the kitchen table.

A flask of cold tea rests on the table. I busy myself with pouring two cups before I start cutting the food for our meal.

Before I've got too far, Nathaniel reaches for a knife and joins me in the task, slicing the bread.

Half an hour later, we've eaten, managed to use the bathroom without embarrassing each other, and found clothing for Nathaniel—a pair of long pants and a warm shirt. The only pair of boots in the bottom of Evander's closet are a little too big, but

Nathaniel pulls on a set of thick socks beneath them to make up the difference.

We operate in silence and I'm grateful that I don't have to say anything or answer any questions, although I'm sure Nathaniel has plenty.

I pause outside Crispin's bedroom door on my way back to the stairs.

Be safe, Dad.

Hurrying on, I lead Nathaniel outside, where I whistle for Treble again.

My thunderbird dives from the clouds, a streak of blazing blue as he drops directly down and lands with a crackle of lightning that's sure to wake everyone within a one-mile radius.

His wings flop to the ground before he snaps them into his sides. I gasp as the cracking sound washes over me. Then I race to his side straight through the streaks of electricity raging around him.

"Treble! Are you hurt?" I try to take hold of his neck, but he wrenches out of my grasp, swinging his head until he's eye to eye with me.

"What's wrong? Where are you hurt?"

He shoves me hard, the flat of his forehead connecting with my chest, knocking me onto my butt.

I stare up at him in shock as he glares down at me, electricity filling his eyes and washing across his head and neck.

"He's angry with you."

Nathaniel appears beside me, picking his way carefully through the rocky snow. He holds one hand out in front of himself as Treble glances askew at him.

"It's okay, buddy," Nathaniel says, keeping his voice calm. "You know she's going to take risks. You knew that when you chose her."

Treble snorts, an angry wash of air that blows across my hair.

Nathaniel continues his approach until he presses his hand to Treble's neck, stroking down Treble's ruffled feathers. "She'll push you away again and again—as many times as it takes for her to protect you. You'll spend your life worrying about her, but you'll love her anyway."

Treble bounces his head up and down at Nathaniel as if he couldn't agree more. When Treble swings back to face me, I'm on the receiving end of an eye roll from him. Then he drops his head and nudges my shoulder. A peace offering.

I wrap my arms around his neck. "I'm sorry, Treble. I told you to fly away when I should have asked for your help. I won't do it again."

If only thunderbirds had eyebrows. I'm sure Treble would raise them in a skeptical arch right now if he could.

He gently removes himself from my embrace, raising his head regally high before he extends and lowers his wing for Nathaniel to climb up.

Settling onto his back, Nathaniel holds his hand out for me, but I give him a smile. "You'd better hold on."

"Huh?"

I turn to Treble. "Want to fly, my friend?"

With another disdainful snort, Treble lifts into the air without me, a single sweep of his wings taking him into the air.

Nathaniel lurches a little but leans low and holds on with the kind of strength that fae take years to build.

Treble rises high into the air above the trees to the left of the clearing before he sweeps down toward me.

I start to run as he dives, timing my stride to the beat of his wings and the friction in the air as he approaches.

My feet leave the ground as he draws level with me.

I leap onto his back, catching hold of the top of his wing

bone and sailing neatly into place behind Nathaniel. Treble adjusts his flight, dipping slightly to make my landing less abrupt. As soon as he senses I'm in position, he rises into the sky again.

"Dark stars, Aura!" Nathaniel says. "How did you do that without killing yourself?"

I shrug as I wrap my arms around his waist and rest my head against his back. "I trust Treble."

At my declaration, I sense my thunderbird finally relaxing, and I know that the faith between us has been restored.

"Whose home *was* that?" Nathaniel asks, turning his head as we leave the Grove behind.

"My adoptive father's. He's a good man. He wanted to raise me when nobody else did." It doesn't hurt as much as I thought it would to speak this new truth aloud.

"Whose clothes am I wearing then?"

"Evander's."

Nathaniel makes a disgruntled noise. "He'll love seeing me in them."

I allow myself to laugh. "He'll get over it."

"Where are we going now?"

My laughter fades. "To the Ball. Where I'm expected."

Where I'll have to pretend that the foundations of my life aren't unraveling.

CHAPTER 31

*W*e soar beyond the mountains, across the peaceful villages and toward the glittering city.

Lamps have been lit all along the streets in honor of the conclusion of the Winter Ascending. Celebrations have already started in many parts of the city, but the main party at the palace is still an hour away.

It's a good thing I'm not worried about getting dressed up. Some fae prepare for days for this event. I'll have a few minutes to slip into... well... my armor.

Treble takes us down onto the empty platform, landing quietly and waiting for us to disembark.

The moment we land, Nathaniel twists toward me. "You've shown me more mercy than you should have. Do what you need to do."

"What are you talking about?"

"I'm supposed to walk free. That doesn't mean you have to treat me fairly."

I do a double-take. "You expect me to mistreat you."

"You need to," he says. "The others aren't allowed to spill my blood, but you can."

My brow furrows. "But... I thought I couldn't harm you until the fight... No fae can hurt you."

He scoffs. "You're supposed to kill me, Aura. We can torture each other as much as we want for the next two days and three nights. It's all part of the fight. Do you understand? The Law requires a fight by a specified time. It doesn't say how long the fight goes on before that."

My disbelieving whisper leaves my lips before I can stop it. "I don't want that."

He gives a bitter laugh. "You thought you had to be kind to me? *No.* You and I will grapple against each other, fight our sense of honor, fight our own hearts, and struggle to do what we need to do, right up until the bloody end."

He grips my arm before I can withdraw from him. His voice turns to an urgent order. "If you don't want your loyalties questioned, you need to show your hatred."

No.

I grit my teeth as I wrench from Nathaniel's grip and slip from Treble's back.

I wrap my arms around Treble's neck. "I'll need you again before the dawn," I whisper to him as he nudges me gently. "Please listen for my call."

Treble bounces his head before his focus suddenly snaps to the platform entrance, his feathers ruffling.

Nadina emerges from the shadows at the doorway, her sharp gaze passing across me, Treble, and finally Nathaniel, who stands a step behind me.

"Commander Lucida," she announces, her boots striking the platform as she strides toward me still dressed in her armor. "The Queen is asking for you."

Four Day Guards follow behind her—a rare sight in the middle of the night when the Night Guard would normally be in control. That either means Mia, the head of the Night Guard, is busy doing her hair or the Queen is now relying on Nadina to carry out her less-than-palatable tasks. Such as bossing me around.

Nadina expects me to jump at her command, so I make her come to me before I speak. "Thank you, Nadina. I'm glad to see the Queen is fully protected this evening."

I give the other guards a serene smile before I peer more closely at Nadina, an overly thorough examination of her face. "Although… you look tired, Nadina. Have you slept at all?"

She doesn't know I saw everything at the cabin.

I quietly dare her to admit what she did.

Nadina returns my cool stare. She doesn't even blink. "I've been running errands for the Queen all night. I'll sleep after the Ball."

"Good. I'd hate for you to be too exhausted to protect her."

She huffs, but I'm already turning away from her to grab Nathaniel's arm and jerk him forward. "Come with me, Fell."

Nadina arches her eyebrow at the way I spoke to him, but a cruel smile crosses her lips. "I'll take him for you if you like?"

Now I cast an arrogant glance up and down her body. "Like I said, you look tired." I lean right into her face. "He'll chew you up for a snack."

She jolts backward. "He isn't allowed to hurt us."

"Maybe he doesn't care about the rules anymore. If he's going to die at my hand anyway, he may as well take as many of us down with him as he can. Isn't that right, *Fell*?"

Nathaniel's dark gaze meets mine, a crazy scary grin growing on his face. He shocks me by leaning in close to me. "Only after I've corrupted you first, Starlight."

Damn you, Nathaniel.

I was trying to make them afraid of him. Now he's gone and

provoked me in a way I can't ignore in front of Nadina and the guards.

My fist cracks across his cheek and my boot collides with his thigh, forcing him onto one knee.

He glares up at me, but I meet the fire in his eyes as I compel him to remain where he landed. He struggles to rise, but I grind my boot harder against his leg, turning his glare to pain.

"Do you see what I have to put up with?" I shout at Nadina.

Damn, damn, damn you, Nathaniel.

"Filthy Fell! I'd hand him over gladly, but it falls to me to kill him. Luckily for me, the rules mean I'm allowed to hurt him as much as I want. If someone else spills a drop of his blood, they'll die." I give Nadina a triumphant smile. "Not me."

She considers me with a new respect. "The Queen was wrong to doubt you, Commander Lucidia."

"I will make her proud." I hold my head high, easing my boot off Nathaniel's knee before I yank him to his feet. "Hurry up," I snap at him. "The Queen is waiting."

He follows me as I stalk away from the women, leaving them far behind. Once inside the stairwell, the silence between Nathaniel and me becomes an unbearable pressure on my chest.

"Please don't do that again," I whisper.

He exhales into the quiet. "That's a promise I can't make."

Damn him for always telling me the truth. Damn him for being so brave. Damn, damn... *"Damn you."*

"I was born damned, Aura," he says. "From the moment I took my father's name, my future was determined."

I'm tired of his secrets. Swinging to him, I demand answers. "Who was your father? *Who are you?*"

"Too many questions, Aura," he murmurs, his dark eyes glinting in the dim light. "Not enough time in the world to answer them."

The strike of footsteps sounds above us and our quiet

moment is over. If I don't want Nadina to catch up to us, I have to keep moving.

I hurry down the stairs and weave through the halls toward the Queen's Tower with Nathaniel close on my heels. I calm myself along the way. The Queen finally wants to see me and I need to be mentally prepared to hide my emotions around her no matter what.

Mia waits outside the Queen's door, guarding it. She gives me a snide smile before she opens it. I won't have to put up with her gloating for long. Nadina will soon tell her what I did up on the platform.

I yank Nathaniel into the Queen's room, and Mia promptly closes it as soon as I step through.

Imatra stands in the center of the room, already dressed for the Ball. She's wearing an elaborate sapphire blue dress with a fitted corset that clashes brilliantly with her blood-red hair.

I can't read anything from her expression as she waits for me to approach her.

Pushing Nathaniel up against the back wall, one hand against his neck, I hold my fist in front of his face. "Stay here. Don't move or I will hurt you."

Turning my back on him, I step only three paces forward before I take a knee. "I'm sorry the Fell creature is here, my queen. Unfortunately, he goes everywhere I go. I'd knock him out for our conversation, but I've discovered that he has a hard head."

"I pity you, Aura," the Queen replies, her voice as soft as the hum of a bee's wings. "Remaining in the creature's presence must be draining."

I don't raise my head, keeping my gaze on the floor, speaking with true honesty. "If I'd known he was the Fell King's champion—if I'd known about the Law—I never would have fought him. I would never risk your life or the lives of my people."

Her dress swishes against the floor as she approaches, dropping to her knees in front of me. "I know, Aura. You have more reason to hate the Fell than any of us."

She places a gentle finger under my chin so that I'll lift my eyes to hers. "I'm sorry that I pushed you away, dear. I was in shock. I needed time to think."

"I will always watch over you," I say. "No matter what happens."

She gives me a faint smile. A gentle nod. "You disappeared this evening. I was worried about you."

All of her statements are so gentle and yet so loaded, ready to explode in my face.

I don't even blink. "With the fight ahead of me, I wanted to make amends with Crispin of the Dawn. He and I didn't part on good terms when I left to become champion."

"Ah, yes." She nods. "He never approved of your loyalty to me. Even with his wife's death, he didn't understand the struggles you went through. He never knew your heart like I do. You and I emerged from that fire forged into the women we are today."

She places her upturned palm under my forearm as she rises, urging me to my feet. Her question is light as she turns away. "What did you and Crispin talk about?"

I choose an answer as close to the truth as possible. "The cabin was dark when I got there. I suspect he was home, but I guess he didn't want to see me after all."

I allow bitterness to fill my mouth, even though my feelings are about her betrayal, not Crispin's. "All those years raising me seem to have meant nothing to him."

"That's a shame, Aura. At least you and Evander have remained friends."

She glides to the far closet as I wait for her to speak again. I thought I'd learned how to interpret her moods. I thought I knew her.

But now, every move she makes, every gentle inflection of her voice and brush of her gaze over me, reminds me of her deception.

"I was wrong to keep you at a distance this afternoon," she says. "I want to make it up to you."

She returns holding a teal-colored dress. The bodice is barely more than two cups held together with sheer lace that dips across the cups and crosses the midriff.

Two thin straps across the shoulders drop down at the back, the bodice joining a long, full skirt made of sheer tulle with a very high slit up the right leg.

Diamonds and flower petals adorn the lace across the top and down one side. The skirt is ombre—teal brightening into turquoise at the bottom.

"I want you to wear this tonight," Imatra says, smiling sweetly at me.

My lips part in surprise. "It's beautiful."

There's also nothing to it. I'd be more protected if I were wearing my underwear.

Before tonight, I would have seen the dress as an innocent gift. Now, I wonder why? After all the years of protecting her, all the Balls to which I've simply worn my armor, why is she offering me a dress now?

She pushes it toward me, urging me to take it, before she turns away to her dresser, retrieving a small box. "I want you to have this as a token of my affection."

I fold the dress carefully over one arm as she holds the box out to me.

It has a glass lid just like Crispin's.

A violet rose lies inside it.

CHAPTER 32

*T*he soft smile on my face doesn't falter. My real thoughts fly high where Imatra won't know them, where they won't show, where she won't hear my soundless scream.

She has given me a poisoned rose.

It's a message. She knows that I lied about speaking with Crispin. She knows that I know about the boys who died.

Now we will play a fragile game, a charade that masks our true feelings.

I press my hand over my heart. "Oh, my queen. One of your precious roses. You've never given me..."

Tears gather in my eyes. Tears that will appear as gratitude, but inside, I'm breaking. All the years I gave my life to her are turning to dust beneath my feet and she's trampling through the wreckage.

"It's one of my favorites," she says. "Imbued with all the courage you'll need for the days ahead."

"I don't know how to thank you..." I take the box and hold it to my chest for a moment before I awkwardly brush away the tears from my cheeks. "I love it."

"I know you do, Aura."

Before I can turn away, she reaches out for me. "Aura. One more thing."

"Yes, my queen?"

"I would like your advice, please. I've ruled Bright for fifty years. It's time for me to consider my line of succession."

My smile fades—just like it should. "You'll rule fifty more. I promise you—"

"I know." She hurries to squeeze my arm. "I know I will, but I need to think about the future. I don't have any children and... it's time to change that."

Our conversation so far has been a dance. Steps carefully taken, but I don't know what music we're dancing to now. She's never spoken about children before.

"The father of my children will have to be strong. The strongest male fae. That way my daughters will be powerful." Her hand tightens on my arm. "You've watched over my lands for seven years. You've trained many of my guards. You've lived among the people. Who is the strongest man, Aura?"

Evander. She means Evander.

"My brother," I say. She will know that any other answer is a lie. She already knows he's the strongest.

"I thought so." She presses her lips together as she sidles closer, lowering her voice. "But I heard..." She clears her throat delicately. "Well... there were rumors..."

I manage to speak. "There's nothing between us."

She smiles, pulling back. "Good. Because I would hate to break your heart, dear one."

"Your happiness is all that's important to me," I say, smiling into her cruel, deceptive eyes.

She leans in and presses a cold kiss to my cheek. "You do

understand, don't you, Aura? As long as the human remains at your side, you can't guard me."

"Of course, my queen. I'll keep him away from you."

She pulls back, her sharp fingers releasing my shoulders. "Thank you, dear."

My expression hardens as I spin on my heel to glare at Nathaniel. I jerk my head toward the door. "Out."

Imatra sighs. "At least he's obedient."

He stops at the door, as if he's about to say something, but anything he says right now could start a fire.

"Open it," I bark.

He swings open the door fast enough that my order sails into the corridor outside.

"Now walk," I order him. "Keep your eyes down. If you look up, I will hurt you. Go back to your room, where you will face the wall."

He glares at me before he strides straight into the corridor, his first sign of rebellion.

Mia backs away from the door as we emerge, flicking her indigo hair behind her shoulder as she watches me with interest.

Nadina leans against the wall behind her with a broad smile on her face. "I told you."

Mia plants her hands on her hips at me. "Tamed the beast, did you, Aura?"

"This creature?" I ask. "He's far too clever for his own good. He's simply waiting to stab me in the back. But we all know what happens to anyone who tries to do that."

I give them a cold smile, satisfied to see the color drain from their faces.

I breeze past them toward Nathaniel's room. Now more than ever, I know that I should have killed Calida today. If I had, nobody would have stepped within a mile of me. Nadina would have brought the entire Day Guard to escort me to the palace today.

They've forgotten what my power looks like and now it's as if I'm wearing shackles around my strength, keeping me tame.

Kicking the door closed with my boot, I cause a loud enough bang to make it sound like I'm in the mood for violence.

All I really want to do is scream.

I gasp for breath as I hold the box tightly while I fling the dress across the room onto the bed as far away from myself as I can pitch it. I place the box carefully on top of the chest of drawers and then I back away from it.

Nathaniel watches me carefully. "You need to tell me whether these walls are thin."

"They're soundproof. This is the Queen's sex room. She likes to be noisy."

He blinks as if I just slapped him sideways, but he shakes it off quickly. "Okay then. Nobody can hear us. Good to know. I guess that's why someone tried to kill me in here."

He shakes his head again, refocusing. "Talk to me."

"I'll talk to you when you start talking to me."

A muscle in his jaw tenses. "I can't tell you who I am."

"Why not?"

"Because then you won't trust me at all."

"But I don't, Nathaniel. I *don't* trust you. I can't even trust my own people right now, let alone a human."

He advances on me. "If you didn't trust me, you wouldn't have curled up and cried next to me. Now talk to me."

My face falls—then blazes with embarrassment. "You were awake."

"I was awake and I don't regret a moment of it." He continues without pause. "Aura. *Dammit.* What just happened in there? She smiled at you the whole time, but it's clear she wants you dead."

She does. And I don't really understand why.

I realize that trying to bargain with Nathaniel just now was a stalling tactic on my part—I'm afraid to speak the truth aloud because that forces me to face reality.

"She made it clear... that if I lose the fight with you, your people won't be my biggest problem," I say. "She threatened everyone I love. That flower is poisonous. She sent one just like it to Crispin. She wants to corner Evander and crush him, and once she does, he'll never be free. She wants me to feel exposed and vulnerable, unable to protect anyone I love."

I rage over to the dress, pick it up and scrunch its flimsy material in my fists, wanting to rip it apart. "This dress! I've never worn anything like it before. It turns me from a warrior into a whore. Any number of sycophants will try to approach me tonight. This dress is an open invitation for them to paw all over me with the Queen's blessing. All they want is the Queen's favor and I'll be a ripe target."

He's quiet for a moment and I guess he's processing everything I just dumped on him.

"Let me see it." He eases my bloodless fingers away from the dress before he smooths it out, running his fingers across the barely-there material.

A slow, lazy smile grows on his face as he studies the lace, the narrow waist, and the high slit.

"Aura... this dress is a weapon." He meets my eyes. "Trust me, if you wear this, you'll control every man in the room. She gave you this dress to make you feel exposed and weak, but she'll regret it."

"She will?"

"Dark stars, Aura." The husky timber of his voice and the intensity in his gaze make me shiver. "She'll wish she never tried to mess with your head."

I can't shake off my skepticism as I take the dress from him.

"Wait," Nathaniel calls as I head to the bathroom "I think I saw…"

He dives toward the closet and rummages through it for a moment before he procures two items of feminine clothing that don't deserve the term 'underwear.'

"You'll need these."

The bra has multiple translucent straps and barely any coverage. The underpants even less so. They're both black.

I snatch them from him. "Fine, but only because I don't have a choice."

I peel off my armor inside the bathroom while Nathaniel leans against the doorframe, not even bothering to avert his eyes as I strip down to my underwear.

He wears an expectant expression, as if he's impatient to see the proof of his theory.

Wrapping a towel around myself, I manage to remove my underclothes and replace them with the black contraptions he handed me.

He's seen me naked—at least I'm pretty sure he looked—but this feels different. Since then, I've cried on his shoulder and breathed in the air across his lips.

My cheeks flush as I reach for the dress, planning to pull it over the top of the towel before I ease the cloth out from under it.

The towel slips. Right off.

So does the impatient mask Nathaniel's wearing.

Left standing in nothing but the skimpy underwear, I hurry to pull on the dress, yanking it over my head so hard that I nearly rip the lace before I reach for the clasps at the side to do it up.

Once I'm done—and as clothed as I'm going to get—I consider myself in the mirror. An unhappy murmur builds. I don't see what he sees, but maybe I just need some color on my face…

Taking a chance, I pull open the drawers beneath the bathroom sink, happy to find them full of powders and creams. Choosing several, I lean forward over the sink toward the mirror to pat powder on my cheeks and carefully dab color onto my lips with my forefinger.

When I look up, Nathaniel is fixated on the curve of my hips as I lean forward, his gaze raking up over my frame to my finger pressed to my upper lip.

"Dark stars," he whispers.

Before I know what he's doing, he strides toward me, ripping off his shirt and discarding it on the floor. He spins me to face him, sweeps one strong arm under my backside, and lifts me up against him.

I gasp in a heated breath. My startled eyes meet his a second before he propels me back onto the bathroom sink, his movements sure and strong as he slides me onto the table, hooks one of my legs around his hips, and tips me backward.

One arm supports my back while his other hand sweeps up under the slit of my skirt. His calloused palm runs the length of my thigh in one sure sweep from my knee all the way to my hip.

The sensation is so intense that I gasp and grip his chest. My responses are purely instinctive, my back arching, my hips rocking.

I inhale. Sink into the caramel scent of his skin and drag his body closer to mine, a moan escaping my lips.

His naked skin beneath my hands is intoxicating, his muscled arms both a threat and a promise, but it's only the promise that burns away at me.

I need him to crush his lips against mine.

He tilts his head, his mouth lowering, his lips whispering across my cheek.

EVERLY FROST

His fingers curl behind my neck, and then, just as suddenly, he holds me there, fixing me onto that spot.

"*This*, Aura," he says, his chest rising and falling rapidly. He refuses to bring his mouth closer, remaining far enough away that I can read his focus: *me*. "Remember this when you walk down the stairs in this dress. This feeling belongs to you. You control it. You can give it or take it away as you please."

He pulls me upright, slipping his arms away from me so rapidly that I can't stop him. He's already turning his back on me and striding across the bathroom by the time I take a breath.

My heart is in my throat as he picks up his dropped shirt and walks away from me to the bathroom door.

No matter what he says, I refuse to believe that this feeling is mine alone, that it was a purely physical action for him, like taking off his shirt and putting it on again. It can't be. The way his breathing caught, the way he dragged me against him...

I slip my feet to the floor, my toes curling against the cool marble like it's the first time I've touched it.

My thigh still tingles, and my lips are parted with quickly indrawn breaths. I take my first certain step since putting on my new clothes, my hips swaying.

A glance in the mirror tells me that my hair is tousled, my cheeks flushed, and my eyes are not so dull anymore.

I whip my hair up into a messy bun, securing it with pins from the bathroom drawer, allowing a few strands to fall across my nearly-bare shoulders. The bra has pushed my bust up so that the inner third of my breasts are visible and the lace pulls in at my waist before the skirt falls across my hips, one leg peeking through the high slit.

I find Nathaniel leaning against the doorframe again.

Throwing my head back, I smile at him, casting him a glance from beneath my eyelashes. "You're right. This dress is a weapon and I plan to use it."

Sauntering past him, I rifle through the closet under his watchful eye and hand him a pair of long, black pants and a one-size-too-small short-sleeved black shirt that will stretch over the contours of his chest and wrap around his muscular biceps.

"I don't need social armor," he says when I offer him the clothes. "The Bright Ones already think I'm wicked."

"Yes," I say, unable to contain my wild, reckless intentions. "But this way we'll look like we're together. That will really drive Imatra crazy."

Nathaniel just opened a locked box inside me that I never knew existed.

I'm not sure if he intended to swing it open so wide, but—*so help me*—I'm walking through it.

CHAPTER 33

*T*he way the Queen's Tower is situated isn't an accident.

This is the one night of the year when the elite in Bright are invited into her Inner Sanctuary. The staircase is designed for maximum impact as she glides down each step to the applause of the high-ranking fae waiting below.

She's surrounded by a handful of select Day and Night Guards—including Nadina.

I was instructed to bring up the rear, but it doesn't bother me, since it leaves Nathaniel free to walk beside me.

The Sanctuary is packed with fae of both major classes—Sunstream and Eventide—some of them milling about, others sitting at the couches and tables that have been brought in.

The side wall has been opened up to expand the room all the way out to the top of the steps leading down to the Spinning Lake. The walls sparkle with lights and the drinks are already flowing.

When Imatra reaches the bottom step, she lifts her voice.

"Thank you, my darlings. Tonight we celebrate all things bright!"

She floats into the crowd, her laughter ringing out across them.

The onlookers focus on her and I can already see them maneuvering. Which one will get to her first, I wonder?

As I reach the bottom step, Nathaniel brushes the back of my arm, and it feels like a warning.

I pause, carefully turning my head to look up at him as he draws close to me. The clothing I chose for him makes him look even larger than he is, the material pulling across his chest and thighs, accentuating the dark flecks in his eyes.

"What's wrong?" I murmur.

He leans down toward me, a slow lean, his lips close to my cheek, as if he's about to tell me a secret.

"Nothing," he whispers, the timber of his voice making me shiver. "But right now, every woman in this room wants to kill you and every man wants to take my place."

His thumb grazes the back of my arm again and the air around us glows as my magic shimmers at his touch.

I'm suddenly aware of a lull around me. The men and women closest to me have turned in my direction, already focused on me.

Just like Nathaniel said, the three women closest to me shoot death stares at me while their male partners look me up and down.

One of the men has the nerve to lick his lips.

The Queen herself half-turns, as if she's not sure what the matter is. Her forehead pinches, her sharp gaze quickly taking in the scene behind her. She definitely won't like losing everyone's attention.

Nathaniel's command is lazy and soft. "Remember, Aura: a weapon, not a weakness."

My eyelids lower as I inhale and allow a smile to settle onto my lips before I raise my hand and curl my fingers around his bicep.

I sway into him for a second. "Come with me."

He focuses entirely on me as I lead him past the Queen toward the slightly elevated platform where couples are already dancing.

The heavy beat thuds through me and the floor lights up under my feet as I move, starlight playing across my feet and casting up across the surrounding dancers' bodies.

I check out the other fae beneath my eyelashes. I don't see Evander or Talsa anywhere—they must still be at the border—but Serena tips her glass at me as we pass by. She's wearing a black dress that covers her body from neck to toe. I guess she's no longer angry at me about my decision to let Calida live.

Unlike Nadina, who is standing guard next to the Queen, Mia—the head of the Night Guard—is dressed in a cobalt blue evening gown and is already hugging both a drink and a man. She's too engrossed in tangling tongues with him to pay any attention to me.

I pull Nathaniel close as the music continues. A group of Eventide fae are gathered at one side of the dance floor strumming instruments and creating a deep beat.

Ignoring the stares from the dancers around us, I whisper into Nathaniel's ear, "I don't know how to dance. I'm just pretending right now."

I must have lost my senses. There's no way I can sustain any attention in an environment like this. Give me a combat arena—I know what I'm supposed to do in a fight. Here, I'm destined to botch the steps and ruin my sultry illusion in two seconds flat.

The light in his eyes grows brighter. "It's just like fighting," he says, immediately catching me around my waist before spinning me around. "Moves and countermoves."

I guess I can do that then.

I catch my breath as he clasps my waist and my right hand, moving me in a slow beat before spinning me again—leisurely this time.

As he pulls me close to his chest, an intent expression grows on his face. I may not know how to dance, but he seems very certain which way he wants me to move—even *how* he wants me to move—communicating using the press and pull of his hands and arms in a way that feels like a building storm.

Moving me backward, he glides his hand down the back of my thigh before he pulls me so close to his chest that I tilt my head back.

Drawing us to a standstill, he hooks my leg around his hips in time with the music, every movement paced and rhythmic. He bends me backward at the waist, causing my back to arch in a way that feels intensely freeing, before he pulls me up again.

It was an intimate move, and... *damn, it felt good.*

I've never partied before. Despite the fact that the Ball is a celebration for everyone who succeeds during the Winter Ascending—which technically includes me—I've always spent the evening remaining dutifully at the Queen's side. My job was always to deflect any unwanted attempts to gain her attention while encouraging the chosen few.

This is the first time I'm free to do what I want.

As Nathaniel leads me around the dance floor, I draw closer to him, matching his steps, my heart growing impossibly light.

His steps follow a pattern that I soon pick up, a rhythmic series of moves and countermoves, just like he said, all of them keeping us close.

Even when he spins me away from him, it's like he only does it so that he can reel me back in, the gaps between our bodies as intense as the nearness.

We remain on the dance floor for so long that the other fae

fade into the background and I forget their intermittent stares in my direction.

Even the Queen's sharp glances stop having an impact. I'm spilling starlight everywhere, but it's soft, not dangerous to anyone, and the more I glow, the lighter I feel.

Nathaniel's steps grow slower, even though the music speeds up. He finally stops moving and brushes a strand of hair from my shoulder.

"I'm sorry," he says.

"For what?"

"For dancing with you like that."

I smile, puzzled by the sincerity of his apology. "It's just a dance. Why would it be a problem?"

His mouth hitches up into a smile that makes my heart do an odd flip. "My people don't have many traditions left, but that dance is reserved for a particular purpose."

Despite the fact that he's keeping me in the dark, his smile is contagious. I find myself smiling back at him. "Then… enlighten me."

"Hmm." He shakes his head, his hands warm and strong around my waist. "No."

I'm not giving up so easily. I run my fingers across his jaw to tuck my hand behind his neck. "It must be an important dance, then."

"Maybe."

I throw out the most outrageous possibility I can think of. "Don't tell me… you just declared your love with that dance."

He shrugs. "Maybe."

My smile falls. *Dear stars...*

The lightness in my heart evaporates. My demand for an answer is sharp. "Why would you dance like that with me?"

He shrugs again, a careful rise and fall of his shoulders. "It's the only dance I know."

I was the one who pulled him onto the dance floor—only to promptly tell him that I didn't know how to dance. I can't be confused or emotional or even angry about his decision to dance the only steps he knows.

I try to swallow, but my mouth is dry. "I think we should take a break from dancing."

Tugging him from the dance floor, I navigate through the press of bodies to an empty couch on the far side of the room beside the open wall looking out over the city.

The couch is conveniently located beside a table laden with food and drinks—cakes and pastries on tiny plates made of edible leaves, and sweet alcoholic drinks in bluebell cups.

I scoop up two oversized flower cups filled with water and hand one to Nathaniel as we sink into the couch.

Fae come and go, snatching up new drinks and food as we sit with silence between us.

Our peace doesn't last long before Mia sashays over to us and slides onto the couch beside me. Her tongue-wrestling companion isn't anywhere to be seen.

She pats my knee in an overly familiar gesture, her breath sweetly intoxicated. "You're having fun with your prey."

She fixates on Nathaniel as she speaks, reminding me of how much interest she showed in him when she first saw him.

Inwardly, I sigh. Maintaining my aggressive guard persona is draining.

Still, I give her the answer she expects.

"I'm stuck with him for the next two days. Just because I'm going to kill him doesn't mean I don't get to play with him first."

"Can I play too?" she asks. Her hungry gaze openly devours Nathaniel. "I could do with a little bit of wickedness in my life."

From the corner of my eye, I discern Nathaniel's dark aggression growing—except that I'm not sure whether his anger is directed at her or me.

There's a fine line between pretending to put Nathaniel in danger and actually putting him in danger. I'm suddenly teetering on the edge of a situation of my own making—a situation I really don't like or want.

I force a laugh. Luckily, Mia seems too drunk to notice how fake it sounds. "Only if you don't mind me watching," I say. "He can't leave my sight."

"Ugh." She makes a face and throws herself into the back of the couch. "I don't like to share."

I take a breath of relief, hiding it behind my cup as I take another sip from it.

Recovering quickly, Mia edges up to me again, dropping her chin onto my shoulder, a conspiratorial whisper on her lips. "You know... I'm not convinced that the Fell are all that bad. Just look at him. He's not monstrous. Imagine the beautiful babies we could make."

"Hush," I say. "You've clearly had too much to drink."

Mia isn't my friend, but to speak like that is treason. Even with the loud music, there are too many fae within hearing distance—not to mention many Frost fae who can pluck our conversation out of the air if they choose.

My senses stretch to a screaming point as I try to tell if we're already being listened to. It's hard to know when the breeze wafts past us through the wide-open wall.

She persists. "You've killed plenty of Fell, Aura. But I've never fought a single one. Are the others like him?"

Nathaniel is so tense beside me now that I can feel the muscles of his thigh and arm pressing against my side.

I'm afraid of what I'll see if I look him in the eye. For nearly a day, I've been able to forget that I killed his people—and that I did it without question or hesitation.

I grit my teeth against the deep regret and guilt I will never atone for. "If you mean are they brave? Yes, they are. Now, how about a drink of water?"

She waves away my suggestion, sinking back into the couch and rubbing her forehead. "I really thought I could beat you. The Queen told me I could."

I'm confused. "What are you talking about?"

"She told me to challenge you. She said I could win. Just like she convinced Calida to fight you. Poor, wretched Calida. Her family have locked her away. They won't let her out until the memory of her shame fades." Mia rolls her eyes. "As if that will happen any time soon."

I'm stiff beside Mia as she leans closer, her breathy whispers so thickly intoxicated that she clearly has no filter, a dangerous verbal stream slipping from her mouth. "The Queen told Calida that she wouldn't heal Calida's niece unless Calida beat you today."

I stare at Mia, confused. "But... *I* healed that girl."

"It doesn't matter. The Queen controls who sees you. Nobody gets your help without giving something to the Queen in return. As soon as you healed her niece, Calida was doomed. She was supposed to hold up her end of the bargain but she failed to beat you. Now her family is terrified that the little girl will get sick again. Children are dying, Aura. Children whose parents won't do what the Queen wants..."

The sudden breeze across my mouth can't be a good thing.

I slap my hand over Mia's lips to stop her speaking, leaning over her as far as I can to hide what I'm doing.

Only the stars know what my gesture looks like. I slip one arm around her shoulders as if I'm hugging her.

"Hush now," I hiss.

Her pale blue eyes widen—a moment of sobriety. She groans when I remove my hand. "I've had too many bluebells."

"You're spouting complete nonsense," I say, loudly this time. "It's time to go find your man and finish the evening with him."

She pats my leg, her overly bright eyes searching the room as she wobbles to her feet. "Good idea. Where did he go...?"

Her sparkling dress drags behind her as she meanders through the thinning crowd. By now, many couples are starting to disappear together.

As reluctant as I am to face Nathaniel, I half-twist toward him. "We need to get out of here. Will you come outside with me?"

"It's freezing out there," he says.

I shake my head. "Trust me."

It's a bad choice of words. I swallow and try again. "There are coats hanging along the wall for us to take."

I can't sit still. Surging to my feet, I catch his hand, grateful when he doesn't fight me.

Pushing through the increasingly intoxicated couples, I catch sight of the Queen sitting on her silver seat on the opposite side of the room. Several men and women lounge around her and Nadina stands guard at her back.

I don't miss being there.

That thought nearly stops me in my tracks.

I've spent every waking moment for the last seven years at the Queen's side, but within the space of a day, my life's goal has been turned on its head.

I don't know whom I was protecting—who my Queen really is—and that uncertainty has brought me a strange new freedom.

My hand closes more tightly around Nathaniel's, the simple act of pressing my palm to his making me shiver and glow.

Veering toward the coats, I snatch two of them and hand one to him. I also choose a pair of sturdy wool-lined boots to cover my bare feet. The boots are specially designed so I won't slip on the ice. The shoes Nathaniel's wearing are already safe to wear outside.

Pulling on the coat and tucking my hair into the hood, I step through the invisible barrier keeping the warmth inside.

As I step into the freezing air outside, I breathe out the prison bars I willingly accepted into my life—the Queen, my purpose, and all of her rules.

CHAPTER 34

*T*urning to Nathaniel, I find his expression shadowed, his emotions hidden.

I can't read his thoughts and... it frightens me. I need to know what he's thinking.

He danced with me in a way that meant something to him... and then Mia reminded him that I'm a killer.

Lamplight spills around us. The palace extends onto an outdoor platform that leads to a wide marble staircase. It's nearly fifty steps down to the frozen lake.

"You asked me about the Spinning Lake," I say, needing to fill the silence. I hold out my hand, this time giving him a choice. "Would you like to stand on it?"

He gives me a silent nod, but it feels forced.

Halfway down the stairs, I can't stand the tension between us anymore. I stop walking, trying to find the words as I stare across the sparkling city. All the glitter hides so much darkness.

"You said I have to mistreat you, but I won't do that anymore," I say. "My people will whisper about me no matter what I do. To some of them, I'm already a traitor. I was tainted the moment that I touched you. I betrayed them the moment that I brought you across the border. All I have for the next two days are my conscience and my heart. I won't destroy who I am."

He stands a pace away from me, a scarily strong man who has allowed me to abuse him when he could have snapped my neck with his bare hands.

And yet... he's taken every verbal and physical beating I've given him.

My voice clams up in my throat, but I force myself to keep speaking. "I'm sorry I never talked to your people. I never asked them why they came to the border. I killed them and I didn't even—"

"Don't."

That single command, spoken with conviction, silences me.

Without another word, he strides ahead of me down the stairs.

It only now dawns on me the number of times he's seen my back and been forced to walk behind me.

We're supposed to remain within each other's sight at all times, but it doesn't seem to prevent one of us from turning our back on the other.

It's my turn to follow him, all the way down to the quiet lake. Sunrise is only a few hours away and most of the celebrations across the city are winding down. We're far enough away from the palace that the music is a faint murmur in the distance.

The lake stretches a hundred paces in each direction, surrounded by intricately designed gardens, but my favorite part—other than the water itself—is the thick copse of whisper willows situated on the right-hand side of the lake beyond the garden.

Nathaniel stops at the edge of the lake, facing away from me.

I can't breathe properly as I come up behind him.

The dress itches. My skin, my heart, my mind—nothing is as it should be and the dress is the last straw.

"I'm sorry," I say as I reach his side.

He looks at me as if he thinks I'm going to restart the conversation he shut down before, but I'm already shimmying around inside my coat as my breath frosts in the air. "I just have to…"

I wriggle around within the confines of the large fleece, unclasping the dress with great difficulty and a good dose of cursing, before I finally manage to rip the damn thing off.

I groan with relief.

Pulling the coat tight around myself to stay warm, I ball up the dress and pitch it into the bushes at the side of the lake.

Someone else can have it.

"I don't care how much that dress messed with everyone's heads, it wasn't me."

"We all wear personas," he says. "Sometimes we are what people think we are. Other times we are what we need to be. Rarely… we are ourselves."

I shiver as I wonder: Who is he right now? Is he acting out a persona or is he actually being himself? How would I tell the difference?

"Tell me again about this lake," he says. His voice is low. A hint of forgiveness.

I point toward the center. "A diamond sits deep down in the middle. The water spins around it in summer and stays frozen in winter. Imatra created both the diamond and the lake to commemorate the fae who lost their lives in the last attack."

"It's an unusual monument."

"Sure, it's strange, but it's also beautiful." On impulse, I step onto the ice. "You can see the diamond if you lie on the surface."

"You'll freeze."

"You'll keep me warm." I pace out onto the middle of the

lake, searching for the slightly brighter glow right in the center. When I find it, I wave him over. "Here."

The coat is long enough for me to tuck my legs into it. Carefully, I curl my knees under myself, making sure the uncovered parts of my shins are lying on the inside of the fleece. Then I tuck my hands into the sleeves. I press them onto the lake's surface while leaning my face close to it.

"You won't see the diamond unless you get up close," I say.

When I glance up, his chest is vibrating. He can't seem to hold in his laughter.

The shred of forgiveness I sensed before expands and the tension in my chest eases.

He told me that humans are capable of both light and darkness. So far he has proven to have a seemingly endless capacity to feel emotion.

"Do you have any idea how silly you look right now?" he asks.

I shrug under the coat. "Unless you're going to offer to lie under me, this is the only way I can see it without freezing my limbs off. Come on. Get down here."

With a final huff-laugh, he tucks his coat under his knees, retracts his hands inside his sleeves, and crouches over the surface.

I wait the two seconds it takes for him to inhale a surprised breath.

"It's beautiful, isn't it?" I ask.

Far below us, the diamond's light flickers through the frozen water.

Even when they combine their powers, the Frost fae aren't strong enough to freeze the lake all the way to the bottom, so a stream of icy water still flows around the diamond, causing the brilliant, white light to shift and flash.

I give a happy sigh. "I could watch it all night."

Nathaniel suddenly reaches out between us. He balances on his other arm, still tucked into his sleeve, using strength alone to remain steady as he strokes my cheek.

His dark eyes are serious. "There's a playful heart locked up inside you, Aura. When you're happy, you're like a dancing star."

I'm not sure if I should be offended that he pretty much told me I was acting like a child. "I... don't get to do silly things very often."

"It wasn't an insult," he says.

I wrench my eyes away from the diamond to turn onto my back, keeping my coat between my legs and the icy surface beneath me.

The hood protects the back of my head and neck as I stare up at the stars above us.

The vast night sky stretches wide, the same kind of deep oblivion that I dream about. Now that the celebrations are dying down, lamps are being extinguished around the city and it only makes the sky glow brighter than ever.

Is pure happiness childish?

Despite everything going on around me, these few seconds lying here are the most peaceful I've felt for a very long time.

Nathaniel's quiet question breaks into my thoughts. "Are you using your power right now?"

I don't look away from the sky, not wanting the moment to end. "No."

He hovers his hand above my cheek, demanding my attention. "You're glowing, but I'm not touching you."

"Hmm." I poke a single finger out of the sleeve of my coat so I can see it. "That's new."

A thoughtful crease appears on his forehead as he leans over me. "I thought I had your glow figured out, but now I'm not so sure..."

I arch an eyebrow at him. "Well, I'm curious. Even if you're wrong... What *did* you think was causing it?"

His smile becomes self-satisfied. "I thought it was because of the way I make you feel. The more intense the feeling, the more intense the glow."

I laugh out loud. I'm probably reading way too much into what he's saying, but I'm prepared to go out on a limb, even if it snaps beneath me. "You thought it was all about sex? Because that's not overconfidence on your part at all."

His thumb grazes my upper lip. "Why don't we test the theory?"

My smile drains away. I should probably be shocked. I consider for a second whether he drank a bluebell while I wasn't looking because intoxication would explain his proposition.

His fingertips graze my temple as he strokes the hair from my face, splaying the strands out across my hood, his hands coaxing me to agree.

"Only a kiss," I whisper. "No more."

Fear strikes through me the moment I give him permission.

Darkness attracts darkness, Crispin said. If the Fell creatures are darkness, then there must be some kind of darkness inside me, too, because right now, all I want is him.

Not just a kiss.

More.

Even if a kiss is all I'll take.

He's still balancing on one hand, his other hand stroking down my neck, his thumb resting against my jaw so lightly that it makes me shiver, soft sensations playing beneath my ear and across my scalp.

His head tilts to mine, hovering above me for the briefest, most agonizing moment before his lips lower to mine, fitting perfectly to the contours of my mouth.

Pleasure strikes through me, hot and intense. More intense than I should be feeling. More desire than I ever expected would be triggered by a kiss alone.

I gasp, nearly breaking the contact.

His hand tightens against my face, his fingers curling into my hair as he nudges my lips apart, only to abandon my mouth for the lower curve of my bottom lip.

His lips trace across mine to the corner of my mouth and back again, branding every miniscule portion of my skin.

My breathing is already out of control. My lips are parted, unable to get enough air to keep me sane. Nothing could keep me lucid right now.

He finally returns fully to my mouth, tasting every curve of my lips.

With every tingle and every shiver, *want* rages through my body, striking straight down into my center.

My back arches up off my coat. I don't care that the edges slip apart. I need to be closer to him, closer to his heart.

My hands slip from my sleeves in a rush, sliding beneath the opening of his coat to tug him down to me. I need the crush of his chest on mine, his heart as close to me as it can be.

His palm drags from my neck to my ribs, curling securely around my hip, not anywhere near enough to my center to ease the ache inside me.

A moan slips from my mouth, an unintelligible wish, but his hand remains where it is, gripping me so tightly, it's like he's mentally shouting at himself not to move it.

Only a kiss.

That's all I gave him permission for and he's honoring my wishes, even though my body is a willing betrayer.

My coat slips apart completely, allowing his chest to press against mine, easing the need inside my heart—but only for a moment.

His tongue touches the tip of mine and I'm lost.

Desire rages from my center to my heart. Shivers run back and forth inside my core, building in a wave I can't control.

The wave tugs at my heart, tearing at me, tearing *through* me.

I kiss him without any inhibition, my mouth opening to his, and he responds with all the intensity I need.

His tongue finally plunges into my mouth and it's a strike all the way through my heart and beyond me. Far, far beyond me.

My stomach tightens low inside me, a cry building inside my mouth. The pressure between us intensifies and a final wave crashes over me.

Starlight bursts from my chest at the same time as I shatter against his lips, a release as complete as if he'd plunged his fingers inside me.

Shock follows relief—and then fear—as light spears between us, flooding our chests.

Too much power.

CHAPTER 35

*T*error that I've hurt him destroys me. "Nathaniel!"

He jolts back from me. His hand flies to his chest, pressing hard, his breathing rapid and shallow, his dark eyes shooting wide as he stares at me in shock.

He's okay.

I tell myself he's okay.

His eyes are impossibly dark as my starlight vanishes, the last tentacles of light dancing up across his shoulders while strands of his hair fall across his face in black lines.

He slowly lifts up into a kneeling position.

"Dark stars," he whispers, dragging air into his chest as if he can't breathe. "What have we done?"

My coat is splayed apart. I'm nearly naked underneath it, but my chest glows right where my heart is, a deep burn that's beginning to feel emptier and emptier the farther he leans away from me.

"I..."

Am confused. Afraid. Lost.

He kissed me. Just a kiss. But my body... *holy stars...* my body responded as if he were part of me, as if we were completely joined and he was stroking inside my center.

It's not possible.

I don't know anywhere near as much about sex as I should, but an orgasm from a kiss is... Not. Possible.

It didn't happen. I must be delusional. The stress of the day and my confused feelings toward him are finally getting the better of me.

I hurry to rise into a sitting position, tugging the coat around myself to cover up.

Nathaniel starts to speak. "Aura, I—"

A blast of heat explodes around us.

Blazing fire roars across the surface of the lake, coming from the direction of the stairs.

Nathaniel dives toward me, snatching me up and rolling with me as the flames strike the spot where we were lying.

A figure covered in black armor runs toward us, her arms outstretched as she releases another plume of fire at Nathaniel.

I grit my teeth, a scream of rage on my lips.

I'm done with being defensive.

Spinning out of Nathaniel's arms, I rise from a crouch, my power an icy burn as it rushes from my chest through my arms and into my hands.

I shove my palms forward. My starlight cuts right through the flames, speeding up the middle and splitting the plume in half so fast that the fire streaks off to both sides.

Our attacker skids to a stop and digs in her heels, increasing her power just in time to stop my starlight cutting right through her chest.

The flames around her build in intensity, forming an instant shield along the length of her body while my starlight widens.

My power pushes at hers, forcing her arms and her flames to stretch wider and wider. The air around us fills with sunlight and starlight, both powers dazzling, lighting up the space for hundreds of paces.

She screams with effort, but my power feels weightless. Stronger than I've ever been.

I stride toward her, drawing my hands apart until the starlight pouring from me covers her entire body and her shield begins to fail, glittering white light eating away at her sunlight.

A pinpoint of my power breaks through her defenses, cutting across her collarbone.

Her scream of pain is too familiar.

I heard it once before in the arena.

I shut off my power so I don't burn her entire body.

She staggers before she collapses to her knees, her head tilted back. Her scream is now full of rage. "He has to die!"

I drop to my knees in front of her and rip off her facemask. "Why?"

Serena's amber hair cascades across her shoulders, her gold-flecked eyes turned up to me. "I'm trying to save you."

I shake my head vehemently. "Not like this."

She grips my arm. "You haven't killed in the arena. Ever. I can save you from that."

"You're trying to get around the Law by burning him—by not shedding his blood—but you won't fool the Law if he dies by your hand. You'll die too!"

Her fingers claw my arm. "I should have died when you beat me, but you wouldn't let me go. You wouldn't let the healers give up until they saved me. It's my duty to kill the Fell."

"Who says?"

I search her eyes. Serena was always a survivor. She fought me hard in the arena, but she wasn't reckless—or desperate like Calida. It isn't like Serena to risk her life without calculating all the risks.

My blood runs cold. "Did the Queen order you to kill him?"

"Imatra doesn't trust you to do it."

My chest fills with bitterness. Imatra has threatened the people I love. Now she's ordering them to kill themselves. "Even though she knows you'll die if you succeed?"

"It's my duty to do right by her."

I stare into Serena's eyes, anger rising inside me. "It's our duty to do right by our people. *Our people*, Serena! Not what suits the Queen's selfish wants."

Her eyes widen. "What's right for the Queen is what's right for our people."

"Threatening our people is not right. Bartering their lives for favors is not right. Clinging to power for the sake of power is *not* right. She has lied and manipulated—how can I trust anything she says?"

As I speak, I can't help but hope that Serena didn't know what was going on, that she was in the dark about the dying children like I was, but my hope is dashed.

Her lips press downward, a disapproving line. "Imatra does what's necessary, Aura. Even if it means that the weakest in our society are eliminated. We're here to carry out her orders. That includes managing our people and killing every Fell we can."

Managing our people. What a way to sanitize Imatra's actions.

I sense Serena's power building again. See the flicker of her gaze to a spot behind me.

Nathaniel is striding up behind me, a perfect target, and I know Serena's next move as surely as if she told me.

I grab her rising hand before she can release her power at him. Wrenching her arm against her chest, I press her palm over the burn I made.

She screams again, this time in pain. "Release me!"

"No."

I've never disobeyed her. Fought her, challenged her, but never defied her.

She shrieks as I fill her chest with starlight. It lights up her body beneath her clothing, her organs and bones turning into gleaming silhouettes.

I ease back on my power moments before every organ in her body would fail, tucking my arm around her shoulders and gently lowering her to the surface of the ice.

She's still breathing, but barely.

Inside, I'm as numb as the frozen lake around me.

Nathaniel reaches me just as I hook my arms beneath Serena's shoulders and prepare to drag her to the side. "I need to get her off the lake or she'll freeze."

When he bends to help me, I stop him. "Don't. She's hurt. I don't want to trigger some twisted part of the Law that implicates you in her injuries."

His expression is unreadable. "You chose not to kill her."

"Like I said... all I have is my conscience and my heart." I drag Serena beneath the whisper willows, quietly fighting my own misgivings.

Serena trained me. She groomed me. She nurtured a desire in me to always obey the Queen. She will never doubt her convictions or ask whether she's doing the right thing. Not like I will.

"You're leaving a string of enemies in your wake, Aura. She won't give up."

"Then I need to become stronger," I say, standing over Serena. *I need to know what really happened on the night my parents died.* That means going back to the burn site.

To do that, I need my armor and I need Treble. Whistling for Treble is easy, but getting my armor is much harder. I can't risk walking through the palace right now, and I can't fly up to my window and leap inside like Evander did earlier because of this

damn Law. If I hit that invisible wall and fall instead...
Nathaniel can watch me plummet all the way to my death.

I consider my coat and Serena's black armor.

She's a similar height and build to me...

Before I think about how cold I'm going to be while I
change, I drop to her side and quickly unclasp her armor,
peeling it off her arms and chest and dragging it down her legs.

As fast as I can, I slip off my coat, throw it over her to keep
her warm, and roll her up in it, making sure it covers her
completely.

My breath frosts, my arms shake, and my chest constricts,
but I manage to pull on her armor moments before Nathaniel
drags me against his chest and wraps his coat around me.

He sighs against my hair as I shiver against him. "You're
allowed to ask for help," he says.

I shake my head, even though I'm grateful for his body heat
while I wait for the thermal properties in the armor to bring my
temperature under control.

Being so close to him again is confusing my body.

As soon as my teeth stop chattering, I slip out of his coat as
quickly as I can and finish doing up the clasps on the armor. I'm
happy to discover that it stretches and conforms to my body
shape, even if the sleeves are a little too long.

I'm also very happy to discover that it comes complete with
liquid weapons: a dagger across each hip and a sword across the
left shoulder, all functioning correctly.

Without delay, I press my fingers to my lips. My whistle is
quick and sharp.

Before I can walk back out into the open so that Treble can
see us easily, Nathaniel halts me with a simple brush of his hand
across my arm. He doesn't grab me, doesn't force me to stop,
merely rests his palm against me.

"Aura."

The sound of my name on his lips sounds like a caress.

I turn my eyes up to his, waiting for him to voice his thoughts. Fighting Serena allowed me to avoid the conversation he and I need to have, but I don't know how to start.

It was a perfect, earth-shattering kiss. Can I start with that?

Whatever he's about to say, it's lost in the crackles of Treble's lightning as my thunderbird soars across the lake. He lands safely on the frozen surface, his talons clawing at the ice to break his flight.

Nathaniel withdraws his hand, but it's slow and reluctant.

"We need to move fast," I say. "You first."

He gives me a nod before we break into a run. He precedes me up Treble's wing, his steps practiced now.

I follow quickly, sliding in behind him, but I take a deep breath before I lean past him to my bird. "Treble, take us to where the ash burns."

Treble knows I mean the burn site where my parents died. We've passed over it a hundred times on my flights to and from the border.

He immediately lifts into the air and spears a path high into the clouds where we won't be seen.

The only way to understand my future is to go back to where my life began.

CHAPTER 36

*W*e leave the city far behind, flying toward the crystal peaks and taking the narrow pass between them.

Gliding beyond the mountains, we soar above the flower fields that stretch between the mountains and the border.

The deadly glitter field that marks the border finally comes into view in the distance.

Evander said that multiple squadrons were being sent out here to defend against a Fell attack. I sense all of the thunder-birds hiding within the clouds in the distance—not only the usual Border Guards but multiple squadrons placed at intervals up and down the border. Possibly as many as one hundred.

I didn't ask Treble to ascend into the clouds that drift above the fields, so we will be fully visible as we approach. There's no point trying to hide when the burned outpost is in plain sight.

I press against Nathaniel's back and he responds to my shifting body language by tilting his head toward me. "What's wrong?"

"There are eyes everywhere," I shout over the wind. "The Queen has sent reinforcements to the border in case your people attack us. The squadrons are concentrated ahead. We're being watched."

He remains half-turned to me, the corner of his mouth hitched up into a rare grin, raising his voice to be heard. "You should stop holding on to me then."

I sigh against his back. I was hoping he wouldn't make too much of the way I've slipped my arms around his waist. "It's easier to travel this way. It has nothing to do with anything."

"They won't see it that way."

At least the Border Guards didn't see the way we danced earlier. I shift away from Nathaniel, holding on to Treble with my thighs. It's hard work sitting apart, but I have no choice.

By the time we circle high over the site of the explosion where my first memories began, my stomach muscles are burning from keeping myself upright.

I'm also fighting the fear growing in my stomach.

Landing on this site is like inviting death into my life.

The glitter field is a highly volatile defense system. Every stem is a crystal blade between waist and chest height and the width of my finger.

The tiny bulb at the top of each stem has the power to explode with a velocity that shoots its broken pieces high and wide. One exploding bulb will trigger the bulbs beside it, resulting in a catastrophic cascade of explosions.

Every few years, the Queen brings all of her guards out here to remind us how powerful the field is. While we remain at a safe distance, she uses her wind power to float a little white mouse across the space between us and drop it into the field.

The moment the mouse's falling body hits the glitter bulbs far below, the grass explodes with such force that the shards travel high into the sky.

It's a barrage of lethal daggers that become airborne and would cut a thunderbird from the air even if it were flying as high as halfway between the ground and the clouds.

Fae do not kill animals, but the Queen declared that the glitter field demonstration is the only time when it is necessary to kill a small creature so that others may be saved.

The field only reacts to living creatures. At any other time, the wind can blow as hard as it likes and it won't trigger an explosion.

The challenge now is that the burn site is only a few hundred paces wide and the outpost's remains take up part of that space.

It's a nearly perfect circle of darkness in the middle of the deadly field.

To land safely, Treble has to circle lower and lower, and tighter and tighter—a death spiral heading toward the widest patch of clear ground.

I've only done it twice before and each time, my heart was in my throat.

That is... until I discovered that the glitter field won't hurt me. It's the same secret that allowed me to steal a stem to tie around Nathaniel's hands yesterday morning.

But that safety only extends to me. I've never tested whether it will protect Treble and it's a risk I'm not willing to take.

I lean into Nathaniel and slide forward to grip his waist again because staying apart only increases the chances of one of us being flung off into the field. "Hold on!"

At my shout, Treble tucks his wings hard into his sides and dives in a sharp, tight circle toward the ashen ground.

The air rushes past us, my stomach plummets, and all I can do is grip Nathaniel tightly, clinging with my thighs around Treble's back as we spiral, round and round at a sickening speed—

My entire body jolts forward as Treble plunges into the ash, digging in his talons and arching his neck so we don't fly right over his head.

The world stops spinning, and I take a moment to breathe.

Nathaniel's heart is pounding beneath my palm. Every instinct must be screaming at him to get off this crazy bird, but he moves in increments. Pressing his hands briefly over mine. Shifting his torso. Swinging his legs toward the wing that Treble has carefully extended so we can climb down.

I follow Nathaniel to the ground, my legs wobbling, trying not to kick up the ash when I take the final step down.

Nathaniel assesses our surroundings while a wary expression grows on his features. He's breathing deeply, taking another moment before he pushes his hair out of his eyes and bends to touch the ash covering the ground.

He draws his fingers back with a sharp inhale. "It's still warm."

All I can do is nod. Suddenly, the flight down seems like the easy part of this journey.

This place...

The outpost's scarred remains are like the shadowed bones of a life I can't remember. The building was burned out so badly that I can't even picture the rooms inside it. It might have contained a rocking chair in which my mother sang me to sleep. Maybe a table at which I ate meals and laughed with my father.

Nothing is left.

I walk to what used to be a door and reach out to press my palm against the tallest burned pillar, the jagged edges calling me to step through into a home that used to be mine.

My fingertips come away sparkling with soot in the moonlight.

The spot I wiped away glows underneath.

Nathaniel takes another quick breath, jolting away from the pillar he stands near. His hand is covered in ash from brushing the burned wood.

"The embers are still burning." He turns to me with a dangerous glint in his eyes. "It happened fifteen years ago. How is it still hot?"

I've asked myself that question a thousand times, but I don't have any answers.

"I honestly don't know," I say. "Nothing grows here. Birds refuse to fly overhead. It doesn't matter how often it rains; the ash never washes away. Whatever dark magic was used to create this explosion... it's still burning."

I point toward the sky. "The Border Guards may watch us, but they don't dare set foot here, and it's not only because of the threat of the glitter field. It's because of the darkness that lingers here. Even Queen Imatra refuses to come back."

"But *you* came back."

"I need to remember." My voice catches. "I... *need*... to know what happened."

"Will you tell me what you know?" Nathaniel's hand drops to his side, but he hasn't tried to wipe away the ash smeared all over his palm. The orange glow from the pillar casts soft light around us.

I press against the jagged wood again, soaking in the burn, fixating on the ebb and flow of the fire inside the pillar.

The heat doesn't hurt me.

I've come back two times—once was the day after I challenged Serena. I didn't stay long. Only long enough to determine that I can't remember anything and that the heat has no effect on me.

This fire did all its hurting when I was seven years old.

"I was born in this ash," I say. "I was born a fully-formed

seven-year-old girl with no memory of the life I lived until the moment I woke up after the battle. I don't remember my mother or my father. I don't remember the attack. I remember... nothing."

I turn to him. "At least... that's what I tell everyone. But the truth is when I say that I remember nothing, I mean I remember a cold expanse, like my mind is filled with..." I struggle to describe my feelings. "Vast, endless space. That's my nothing."

The same nothing that surrounds me when I sleep.

"What about when you woke up?" he asks, still keeping his distance.

I shiver against the wood, curling my fingertips around the pillar. "Right before I woke up, I felt more fear and pain than I thought I could survive. My chest hurt... so badly... and I..."

My hand shoots from the burning pillar to my heart. I press the heel of my palm to the space below my collarbone, trying to ease the ache.

Just an hour ago, I felt more happiness in my heart than I'd ever felt before, but now...

"I still feel it. It still hurts."

I force air in and out of my chest, focusing on continuing to breathe.

Nathaniel takes a step toward me, an intense concern filling his face, but my hand shoots out—*stop*—because I don't want help right now.

I just want to get the words out, get it all said, and then I can lock it all away again.

"I woke up huddled in the scorched ash. Right there." I point at an empty spot in the dirt five paces away from the wreckage of the front door. "Fiery embers floated around me. My clothes were burned away. My skin was coated in ash. I looked up and I saw her... Imatra was kneeling in the ash closer to the glitter field. She was reaching for me, begging me to come to her, to come away from the fire. So I crawled through the ash to her."

I stop speaking. The images flash through my mind quickly now.

The ash had smudged Imatra's bright skin, leaving smears like insults against her perfect neck and arms. I buried my head against her shoulder and curled up in her lap, crying. Not because I was sad, but because I was in pain. Too much pain.

Tears had sparkled in her eyes, forming into tiny pearls as they rolled down her cheeks.

"She let them fall to the ground," I whisper, swaying against the pillar.

"Let what fall?"

"Her perfect tears." I shake my head. My gaze narrows. "She told me she was the one who pulled me from the flames, but..."

I cast a narrow-eyed gaze across the ash. "I was here and she was there, farther away. I crawled through the dust to her. I pulled *myself* from the fire."

I lift my hand from the wooden pillar and stare at my glowing skin.

This fire.

Why doesn't it hurt me? And why was she kneeling so far away from me, reaching out desperately for me to come to her?

Her grasping hands had pulled me tight, her silver voice whispering to me: *I'm sorry, child. I couldn't stop the Fell. They took everything from you, but one day you will take everything from them.*

Nathaniel finally crosses the distance to me, stopping closer than he should. "You don't have to remember anything else. We can go now." He glances at Treble urgently. "We need to go."

I study the tension around his eyes, the way his gaze rushes across my face and his hands hover around my frame as if he's expecting to need to grab me at any moment.

He carefully laces his fingers through mine, covering my burning palm with his, even though he winces.

The heat is hurting him.

He tugs me toward Treble, but I refuse to budge, forcing him to stop as I dig in my heels.

"Why are you looking at me like that?" I demand.

"Because you're paler than you should be."

"I feel fine."

"You're not fine. We have to go. Something is very wrong with this place. We're leaving. *Now.*"

I never thought I'd see Nathaniel close to panic. He's cycled through all the emotions. Been angry. Insulted. Raging against my misconceptions about his people. Deadly calm. Quiet when I didn't expect him to be. He's challenged me when I made claims he disagrees with.

But now he's tugging me toward Treble in a way that tells me he's two seconds away from throwing me over his shoulder if I don't move fast enough.

It only makes me angry. "You've never shown any weakness. Why are you afraid of this place?"

He stops and stares at me. "I'm not."

"Then why are we leaving?"

"Because if you could see yourself right now, you'd run too."

He's deadly serious. The pulse at his wrist is racing. I can feel it beneath my fingertips.

I throw my head back, my own self-loathing roaring to the surface. "What would I see? A washed-out woman with dull eyes and hair the color of the dead?"

He holds up our intertwined hands. "Tell me, Aura: What *don't* you see?"

My forehead creases as I stare at our hands. He's touching me, but... I'm not glowing. The back of my hand is dusted in ash, a gray color seeping through my fingers, but when I brush at it, the ash doesn't come off.

I suddenly realize what Crispin said to me that I should have contradicted.

He said that Nathaniel would wake up angry... if Nathaniel thought that Crispin had hurt me.

Nathaniel would be angry if I was hurt.

He's not afraid for himself right now. He's afraid for me.

CHAPTER 37

*N*athaniel is trying to protect me.

"No!" My shout echoes around us. "You aren't allowed to feel like that." I try to wrench my hand from his, but he holds on tightly.

I shove him instead. "You're destined to kill me. You're not allowed to care."

I smack my fist at his face, but I have no strength or speed, and he easily evades the blow.

My legs wobble and his shoulder is suddenly angled under my stomach and he…

Oh no, he wouldn't dare.

He swings me up over his shoulder like a sack of wheat.

I kick my legs, fighting everything inside my heart and mind that tells me to stop lashing out—even my survival instincts are screaming that I need his help right now.

But I can't allow him to worry about me because then I have to face the feelings that have crept into my own heart.

The dragon warned me that by the time Nathaniel and I fight, we won't want to. I'm already full of confusion and doubt.

I don't need Nathaniel's feelings to add fuel to the war inside my heart and mind.

He strides toward Treble, warding off the blows I land on his back, ignoring the kicks I aim at his legs. "Aura, don't fight me! Please! You're turning to ash!"

Shock makes me stop struggling. As my body bounces across Nathaniel's shoulders with every step he runs, I try desperately to wipe the dust off my hands, but it doesn't move.

It's like it has sunk into my skin and I can't get rid of it.

A new panic takes hold of me because my whole world is turning gray.

Lifting my head to look behind us, I can see the ash that Nathaniel's boots are kicking up. It flies into the air and hovers, rising as if it's coming for me. As if I'm some kind of ash-magnet.

Suddenly, I can't breathe and the scenery swims around me, a glittering blur of color bleaching pale.

I'm aware of Nathaniel running up Treble's wing before he drops into position on Treble's back. At the same time, he drags me down in front of him, scissoring my legs and pulling them around his hips so that I'm facing him, my arms curled against his chest. He's hugging me as close as possible.

His voice thrums through me. "Fly, Treble," he shouts. "Now!"

Treble sweeps his wings in one strong beat that propels us into the air in a rush.

The wind generated by Treble's movements ripples through the glitter field, making the stems at the edge of the burn site shriek and clash.

My heart is in my throat as I wait for the glitter field to explode and the shards to cut through us.

Treble's wings crack, lightning spearing across the night sky and lights up the air around me, but the glitter field doesn't shatter.

I don't know if that's because Treble is carrying me, or if we just got lucky.

We burst high into the sky, rapidly ascending before we streak through the air. Treble continues to beat his wings in panicked movements while Nathaniel speaks to him, but I'm having trouble hearing anything now.

I don't know which way we're facing or what's going on around us. Treble's blue lightning is the last color I see before darkness closes in and my vision doesn't extend beyond Nathaniel's face.

Cradling my head, he returns his focus to me. He lowers his cheek to mine, tilting close to my mouth and nose as if he's trying to sense whether I'm breathing.

I read my name on his lips: *Aura?*

I can't answer him. Despite the wind rushing past me, I have no air.

"Breathe, Aura!" Nathaniel's command breaks through the silence. His voice is deep and angry, the kind of anger that only panic can bring.

He tilts his lips to mine. The hand that was supporting my waist rises to my chest, pressing against my heart. He curls his other arm behind my head, a precarious balancing act.

He takes a deep breath before our lips connect.

It's not a gentle kiss. His mouth seals against mine as he exhales, blowing air into me. Oxygen rushes from his mouth, forcing its way into my throat. At the same time, he presses his palm against my heart.

One press. Then two.

He's trying to breathe for me. He's trying to make my heart beat.

The burn site was stealing my life away from me and I don't know why.

But I do know that I should already be dead. I've gone too long without air. Only the stars know how I'm still awake.

Tears burn behind my eyes as he releases me to shout, "Aura! *Breathe!*"

He could let me die—the nightmare would be over for him—but he's trying to keep me alive.

His mouth crashes against mine, and his fist hits my heart so hard that I thud against his supporting arm, a sliver of air gets through, and then—

Oxygen rushes into my chest, a sweet inhalation.

Starlight bursts between us and the constriction inside my throat vanishes.

I scream as I suck air into my starving lungs, dragging oxygen in and out of my mouth, choking and shuddering against his chest. I grip his sides with my weak hands as his heaving chest rises and falls against me.

He gave me air, helped my heart to beat again, and now all of the emotions raging through me are too much to process.

I start to speak, but his arms close around me, crushing me so close that I have to tip my head back to see him. "Nathaniel?"

The wind destroys my whisper.

His focus has shifted to my right. The muscles in his arms tense up while darkness grows in his eyes.

My vision finally widens far enough from the pinpoint of Nathaniel's face to see the squadron of thunderbirds diving toward us from all sides.

Crackles of lightning fill the air behind me, telling me that more thunderbirds are dropping from the clouds, but I can't turn to see them.

Evander flies at the head of the squadron soaring toward us

on my right. Cadence dives in our direction, her crimson lightning casting violent electricity ahead of her.

I'm sure Evander is coming to make sure I'm okay, but my eyes widen when Cadence doesn't slow down.

Evander somersaults off her back as she flies overhead. He lands with a thud on Treble's back directly behind Nathaniel, upsetting Treble's balance so that we wobble in the air.

A dagger glints in Evander's fist.

Before I can scream, he crouches behind Nathaniel, grabs Nathaniel's hair, pulls his head back, and presses the blade to his throat.

"Move away from Aura!" Evander shouts. He isn't wearing a facemask and his blue-gray eyes light up sapphire as the lightning from Treble's wings mixes with Cadence's. She's rapidly circling back to us while the other thunderbirds take up formation at a safe distance.

A muscle ticks in Nathaniel's jaw. "If I let her go, she'll fall," he shouts. "Do you want her to die?"

Evander's eyes widen before they narrow with fury. He curses at Nathaniel more vehemently than I've ever heard him speak, telling Nathaniel to go to hell in as many different ways as he can. For Nathaniel to imply that Evander would ever want to hurt me is more than my brother will tolerate.

But Nathaniel isn't lying. My legs are weak. I'm still recovering. The amount of weight I'm leaning against Nathaniel is telling him that.

"Evander! Stop!" I rasp.

My fear is for both of them. If Evander sheds Nathaniel's blood, he'll die.

CHAPTER 38

*a*t the same time as I shout, another thunderbird darts toward us, closer than the others. Its rider pulls back her facemask, allowing strands of coral hair to escape from beneath her hood.

"Evander!" Talsa screams. "Remember the Law!"

Evander's fury turns to worry as he glances at her.

I take advantage of Evander's distraction to reach out and grab the dagger's hilt, my hand closing over Evander's. My legs are still like jelly, but my arms are finally working fully again.

I grip the dagger hard, refusing to let Evander do anything with it.

"Aura, what are you doing?"

I glare back at him. "I'm stopping you from killing yourself."

The wind snatches at my mouth. Evander's expression shifts as he pulls my speech to his ears. The corners of his lips turn down, intensely unhappy.

"You need to tell me what's going on," he says, his power carrying his voice to me. "You're flying toward the border. Why are you doing that?"

Toward the border?

I shake my head—*no*. Treble was rising into the air away from the burn site. Nathaniel shouted at Treble to fly and that was all I heard.

Nathaniel wouldn't tell Treble to fly to the border. That would mean he was taking me into Fell country.

I adjust my focus beyond Nathaniel and Evander, who are both facing me, both of them tense. In the distance, I can see Bright's mountains. But I'm facing backward, so that means...

Twisting, I can just see the foggy marsh where I fought Nathaniel yesterday morning. It's in the direction that Treble is flying.

I'm filled with confusion. Why would Nathaniel take me this way?

Nathaniel's dark eyes reveal nothing as I turn back to him.

Still gripping Evander's hand so he can't use his dagger, I lean close to Nathaniel. "Were you taking me to the border?"

Slowly, very slowly, he takes a breath and starts to speak. "I need to tell you—"

An ear-shattering crack of wings echoes around us. Four more squadrons of thunderbirds burst from the cloud cover, descending to fan out and cover the airspace between us and the mountains.

My eyes widen to see the Queen herself riding her crimson thunderbird, streaks of lightning glittering around her slender form. She has swapped her ballgown for armor that catches the last of the moon's light, her hair tucked away into a tight hood.

Nadina rides at the head of the oncoming squadrons, still wearing the golden rose that gives her power at night. She and the Queen must have come straight from the Ball.

Imatra leaves the main group, drawing level with us. Her thunderbird coasts on one side of us while Cadence flies on the other, waiting for Evander to return to her.

I sense the tug of the Queen's magic as she uses it to slow our flight, manipulating the air to keep us aloft, but also to stop Treble from speeding away.

I sense the tug of the Queen's magic as she uses it to slow our flight, manipulating the air to keep us aloft, but also to stop Treble from speeding away.

The tension in Treble's body tells me he's afraid, especially now that the wind around him is being manipulated, taking away his control of our flight.

He bounces his head at Cadence, but she doesn't look at him. He must be trying to talk to her, but she must not be listening.

All of the other thunderbirds are avoiding looking at him too. My heart sinks at the possibility that they've closed him out.

As soon as we slow down, all of the other thunderbirds begin to circle us, maintaining their flight by spiraling around us like predators.

My ears pop as Imatra reduces the wind to a whisper, dropping us into silence. It reminds me of the silent wind tunnel we were caught in before the Vanem Dragon sealed the Law.

She gives us a serene smile, her voice effortlessly audible now. "Evander, remove your dagger and return to your bird. I would hate for Aura to get hurt."

Evander gives her a reluctant nod. "As you wish, my queen."

I ease open my fingers to allow my brother to slide his weapon free. He can't be aware of what's going on at the Grove or the threats against his father, or he wouldn't be so trusting of the Queen right now.

With a nimble leap and flip through the air, he leaves Treble's back, his flight powered by his magic as he lands comfortably in Cadence's saddle.

Imatra gives him an indulgent smile across the distance and I sense the quiet space around us expand to encompass Evander and Cadence. "You're one of my best warriors, Evander of the Frost. A blessing to me."

Evander gives her a stoic nod. He hasn't had as much practice reading the subtext in everything Imatra says, but I'm sure he doesn't miss the way her gaze flickers to Talsa.

Unlike the circling birds, Talsa's thunderbird is coasting high above us, dipping when it needs to maintain its position. She won't be able to hear anything we're saying, but she seems determined not to take her eyes off us.

My heart turns cold. If Imatra is serious about her intentions toward Evander, then Talsa is in her way.

Still holding on to me, Nathaniel remains quiet, but the tension in his body and the flicker of his gaze tells me he's counting every thunderbird surrounding us, every guard, and every possible blade that could cut us down.

Imatra leans in my direction with a conspiratorial whisper that travels with her power. "Talsa has such beautiful hair, don't you think, Aura? I should give her a violet rose to wear in it. It would suit her perfectly."

I grind my teeth, my hand easing toward my hip and the dagger that rests there.

I suddenly find myself the center of Nathaniel's attention again. He knows that the violet roses are poisonous so he won't have missed the Queen's threat, but he gives me a quick shake of his head. I shouldn't engage her in battle.

I snap, "What do you want, Imatra?"

At the side, Evander jolts in alarm. Speaking to the Queen like that is a punishable offence.

Imatra gives me a sweet smile. "I want you to come home, Aura. That's all. I just want things to go back to the way they were."

She reaches out across the distance, even though she's too far away to touch me. Even wearing armor, she's covered her hands with rings, dripping rocks that glitter and distract from the way her fingers form claws that want to latch on to me.

"Come, dear," she says. "Come away from the Fell creature.

266

Evander can help you across the air safely. You can ride with me. You don't need to worry about the Fell anymore."

Around us, the thunderbirds circle more closely, ready to strike.

I suddenly see Imatra's plan too clearly. She sent reinforcements to the border, but she didn't do it to keep Nathaniel's people out.

She did it to keep Nathaniel in.

Somehow... she knew he would try to bring me here.

The way we're sitting, Nathaniel is facing his home while I am facing mine. Two polar opposites, light and dark.

Behind him, Nadina's thunderbird is drawing into position. So are the other Solstice fae. Flames grow around their hands and arms, an unnatural fiery glow in the dark of dawn.

The moment I leave Treble's back, they'll strike Nathaniel dead.

It doesn't matter that whoever kills him will die. The Queen has ordered them to do it, and they're prepared to die to carry out her wishes.

Imatra isn't here to take me home.

She's here to have Nathaniel killed. This time, she's not taking any chances that she'll fail.

CHAPTER 39

S trands of my white hair trail across the space between us as I leave my dagger on my hip and slide my arms around Nathaniel's waist.

He tilts his head to mine, the dark threads of his hair pressing to my cheeks.

We are both darkness and light, somehow connected despite our differences.

My starlight bursts around us as soon as our foreheads touch, my power glowing across the night sky.

Imatra recoils, retracting her hand before my light can touch her skin.

Evander, too, leans away, urging Cadence to float farther from us.

I've bought us a little space, but it won't last long.

"Nathaniel," I whisper in the quiet. "You made me a promise."

He grips my shoulders, a firm hold. "I promised you I'd tell you what I really planned." The flecks in his eyes always seem to darken in my light, while the depth of his thoughts remain a mystery to me.

"I didn't come here for revenge," he says. "I didn't come to kill your Queen. I didn't plan to invoke the Law. I had the spells cast on my hands because it was the only way I could think of to force you to come with me. To make you *choose* to come with me. I was going to take you into Fell country and then come back to the border to heal your friends."

The darkness in his gaze draws me in and won't let me go. "I came here for you."

My breath catches. "Why?"

"Because I promised my father I would."

Imatra's angry shriek cuts through the quiet. She surges forward, crimson light growing around her fingertips.

It pushes at my starlight, carving enough safe space around herself to move closer to us.

"I knew you were going to try to steal her the moment you reminded me of your father," she screams. "Where do you plan to take her, Nathaniel? Into the darkness, where she'll suffocate without the light?"

Nathaniel's arms tighten around me as he turns toward Imatra. Other than the way he holds me, he appears unaffected by her rage.

He wears the mask of a man who knows he's about to die and all he wants is the truth before he goes.

"Did you hold the dagger that struck my father in the back?" he asks her.

Her upper lip curls. "You're too much like him. You believe in truth and goodness. You think peace is possible—"

"No," he says. "Peace is impossible. All I can do is tip the balance in favor of justice."

She lets out a disdainful breath. "You *are* your father's son."

Nathaniel's indifference disappears. "Were you the one who struck him?" he roars. "Three blows to his back. Shallow enough for his horse to drag him back alive. Deep enough that he couldn't be saved. Did you kill him?"

"Me?" She laughs. Loudly. Her giggles rise into air, elevating the tension around us.

Behind Nathaniel, Nadina's thunderbird edges closer as it circles, the flames growing around her sun-kissed hands. The other Solstice fae follow her lead. Soon, the first rays of daylight will strike across the horizon and they won't need the Queen's power anymore.

Imatra laughs so hard that she grips her side, but she stops just as suddenly, raising her voice as if she's announcing crimes to the world. Her shout echoes out and beyond the cocoon of silence she created for us, far enough that the fae circling us turn their heads to listen.

"I didn't kill your father or his army," she shouts. "I wasn't the one who burned a thousand human warriors to dust. I didn't shatter the bodies of Evander's mother and her squadron."

She shakes her head. "It wasn't me."

Her gaze settles on me.

She smiles.

The lifting of her lips is like a knife through the foundations of my world.

Nathaniel turns to me, his neck stiff.

Evander is frozen on Cadence, snow gathering around his hands, his power rising as he stares at me.

Every fae follows Imatra's gaze to its unnerving point of focus.

Me.

"Only one other person survived the blast," the Queen shouts. "Only one other... *powerful*... girl."

CHAPTER 40

$\mathcal{I}$ taste ash in my mouth as Nathaniel draws away
from me, the smallest distance that feels like a chasm
opening up between us.

I struggle to find my voice, to think clearly. My heart hurts, a
sharp pain, an endless ache.

"Oh, but you don't remember," Imatra says, lowering her
voice again. "Let me tell you what I've been keeping to myself all
these years, Aura."

Her thunderbird coasts closer as she speaks. Dangerously
close.

"Your parents came to me when you were born, afraid of
their newborn daughter's uncontrollable power. I helped them
put you into a deep sleep in which you would continue to grow
until you were old enough to learn control."

Her soft voice turns into a snarl. "They failed to tell me that
the spell was wearing off. The night that the human army came
to negotiate peace here at the border, you woke up. It was
sudden and catastrophic. You destroyed everything."

I press my hand to my forehead, rubbing hard, needing the

memories to surface, but all I remember is the pain in my chest, sudden and sharp. Even the Vanem Dragon said that his sight went dark for hours—that he couldn't move until the explosion happened.

All I remember is ash and heat.

"No." I shake my head.

"You killed them, Aura," Imatra says, her eyes gleaming. "All of them. Even your own parents."

"Please, no."

Around me, the fae are closing in. Nadina soars closer and the accusing stares of the Border Guards who used to trust me are like knives cutting through me.

When I look to Evander, he has withdrawn, his cheeks ashen with shock. Imatra said I killed his mother—a mother he mourned with his father. She said that I destroyed an entire army. Killed my parents.

I have no memory of the event to dispute what she's saying. I have no defense, no proof, no claim to innocence, but there's one thing I do know.

One glimmer of hope.

I've lost Evander's trust, but I close my eyes, hoping that Nathaniel will hear me. "I didn't have a dagger."

Nathaniel said his father was stabbed in the back three times. His father was left alive for his horse to drag him home.

I wait for his response, my shoulders slumping with every passing second.

Nathaniel's voice washes over me like a lifeline. "You didn't kill my father. He didn't have any burns on his body."

Warm, gentle hands slide across my cheeks. His thumbs graze my temples and coax me to open my eyes.

"When I walked out of the fog yesterday morning, you didn't strike first." His eyes search mine. "The past is complicated. *You're* complicated."

He turns a hard glare at the Queen. "The past can be fabricated when only one person remembers it."

Imatra recoils. "Are you accusing me of lying?"

"You're a practiced liar, Imatra. You lured my father here by lying about wanting peace. Why not go farther and wake a sleeping girl to destroy an entire human army for you? Even if it means losing a squadron of your own people. *You're* still alive. That means you were prepared."

At the side, Evander's focus shifts to the Queen, a darkness entering his eyes.

If what Nathaniel is implying is true, then the Queen chose to wake me and willingly risked his mother's life.

Nathaniel slides one arm around my waist, gripping tightly as he places his other hand on Treble's neck. It's the kind of move I make when I'm telling Treble to prepare to fly.

"I came for you, Aura," he says, brushing a kiss against my cheek. "I don't intend to fail."

How can he still believe that I have any goodness inside me now that he knows what I did?

Even if the Queen woke me deliberately, my power apparently burned through a thousand humans. How is Nathaniel still so determined to walk the path he chose for himself?

"Enough!" Imatra screams, her features twisting. "If you want to die, then so be it."

Her thunderbird rears up as she drags at its reins, driving it abruptly to the left and away from us.

Her power over the air breaks and the wind suddenly rushes in.

At the same time, flames rage toward Nathaniel's back as Nadina and the Solstice fae let their power loose.

I jump to my feet, both of my hands shooting out above Nathaniel's head, my power shrieking through me and bursting across the air.

Fire and starlight collide, tearing at the sky. My heart pounds with my fear—fighting one Solstice fae is far less daunting than fighting ten. What's more, my back is vulnerable.

"I need a weapon," Nathaniel shouts.

"Daggers at my hips. Sword at my shoulder," I cry.

Remaining low, Nathaniel grabs the weapons, not as practiced as me at peeling them off, freeing them just in time to duck past me and deflect the downward cut of a Dusk fae's blade.

The Dusk fae control animals. They move as one with their thunderbirds, giving them supreme agility in the air, but their only attacking ability is their blades and physical skill.

One of them has already jumped off her bird to land on Treble's neck, viciously swiping at Nathaniel before she leaps off again.

Her jump is perfectly timed so she can land in her bird's saddle as it flies beneath us. Another Dusk fae immediately takes her place.

Nathaniel and I stand back to back, our knees bent to keep our balance as Treble takes control of our flight once more, darting between attacking birds.

The sound of clashing steel is the only indication I have of how the fight at my back is going.

The danger for Nathaniel is if he hurts one of the fae—a danger they will no doubt be counting on. If they can force him to cut one of them instead of only deflecting... he'll die like they want him to.

We need a way out—and fast.

Keeping one arm outstretched to maintain my starlit barrier and repel the flames, I thrust my other arm lower, aiming a burst of starlight at the space beneath Nadina's thunderbird.

The burst upsets her bird enough that it bucks and Nadina

loses her balance. Her power falters for a moment, giving me a few seconds of reprieve. It's not much, but it's a start.

Before Nadina can recover, I stream power into the air beneath the other birds. It doesn't burst anywhere close enough to harm them—I don't ever want to hurt a thunderbird—but the explosions cause them to buck and rear, their wings colliding, making them panic.

The rider on Nadina's left bounces off to the side as her thunderbird jolts. She slips from the saddle but tries to cling on...

Her falling scream makes my heart stop. She's dropping straight toward the glitter field and she's far bigger than a mouse.

In our efforts to evade the other birds, we've descended too close to the field, well within the reach of its explosions.

"Treble!" I scream. "*Up!*"

One arm still outstretched to deflect the last flames spearing my way, I twist and grab Nathaniel's arm, pulling him down into a crouch beside me so he won't fall off.

Two riders send fire streaming at us, leaning over from the side of their birds. I deflect their power at the last moment as Treble soars past them into the sky.

Below us, the falling woman hits the field.

CHAPTER 41

*G*litter shards explode up into the air so high and so fast that they cut right through the riders who were leaning across their birds.

The women slide off, their dead bodies plummeting toward the glitter field. The rider-less birds try to rise higher, their wings damaged and bleeding, but they can't fly fast enough.

My heart sinks as the fallen riders hit the field, triggering more explosions of glass. The air sparkles with the deadly shards, turning the space below us into a flurry. The flailing birds scream under the new barrage of glass daggers flying upward.

Tears stream down my cheeks as the birds also fall.

Treble's wings beat in strong, panicked sweeps, lifting us above the reach of the explosions just in time.

I crouch low, holding on to Nathaniel as Treble darts between two thunderbirds ridden by Solstice fae, who try to block our path. I fling my power left and right, blocking the flames they aim at us while I balance on Treble's back.

My name is shouted from above us. I catch sight of Talsa in

the distance. It looks like she was staying high, but her bird suddenly darts to the left, colliding with a Solstice fae who was about to dive at us from above.

I don't have time to decide whether Talsa deliberately got in the way of the attacking fae or whether her bird was simply spooked by the explosions below us.

A flame sizzles past my face, close enough to singe my hair. Nathaniel spins, my sword raised in his hands. "Aura! Behind you."

I turn just as another plume of fire skims my shoulder.

Nadina's thunderbird soars toward us, her attacks dangerously close. Treble banks left, but Nadina's bird tracks our path, its flight quick and agile.

I stay in a crouch and raise my hands, preparing to defend us when Evander appears off to the side.

He drives Cadence toward us. Ice streams from his hands but narrowly misses us and—somehow—hits Nadina's flames instead. The impact forces Nadina off-balance and her thunderbird swings to the side.

Evander draws alongside us and leaps onto Treble's wing bone. I sense he's using his power over the air to keep his balance as he takes a swipe with his fist at Nathaniel. His blow flies wide, far wider than it would have if he were serious about making an impact.

I shout, "Brother, please—"

He doesn't let me finish, following up with another punch aimed at Nathaniel's stomach, but he pulls the hit before he connects. Relief fills me. He's making it look like he's fighting us so he won't be branded a traitor.

"One day you'll remember what happened that night, Aura," Evander whispers, between pretend swipes. His magic carries his murmurs directly to my ears. "When that day comes, you can clear your conscience and atone if you need to. Until then, you're still my sister. Now go!"

He somersaults back into his bird's saddle, gathering his power in front of his chest as if he's going to blast us with it, but waits the split second it takes us to rise higher into the sky.

Deadly ice explodes across the space beneath Treble's belly, just missing us. It was a powerful enough strike to make anyone think that he was really trying to hurt us.

We're still flying above the glitter field and pure chaos exists between us and the border. As other Frost fae dart into the fight, ice and fire streak toward us in turns. My reflexes are stretched and my muscles scream, but I spin and turn, deflecting the attacks with my power while Nathaniel blocks anyone who gets in close enough to stab their weapon at us.

Suddenly, Treble screams.

The awful sound tears through my heart.

The wind snatches at my hair as I whirl toward the flames rising from his left wing. "No!"

Nadina flies above us, leaning over her bird, a satisfied smile on her face. She couldn't hit me, so she hit Treble's wing instead.

"Your turn to fall, Aura!" she shouts, tugging on the reins so her bird lifts high into the air, evading the burst of starlight I fling at her.

She screams an order at the other fae. "Rise up! Let them fall to their deaths together."

Every thunderbird near us darts upward, every rider racing to fly to safety beyond the reach of the glitter grass that will shatter when we hit the field.

"Treble! No!" Tears blur my vision as Treble continues to shriek in pain. Of all the low moves Nadina could make...

Nathaniel grabs me. He points upward.

I follow the direction of his finger. Evander is the only one who hasn't abandoned us. Ice is already forming around his hands, but if he puts out the flames, he'll be a traitor. The Queen will have him put to death.

Far above us, I catch sight of Imatra watching us fall.

Treble is losing height rapidly, but maybe if we get off his back, he'll have enough strength to coast clear of the field instead of crashing into it. Then Evander can help him without being branded as a traitor.

Nadina told me it was my turn to fall.

It finally is.

I spin to Nathaniel. "I don't expect you to trust me, but will you believe me when I say I don't want you to die tonight?"

His forehead creases, but he's holding my arm, his grip firm and certain. "Yes."

I gasp in a breath at his unexpected trust, my heart glowing beneath my armor so brightly that it casts light between us.

Before I can doubt myself, I slip my arms around his chest and pull him close. Easing my sword from his fingers, I tap it to my shoulder, where it conforms with my armor again.

Nathaniel allows me to drag him down onto Treble's back. I slip into his lap and hook my legs around his hips, preparing to curl them around the backs of his thighs, wrapping myself around him as tightly as possible.

"We call your people Fell: the fallen ones," I say to him. "It's time for me to fall too. Will you fall with me?"

The crease in his forehead clears as he wraps his arms around me, holding me close. An expression of acceptance grows on his face. "I will."

I close my eyes, filling my lungs with the scent of his skin. "Okay then."

I tug us to the side, leaning my weight into thin air.

The world is quiet as we slip from Treble's back and plunge toward the glitter field.

CHAPTER 42

$\mathcal{T}$he wind is fierce. It rips and tears at us, trying to pry us apart as we fall.

Screaming with effort, I hold onto Nathaniel, twisting so that I'm beneath him, refusing to let his body part from mine. He fights me. He wants to hit first and cushion my fall, but I won't let him.

At the last moment, I fling us sideways, driving my body into the ground.

We hit the glitter fronds and I brace for every limb to break and every bone to shatter.

The grass thickens beneath my back, a wild thicket forming that bends, catches us, and flings us back up into the air.

I gasp as we lift up before we drop and bounce onto the platform of grass again, up and down until the thicket sinks beneath us, depositing us gently onto the earth.

I lie beneath Nathaniel as the glitter grass rises up around us, curving over to form a green canopy that blocks out the sky and all the thunderbirds sailing through the air far above.

Right before the grass closes over us, I see Treble rise higher without our weight on his back. I close my eyes and wait, my heart beating hard, praying that I don't hear him hit the ground.

Praying that Evander will get to him in time.

All is quiet.

No explosion.

Nathaniel's chest rises and falls rapidly against mine, one hand resting under my head, his other hand pressed to my shoulder. "Aura... how...?"

I bite my lip. "I had a bad day when I was fifteen years old."

He waits for me to continue, his lips pressed together in a quizzical line. "And?"

"After I nearly killed Serena, I flew out to the burn site and I was so angry... and reckless. I ran toward the glitter field, daring it to hurt me." I close my eyes as he rubs my shoulder. "I ran right through it. Don't ask me how or why. That burn site is like death to me, but the glitter field is like life."

"So this is how you bound my hands yesterday morning," he says.

I reach out to run my fingertips along the nearest stem. "It will turn back to glass once I'm gone," I say.

I'm still wrapped around him and I find myself suddenly frozen. I didn't think past this moment, didn't expect to survive.

I don't have a plan, can't see the future.

"We need to run now, Aura," he says. "They won't give up until we're well into the marsh."

I shiver. I've never gone beyond the immediate border, never ventured past the misshapen trees. They've always marked a safe zone for the fae.

Anywhere past the trees is the land of darkness. My people won't follow us past that point.

Nathaniel rises back onto his heels and pulls me with him. The canopy stretches above us, but it won't be high enough to cover us once we're standing.

"I'm ready," I say, preparing to rise. "Promise me you won't let go of my hand. I don't know what the field will do if you aren't touching me."

He gives me a crooked grin. "I won't let go."

As soon as we push through the canopy, shouts fill the sky. Nadina and the Solstice fae are driving their birds through the air, dangerously close to the glitter field, coming after us.

The Queen's scream rises above the other shouts. "Kill them! Don't let them get to the border."

Nathaniel's grip is strong as I break into a run. He times his steps with mine, keeping pace beside me, our arms pumping in unison. The glitter grass parts, glistening emerald stems bending aside to allow us to run through it.

Seconds later, fire strikes the ground behind us, missing us by inches.

We don't stop. The edge of the field is a hundred paces away and the foggy marsh beckons in the distance, a shrouded freedom waiting for us.

Another ball of fire hits the glitter field on my left-hand side. I flinch away from it, but Nathaniel keeps me steady, his grip on my arm urging me forward.

Three more fireballs hit the ground, one right in front of me. I don't have time to scream.

I veer to the left, tugging Nathaniel with me, our feet flying across the earth as flames explode around us, but the grass remains green and soft, impervious to the heat.

The edge of the field is twenty steps away. Then ten.

We burst through it and keep running, still hand in hand. There's no reason to hold on to each other now, but I don't want to let go.

"Stay with me, Aura," Nathaniel shouts, tugging me faster along the muddy ground, our feet kicking up sludge.

A final blast of flames sizzles behind us and then there's

silence. Even the shouting stops. They won't admit it, but the fae fear the mist and all the monsters they believe hide within it. They won't pursue us now.

We race into the fog toward the tormented tree where Nathaniel first appeared, but I dig in my heels as soon as we reach it. "Stop. Please. I need to stop."

My chest heaves and the silence fills with our rapid breaths. He doesn't let go of my hand, the glow between us casting shadows through the haze.

My senses tingle and my skin prickles. A breeze eases across my cheeks, wiping away the tears I didn't know I was shedding.

"Evander," I whisper, my heart in my throat as I pray for him to hear me.

My brother's response is a soft burst of sound on the wind. "Treble lives. Go, Aura."

His voice vanishes, the last traces of the life I knew disappearing too quickly.

I'm about to follow Nathaniel—a man I know almost nothing about—into darkness. I don't know what will happen to Evander, Talsa, or Crispin after I leave. I don't know what waits for me beyond the marsh.

The rays of the new day lighten the sky behind us, but the sunlight doesn't touch the ground where I stand.

It's dawn.

The second day of the Law has begun.

I have two more days to live.

I spin to Nathaniel, close my fingers tightly around his, and run with him into the misty woods.

Continue Aura and Nathaniel's story in Radiant Fierce (Bright Wicked 2).

RADIANT FIERCE (BRIGHT WICKED 2)

One lie began it all.

I have become a traitor to my people, hated and feared by the ones I once protected, driven to destruction by the lies on which my life was based.

Two traitors.

Now, I have no choice but to escape with Nathaniel Shield into the heart of Fell, a land of dark creatures and brutal laws ruled by a cruel King, who wants us both dead.

Three chances to survive.

With every step we take, Nathaniel's secrets grow.

Every move he makes to claim me destroys my heart, piece by piece, until the truth he's hiding threatens to tear me apart.

When the Fell King comes for us, I must choose between love or survival.

But how can I follow my destiny when I'm fated to kill the man I love?

I have three days to live. The second day has begun.

Content information: Radiant Fierce is a fantasy romance, the second in the Bright Wicked series, a trilogy told over three consecutive days. Recommended reading age is 17+ for sex scenes and language.

STORM PRINCESS

A COMPLETE FANTASY ROMANCE

"Will you wait for me?" he asks.
I whisper, "I would wait a lifetime for you."

The last warrior in the House of Rath...

I thought he died. I watched him bleed out on a cold
mountainside while thunder and lightning formed a cage
around me, trapping me in a power I never wanted.

The Storm...

It chose me. A furious force unleashed in vengeance, the Storm's
destruction would rage across the kingdom if not for me.

Day after day, I survive its wrath, taking the lightnings strikes,
the icy needles of rain, and absorbing its deadly force, stopping
its fury.

Through it all, I bury my memories, and force myself to forget the promise I made, denying what I want most.

My heart...

Now, Baelen Rath has returned, wearing the scars of battle, and vowing to fight for me.

He burns through the walls I've built around my heart, drawing me in, body and soul.

But the closer he gets to me, the clearer it becomes that he has secrets he didn't have before.

So do I.

Because the Storm is changing and its power is growing.

Like the fire Baelen ignites within me, soon it will be beyond my control.

Content information: Storm Princess: Book 1 is the first in a complete romantasy trilogy.

Recommended reading age is 17+ for sex scenes, mature themes, violence, and language. Ends on a cliffhanger.

Tropes for the series include:

Touch her and..., second chance romance, forbidden love, high fantasy, elves, gargoyles, and magical creatures.

*This is a revised edition. Now including alternate point of view chapters previously only available in the complete collection.

ALSO BY EVERLY FROST

BRIGHT WICKED - COMPLETE

(Fantasy Romance)

1. Bright Wicked

2. Radiant Fierce

3. Infernal Dark

STORM PRINCESS - COMPLETE

(Fantasy Romance)

1. Book 1

2. Book 2

3. Book 3

ASSASSIN'S MAGIC

(Dark Urban Fantasy Romance)

1. Assassin's Magic

2. Assassin's Mask

3. Assassin's Menace

4. Assassin's Maze

5. Rebels

6. Revenge

7. Rogue

8. Assassin's Match

SOUL BITTEN SHIFTER - COMPLETE

(Dark Urban Fantasy Romance)

1. This Dark Wolf

2. This Broken Wolf

3. This Caged Wolf

4. This Cruel Blood

DEMON PACK - COMPLETE

(Dark Paranormal Romance)

1. Demon Pack

2. Demon Pack: Elimination

3. Demon Pack: Eternal

SUPERNATURAL LEGACY - COMPLETE

(Angels and Dragon Shifters)

1. Hunt the Night

2. Chase the Shadows

3. Slay the Dawn

4. Claim the Light

DARK MAGIC SHIFTERS

(Dark Urban Fantasy Romance)

1. Wolf of Ashes

2. Bond of Flames

3. Crown of Fate

KINGDOM OF BETRAYAL

(Fantasy Romance)

1. A Sky Like Blood

2. A Sin Like Fire

3. A Storm Like Iron

4. A Soul Like Glass

MORTALITY - COMPLETE

(Science-Fantasy Romance)

Mortality Complete Set: Books 1 to 4

1. Beyond the Ever Reach

2. Beneath the Guarding Stars

3. By the Icy Wild

4. Before the Raging Lion

<u>Stand-alone fiction - dark romance</u>

Corrupt Me: Immortal Vices and Virtues

ABOUT THE AUTHOR

Everly Frost is the USA Today Bestselling author of fantasy romance, urban fantasy and paranormal romance novels. She spent her childhood dreaming of other worlds and scribbling stories on the leftover blank pages at the back of school notebooks. She lives in Brisbane, Australia with her husband and two children.

- ⓐ amazon.com/author/everlyfrost
- f facebook.com/everlyfrost
- ⓞ instagram.com/everlyfrost
- BB bookbub.com/authors/everly-frost
- g goodreads.com/everlyfrost